GIVE IN TO ME

Praise for Elle Spencer

The Holiday Treatment

"If you are looking for the perfect Christmas read, *The Holiday Treatment* should be top of your list for Santa. Light-hearted, laugh-out-loud funny with all the right ingredients for a perfect Christmas rom-com, it would make the ideal screenplay for a Netflix special… It's well written, well-paced and brings welcome relief after a difficult year. Perfect reading for the holiday season and a great stocking filler for your friends."—*Curve Magazine*

"The whole book is funny. Holly, our main character, is a hot mess. She is adorable, witty, and keeps you in stitches. Meredith is 100 percent taken with her and the chemistry is palpable. The push-pull of their love story keeps you engaged the whole time. At times it is so sweet and the other times, well it is super sexy. Great read, highly recommend. If you need a book to escape, this is it. You will love this adorable read that gives you a ton of fun."
—*Romantic Reader Blog*

"Do you ever read a book, and when it comes to writing the review, you just don't know if you could possibly do the book justice? That's how good this book is. [It] was the warm Christmassy hug I was looking for. I did not stop to put this book down when I was reading it. It just pulled me in from the first chapter…The best way to start the festive season is with this fantastic Christmas rom-com! You won't regret adding this to Santa's list!"—*Les Rêveur*

"As always, Spencer comes through with a novel that's engaging on all levels. It has everything I want in a story—great characters, witty dialogue, an original plot, hot sex, a fair amount of angst, and an ending that got me all verklempt. It's got all the elements to get you in the mood for Christmas. It even smells like chestnuts roasting on an open fire. (Really, Victoria?) I think you'll delight in it. I'm ready to break out my ugly Christmas sweater and start humming Christmas carols."—*Lesbian Review*

Waiting for You

"I laughed, I cried, I fanned my face (hot, sexy scenes)...Elle Spencer is becoming one of my favorite writers!"—*Marcia Hull, Librarian, Ponca City Library (Oklahoma)*

"This book is so much fun to read. The dialogue is fun and funny... This is definitely recommended: lovely ladies, excellent chemistry, great supporting cast and high fun factor in the writing."—*Best Lesfic Reviews*

"I do have to give it to Spencer: she is really, really good at writing chemistry between romantic leads...This is a book that has just about everything, comedy, feelings, sexy scenes, a great supporting cast and past lives. Fans of rom coms or dramadies will love this."—*Colleen Corgel, Librarian, Queens Public Library*

"I've come to count on Spencer to take me away from whatever drama is going on in the world to a place where sharp, attractive women will entertain me with their wit and warmth."—*Lesbian Review*

"I love the books Elle Spencer writes. Ever since her first novel, *Casting Lacey*, I have gravitated to everything she has written. BIG FAN! Spencer does a great job with this book, the story reels you in and holds you captive chapter after chapter."—*Romantic Reader Blog*

30 Dates in 30 Days

"I'm an Elle Spencer fan. I want to say that this was surprisingly good, but I guess I shouldn't really be that surprised. She generally delivers on everything I love about reading romance. Feelings, chemistry, conflict, angst, tears, and happiness. The characters were likable. Fun situations. Great chemistry. A slow burn romance that satisfies in the end."—*Bookvark*

"As usual with Spencer, the characters are wonderfully layered and flawed, [and] the chemistry is out of this world."—*Jude in the Stars*

"Spencer imbues the story with some great humour and witty banter that brings the characters to life, and the romance works wonderfully. I really enjoyed this one–it hit all the right notes for me and left me with a bit of an aw, shucks smile on my face when I finished."
—*C-Spot Reviews*

"Ms. Spencer knows how to build the tension so thick that you could cut it with a proverbial knife. The intimate scenes are really hot… Overall, a clever, funny and light romance with great chemistry and a superb cast."—*LezReviewBooks*

Private Equity (in *Hot Ice*)

"This story had a lot of heart and quite a bit of depth for so little time. This was the strongest among the three novellas."—*Bookvark*

The Road to Madison

"The story had me hooked from its powerful opening scene, and it only got better and better. I feel like Spencer tailored this book just for me. For anyone who has read my reviews, it's no secret that I love romances that include lots of angst, and *The Road to Madison* hit the bull's-eye."—*The Lesbian Review*

"Elle Spencer weaves a tale full of sadness, remorse but one filled with those little moments that make you have the flutters. Her characters are well developed, the dialogue is seamless and natural, you really get thrown right into Madison and Anna's world. You feel what they feel. This book grabbed my attention and had me turning the pages through the night. A delightful story that I thoroughly enjoyed. I cannot wait for the next adventure Elle Spencer takes me on."—*Romantic Reader Blog*

"Elle Spencer is fast becoming one of my favourite authors. She transports me into the story and I feel like I'm living vicariously through the characters."—*Les Rêveur*

Unforgettable

"Across both novellas, Elle Spencer delivers four distinct, compelling leads, as well as interesting supporting casts that round out their stories. If you like angsty romances, this is the book for you! Both stories pack a punch, with so much 'will they or won't they' that I kind of wondered how they'd turn out (yes, even though it's marketed as romance!)"—*The Lesbian Review*

"I was stunned at how Elle Spencer manages to make the reader feel so much and we end up really caring for the women in her novels…This book is perfect for those times you want to wallow in romance, intense feelings, and love. Elle Spencer does it so well."
—*Kitty Kat's Book Review Blog*

Casting Lacey

"The characters have a chance to really get to know each other, becoming friends and caring for each other before their feelings turn romantic. It also allows for a whole lot of angst that keeps things interesting. *Casting Lacey* is a compelling, sexy, angsty romance that I highly recommend to anyone who's into fake relationship books or celebrity romances. It kept me sucked in, and I'm looking forward to seeing more from Elle Spencer in the future."
—*The Lesbian Review*

"This is a very good debut novel that combines the fake girlfriend trope with celebrity lifestyle…The characters are well portrayed and have off-the-charts chemistry. The story is full of humour, wit, and saucy dialogues but also has angst and drama. I think that the book is at its best in the humorous parts which are really well written…an entertaining and enjoyable read."—*Lez Review Books*

"This is the romance I've been recommending to everyone and her mother since I read it, because it's basically everything I've been dying to find in an f/f romance—funny voices I click with, off-the-charts chemistry, a later-in-life coming out, and a host of fun tropes from fake dating to costars."—*Froli*

By the Author

Casting Lacey

Unforgettable

The Road to Madison

30 Dates in 30 Days

Waiting for You

The Holiday Treatment

Give In to Me

Private Equity in Hot Ice
(with Aurora Rey and Erin Zak)

GIVE IN TO ME

by

Elle Spencer

2021

CREDITS
Editor: Barbara Ann Wright
Production Design: Stacia Seaman
Cover Design by Tammy Seidick

Acknowledgments

A huge thanks to Rad, Sandy, and the entire Bold Strokes crew for all you do in front of and behind the scenes.

Barbara Ann Wright, thank you for your patience, guidance, and always gracious commentary as you help me to make every book better.

Stacia Seaman, your eagle eye is amazing.

Thank you to my amazing wife, Nikki. Five years and counting. You and me, baby.

Paula, as always, your support and friendship is everything.

To my friends and family near and far, I am so grateful to have you in my life and will be ever more grateful when we can be together again in person. Miss you all.

Finally, thank you to the people who continue to buy my books. Your support and encouraging messages along the way mean the world to me.

CHAPTER ONE

Whitney spotted her agent sitting at a small table in the hotel bar. Perfectly made-up face, unimaginably expensive hair. A suit that fit so well she might as well have been born in it. That was Liz. For her, the effort—and the cost—made the girl.

Liz had already ordered the margaritas along with what looked like homemade tortilla chips and a bowl of guacamole. The perfect bar food. The only thing that would've made it even better was a booth Whitney could slide into and fully relax in after her massage. One that faced the entrance and anyone who might approach them. Instead, they'd be sitting at a high-top table with hard wooden chairs.

After a quick scan of the place, Whitney realized Liz had chosen the best option available. A table in a quiet corner with a view of the entrance beat sitting at the bar with a bunch of sweaty, sunburned golfers. She noticed a woman sitting alone at the end of the bar far away from said golfers. She kept her gawking to a minimum—it was nothing more than a quick glance—but it took some effort.

She had no idea what they were doing there. Her plan—and it was a good one—had been to drain the minibar of whiskey while watching *Notting Hill*. She already knew the hotel had it on pay-per-view. She didn't care if it was old. Or straight. It took her out of her head, and that was enough.

She chose to sit with her back against the wall so she could see who came in and out. She said it was for people watching. And that was true. She was people watching. Some of her best side characters were based on actual people. She'd study their movements, their speech patterns, their facial expressions. Even though she wasn't currently writing, it was a habit she'd always enjoyed. People were interesting from a distance. She could draw her own conclusions and make up her own stories about who they were, where they lived, who they loved.

But it wasn't quite so simple. It wasn't just people watching. Whitney always sat with her back to the wall. Was she protecting herself? Obviously. Paparazzi? Sure. At least some of the time. Did she need to know who was coming? Absolutely. One hundred and ten percent. For sure. She wanted to be prepared.

"How's your room? Mine is fabulous." Liz held up what little was left of her margarita and signaled the server that she was ready for another.

Whitney took a sip. It went down so smoothly, she knew Liz had ordered the top-shelf tequila. God, she loved her friend. Because really, Liz had become more friend than agent. "King bed," Whitney said. "Fireplace. Big tub. I can't complain."

"What?" Liz said with surprise in her voice. "Is this a come-on? Finally?"

"No. Never." Whitney shook her head for effect. "Not ever."

Liz took a sip through her straw. She smiled and shrugged. "If you say so."

"You asked how my room was. I was answering."

"Right. Of course." Liz transformed into the consummate professional once again. It was so fast and effortless, a normal person might have found it disconcerting. But Liz never encountered normal people. Liz wasn't normal people. Hell, she wasn't even human. Liz was an agent. "Truth be told, this resort doesn't have a bad room," she said. "I upgraded to one with a whirlpool on my patio. You can join me later, but a word of warning, I'll be naked."

Okay, so maybe the consummate professional thing was an overstatement. Whitney didn't really mind. When it came to speaking engagements, Liz only accompanied her if they were held in a posh hotel. Granted, that was almost always. She'd never had to book a conference at the airport Ramada, but she imagined it for a moment nonetheless. She pictured a coupon for two-for-one appetizers at Applebee's on the back of the ticket. At the rate she was going as an author, her need for that coupon might not be that far off.

So it was no surprise that Liz had offered to make the three-hour drive to a beautiful resort east of Palm Springs with Whitney. She loved being pampered. She loved the finer things. It also wasn't a surprise that once they were there, Liz had gotten the best room available. Fortunately, Whitney had already done her one better. It turned out the booker was a fan. She'd gone on and on about how the Piper Kane books had changed her life. Needless to say, Whitney had a very nice room. She made a mental note to send over a signed copy of the Piper Kane series box set. She'd even send the shitty one with the shitty reviews. God knew there was no other way she'd ever get rid of them.

"Whitney? You with me?"

"What? Oh, right sorry. Naked. Hot tub. That's a hard pass."

Not that Liz wasn't in tip-top shape for her sixty-plus years. Nobody wore a pantsuit better. It was just that they weren't quite *that* comfortable with each other. It didn't matter that Liz was straighter than any woman Whitney had ever met. It was that hanging out with Liz in that way was kind of like nude hot tubbing with your bossy older sister. It just wasn't done.

The way she eyed one of those sweaty golfers was proof positive of just how straight she was. Of course, she'd chosen the youngest of the bunch to undress with her eyes. He was probably the hired pro, yukking it up with the older rich dudes so he'd get a better tip. Actually, he was perfect for Liz. "Why don't you invite short, tanned, and handsome to your hot tub?" Whitney said.

"He's not that short. And don't think I haven't mulled that idea over in my well-coiffed head, but I fear I'll have to settle for you."

Liz punctuated the insult with a wink, then thanked the waiter for his quick delivery of her second round. Whitney took a long sip and glanced over at the bar again. The gorgeous woman with long brown hair lowered her gaze when their eyes met.

"She hasn't taken her eyes off you since you walked in," Liz said.

Whitney huffed. "Well, then, she's about to watch me eat a salty chip slathered in guac." She moaned her approval a little louder than she normally would. "Oh my God, where has this guac been all of my life?"

Liz raised an eyebrow. "You think I'm kidding. Well, go ahead and stuff your face, but I'm telling you, she's into you." She gestured toward the woman with her head as if Whitney didn't know who she was referring to.

"I know who you mean, Liz. You don't have to be so obvious." She wondered if the beautiful brunette was also a people watcher, and if so, what conclusions she was drawing about Whitney. Was she making up a story for her? Something along the lines of bored, lonely lesbian bemoans the loss of her charmed life over what was sure to not be her last margarita of the evening. She'd be spot-on, but Whitney was too good at disguising her pain. And she'd mastered the art of the deflection.

"How long has it been since you've had sex?"

The question, which had been asked a little too loudly for Whitney's liking, startled her so much that the guacamole-covered chip she was about to shove in her mouth took a tumble down the front of her white blouse, leaving a trail of green goodness. "Shit."

Liz held up her glass. "If I actually manage to get you laid tonight, it'll be my greatest achievement in life. Here's to me."

Whitney wiped the avocado chunks off herself while swearing under her breath. Her ability to gracefully deflect the rude question with a snarky comeback got lost under the table with the chip. No five-second rule for the chip, and snarky comebacks tended to lose their bite after about ten. "You don't just ask someone about their sex life like that, Liz. And besides, I'm doing just fine, thank you very much."

"Uh-huh."

Whitney gave up on her blouse. She couldn't do anything more with it until she got back to her room. She took another sip and willed herself to not look at bar-woman again. "Look," she said. "I know you think your gaydar is extremely reliable."

"I've never been wrong," Liz said.

"Fine, but I'm still not ready to jump into anything serious."

Liz leaned in and lowered her voice. "Honey, I'm only suggesting you jump into her panties."

Whitney rolled her eyes. "Now you're just being crass. And you're ruining my post-massage buzz. I'll have to get an alcohol-induced one." She picked up her glass and licked some salt before taking a good long sip. She smirked to herself because now she could blame her desire to drink the night away on Liz. *Clever, Whit. Very clever.*

"Well, excuse me if I'd rather see you in love again and happily typing away on your next best seller," Liz said. "This is all Reece's doing. If she hadn't—" She seemed to notice the glare Whitney shot at her for mentioning her ex-wife's name. Liz leaned back in her chair and folded her arms. "I'm going to shut up now."

Whitney sighed. Liz rarely stopped mid-sentence. In fact, she rarely stopped talking at all. And how perfect that she'd bring up Reece right after Whitney had spilled guacamole on herself. Hell, maybe she should break down crying right there in the bar so the humiliation would be complete. She looked Liz in the eye and said, "You were about to say, if she hadn't cheated on me while I was finishing the final draft."

Liz put a hand on Whitney's arm. "I'm sorry. I know you don't like to talk about it."

Whitney shrugged. "I finally did the math. We were in talks for months on the movie deal for the first book. I think her affair with one of the producers had been going on for at least that long."

"Well, sure. How the hell else was she going to get the lead role?" Liz put her hands up. "Sorry. I realize that insulting Reece's acting abilities doesn't help the situation. We want the movie to be a big hit." She softened her tone and said, "But I know how much you love that character and how hard it must be for you knowing you'll have to watch Reece on the big screen speaking Piper's words. Being...Piper."

Whitney held back her emotions. It was not the time or the place to discuss why she never should've left her famous wife all alone while she toiled away in her writing cabin for the entire summer. Nor was it the time to discuss how angry she was that she was powerless to change who would play Piper on the big screen. She put on a fake smile and said, "Let's talk about a happier subject."

Liz held up her glass. "Good call. Here's to happier subjects, like the fact that she still can't take her eyes off you, guacamole-stained shirt and all."

Whitney shook her head. "You don't give up, do you?"

Liz swung her head the woman's way and then back again. The second margarita appeared to be taking effect. "If I were gay, I'd be all over that gorgeous girl. Tell me I'm wrong."

Whitney risked another glance. Liz wasn't wrong. Of course she'd set her sights on the hottest girl in the room. Liz would probably take her back to her room too. But Whitney wasn't Liz. At least, not since her confidence had taken a nosedive off a thirty-foot cliff. Being left for another woman would do that to a person.

Whitney watched the woman tuck her hair behind her ear and give the man who'd just stepped up to her a tight, obligatory smile. It was clear she didn't want his attention. For a fleeting moment, Whitney wondered what would happen if she were the one who'd stepped up and offered to buy her a drink.

With the woman's attention focused elsewhere, Whitney took the opportunity to get a good look at her. Her pink sleeveless dress hit her at about mid-thigh, leaving lots of smooth, tanned goodness to admire. Same with her toned arms. Her fingers were long and slender. Short, manicured nails. She laughed at something the bartender said, and Whitney found herself wanting to join in the laughter too.

"What are you smiling about?" Liz asked.

"Nothing," Whitney said. But it wasn't nothing. Her imagination had taken her from buying the woman a drink to running her fingers under the hem of that dress until she found what was surely a pair of matching panties. Because if the dress, sandals, and toenail polish were all pink, everything had to be.

In her mind, she slid the dress up those thighs so she could confirm it. Of course, that meant she'd have to ease those legs open so she could get closer, and when her fingers found lace—wait, make that *moist* lace—she'd definitely have to lean in and taste those pink lips too.

She shook her head to clear that image from her mind. Okay, so maybe it had been a while since she'd had sex, but she wasn't about to admit it out loud. She simply crossed her legs a little bit tighter and hoped she hadn't turned bright red with how hot she was making herself. She looked at Liz and said, "What? Stop staring at me."

"I'm just staring at you staring at her, and as soon as she gets rid of Mr. Three Bud Lights and Counting, she'll go back to staring at you again. Isn't this fun?"

"Liz, even if I wanted to—"

"Stop," Liz said, cutting her off. "It's time to rev up your love life, Whit. You don't have to put your heart out there right away, just get some action. Have some sex. Get some inspiration. Remind yourself that you're still alive and kicking."

Whitney put up a hand. "Okay, I get it. Believe me, I do." She paused. Could she even do casual sex? It sounded kind of nice. No emotions. No baggage. Just the touch of a beautiful woman who she could kiss good-bye and mean it. Whitney had never had a one-night stand. She wasn't even one for brief flings. On the other hand, maybe it was time to do things differently. Judging from the shambles of her current life, the old way clearly wasn't working. She stole another glance at the woman. "What do you want me to do? Go ask her to dance and hope she doesn't laugh me out of the bar?"

Liz glanced around. "If she were to laugh, it would only be because this isn't that kind of bar." She cupped a hand around her ear. "I can barely hear the elevator music coming from the lobby. I think it's the easy listening version of 'These Boots Are Made for Walkin'.' Then again, there's nothing sexier than two women making their own music, am I right?"

The big wink let Whitney know that Liz had no intention of letting this go. In fact, it would only get worse the more she drank. She'd get bolder and louder, and Whitney wasn't in the mood for that. Nor was she in the mood to walk up to a beautiful woman while wearing her appetizer on her blouse.

In the past, the fact that she'd been married had saved Whitney from Liz and her infamous matchmaking shenanigans. Liz could claim a few success stories on that front. Or rather, she could brag endlessly about hooking this or that friend up and how great it was that they were still married. Right up until they'd announce their divorce.

A group of men walked into the bar, all wearing lanyards around their necks. "Tomorrow's audience just arrived," Liz said.

"I need to leave." Whitney took a final sip of her margarita and stopped Liz before she could say anything. "Look at my blouse, Liz. I can't mingle with anyone right now."

"Right. Okay, go change and hurry back."

Whitney shook her head. "No, I think I'll just chill in my room tonight. Maybe get some work done." Whitney hoped that would be the end of it. After all, Liz-the-friend might have wanted her to get laid, but Liz-the-agent wanted another Piper Kane book to be written.

"What about…" Liz rolled her head and eyes so hard, Whitney frowned at her.

"Are you okay? You look like you're about to have a seizure."

She threw a thumb in the woman's direction and whispered, "What about her?"

"Oh." The head rolling made sense now. Whitney leaned in and said, "I think I'll leave this up to my *wingwoman* to figure out."

Liz froze. She blinked a few times, glanced at the woman, then blinked again. "Is that code for—"

Whitney stood. "Text me if anything interesting happens."

Liz grabbed for her sleeve. "Whitney, wait."

Whitney pointed at her feet. "Boots. Walking." She smirked as she sauntered away because unlike Liz, she had one hell of a saunter. There were a few perks that came with having been married to a model turned actress. Long legs that wrapped around you with ease was one of them. So was having her teach Whitney how to walk like a boss, even when it felt like the world was crumbling around her.

❖

The hotel bathrobe felt soft against Whitney's skin after her hot shower. She could count on the amenities being nice when she was the keynote speaker, but that wasn't the case this time. She was one of several speakers at the large conference, so the bathrobe was a nice surprise.

Calling an early night had been the best decision she'd made all week. And even though she had a light buzz from the margarita, she knew a nightcap would help her fall asleep. A good night's rest had become a thing of the past since her divorce. She still hadn't adjusted to sleeping alone in a big bed. She probably needed to downsize to a queen so the empty space didn't feel so huge. In-room minibars rarely had anything interesting, but she bent down to take a look anyway. "Leave me alone," she shouted at her phone vibrating on the bed. She grabbed a little bottle of the only whiskey they had and sighed as she looked at the label. "I wish your name was Jill Daniel's. Or Jane. Or Jodi."

Her phone started up again with a barrage of text alerts. "Oh, for fuck's sake." She marched over to the bed, bottle in hand.

The sexy Gabriela is on her way.

You're welcome.

She has a sexy voice.

So does short, tanned, and hung. Bahahaha.

"What the..." Whitney put the phone to her ear. "Answer, damnit. Liz. What the hell did you do?"

"I told you my gaydar was pinging like a submarine under Russian attack. She's totally into you, so don't blow this, okay? Just relax and enjoy yourself."

Whitney threw a hand in the air. "I was joking, Liz. Joking. Did you seriously think I wanted you to be my intermediary?"

"You don't have time for six-syllable words, Whit. Neither do I, come to think of it." Liz chuckled. "One-syllable words for the rest of the night. Mostly just 'fuck' and 'yes.'" Her laugh was cut short when the line went dead.

Whitney lowered the phone from her ear and stared at it for a few seconds. This wasn't really happening, was it? She turned and set her eyes on the door, waiting for the knock. "Oh God," she whispered before she sprang into action. She needed to check herself in the mirror, so she raced into the bathroom and ran her fingers through her damp hair. Her face was bright red because of course it was. Anyone in their right mind would have a blush in their cheeks in this moment. And possibly red streaks on their neck.

She still had that little bottle of Jack in hand. She couldn't do this sober. No fucking way. She twisted until the stubborn little cap finally gave way and downed it in one swallow. She grimaced and wiped the back of her hand across her mouth. "I could just not answer the door," she said out loud.

That was one option. She could shout that she was busy and sorry for any confusion. She ran through a few other exceptionally good ideas. She could hold a lit match up to the smoke detector to trigger the fire alarm. But she didn't have any matches, damnit. Maybe she could sneak out the window. The second floor wasn't that high up. She was pretty sure there was some sort of vine growing on the building that she could shinny down.

She finally landed on what might have won the best-idea-of-the-day award. She, Whitney Ainsworth, could spend the night with a beautiful woman. Okay, fine. Maybe it was Liz's idea, but it had some merit. Nice hotel, comfortable bed, an orgasm or two. What would be so bad about that? She huffed at her own image in the mirror, then leaned in so she could check her roots. Even if it seemed like a nice idea, when push came to shove, could she really do this? Would sex with a complete stranger really make her feel better? She reviewed her mental image of the stranger at the bar and concluded that casual sex could in fact make her feel better. Besides, people did this kind of thing all the time, right? It would be fine. She'd still be the same person in the morning.

Once she was sure her hair was still the three shades of dirty blond her colorist meant it to be, she leaned on the sink and looked herself in the eye. "Everything about this is bad," she said. "Because you don't do this, Whitney Ainsworth." She took a deep breath and blew air through her lips while she continued to scrutinize herself.

Had it really come to this? Was she really so desperate for a little bit of human contact that she'd actually consider answering if someone knocked? She opened her robe and put her hand on her chest. Sure, the whole thing felt a tad desperate and creepy. But Whitney knew the pace of her breath didn't have a damn thing to do with desperation, creepy or otherwise. The truth was, it felt exciting. She let the robe fall back on her shoulders enough to expose her breasts. Her nipples had hardened, and for a moment, she let herself remember what it felt like to be naked in the presence of another human being. How long had it been since she'd experienced that kind of vulnerable, unrestrained passion? Afraid to do the math, she tightened her robe. "Too long," she whispered.

The soft knock on the door brought her back to reality. What would it be? An apology through a closed door, or would she open that door and let fate rule the night? She tucked her hair behind her ears and gave herself a final look in the mirror. "You want this more than you don't want it," she said. And with that, she marched over to the door, threw it open, and in the most seductive voice she could muster, said, "Hello, I'm Whitney."

Okay, so maybe it came out over-the-top seductive. Just this side of Kathleen Turner voicing Jessica Rabbit. The woman stared at her wide-eyed for a few humiliatingly long seconds before her eyes fell to Whitney's chest. "Should I come another time?"

"Now is perfect," Whitney said with a little less Jessica Rabbit. Judging from yet another glance at her chest, the robe must've slid back open a bit. She chose to leave it that way because that was what Sharon Stone would do in a situation like this. She'd also open the door a little wider and say, "Please, come in."

Whitney barely got the words out before she screamed different words in her head. Words like, *This is insane. Since when do you let total strangers into your hotel room? This woman could have a gun in her purse. Or a big butcher knife. And don't forget, you're not actually Sharon Stone. Even Sharon Stone isn't Sharon Stone. In real life, she wears underwear and bakes cookies for her kid.*

On closer inspection, she could see that the purse was too small to hide a butcher knife. It was one of those shoulder bags that could hold a wallet, phone, and maybe one tampon. Definitely not even roomy enough for the compact Glock 33 that Piper Kane favored in her books.

Whitney double locked the door and turned. When she found herself face-to-face with her apparent date for the evening, she leaned back against the door. She felt slightly light-headed due to the alcohol hitting her empty stomach, so she stayed where she was while she planned her next move. Should she saunter over to the bed and let her robe fall away as she went? Or maybe she looked sexy right where she was, against the door with her hands behind her back, her robe gaping open but not revealing too much too soon.

"Thank you for seeing me," the stranger said. "I wondered—"

Whitney put a finger to her own lips in an attempt to get her to stop talking. Too much small talk and she might lose her nerve. Pleasant conversation could be, well, pleasant, but that was not what Whitney needed. She could get that anywhere. Even Liz could be pleasant when she wasn't channeling a matchmaker from a different era. What she needed, she hadn't been able to admit to herself until that very moment. "You don't have to wonder about anything," she said "I want what you want."

"You do? Wow, that's a relief. I mean, your agent said you'd like to get to know me better, but I wasn't so sure after—"

Whitney pushed off the door and stepped closer. Their sudden proximity seemed to silence her would-be lover again. Was she nervous too? Was her mind reeling with the possibilities? Could she feel the tension building between them? All physical signs pointed to yes, she felt it too.

Whitney was able to relax a little once she realized she wasn't the only one in the room with red streaks on their neck. What was the name Liz had texted? Oh, yes. *Gabriela.* Gabriela was even more beautiful up close. She had a smooth voice that leaned toward seductive. She smelled nice too. Something light and floral. Jo Malone, maybe? Good taste in perfume was always a plus. Her chest heaved under her dark locks. She started to say something but stopped. It was now or never. Whitney could lean in or she could back away, but nothing in Gabriela's demeanor was telling her to back away. And her own body was screaming at her to just kiss the girl already. She put her finger under Gabriela's chin and whispered, "My agent was right."

Their lips met, and Whitney both heard and felt the air leave Gabriela's lungs. Her breath had a tinge of sweetness to it, probably from the Cosmo she'd been sipping at the bar. Her lips were soft and surprisingly responsive given that they'd only just met.

Gabriela's hands landed on her shoulders with a light thud. She wasn't pushing her away, but she wasn't pulling her closer either. Whitney pulled back from the kiss but just barely. She wanted this. It had been so long since she'd felt the touch of a woman. Kissed her soft skin. Ran her fingers through her hair. Her body remembered. With just that one kiss, she felt a fire in her core. But Gabriela needed to want it too. So she waited while their breath mingled, and their eyes searched for answers.

Gabriela's chest heaved. Her fingers still gripped Whitney's shoulders when she said, "I seem to have lost the ability to think."

Whitney lifted a hand to Gabriela's cheek and caressed it. "I'm not thinking very straight right now, either."

"Mmm. Good thing," Gabriela murmured. Her grip loosened, and with a sense of wonder in her voice, she said, "My God, is this really happening?" Her eyes were full of questions, but they were also exploring. Taking in all of Whitney, dropping to the gap in her robe and then back up again.

Whitney couldn't believe it either. Had she really just kissed a complete stranger? "Let me guess," she said. "You don't make a habit of this sort of thing?"

"Not usually. Or like, ever." Gabriela ran her fingers along the opening of Whitney's robe. A bold move that she seemed to regret since she pulled her hand back as if she'd been burned.

"Me either. Not even once." Whitney's eyes were firmly planted on those lips she desperately wanted to taste again. With a featherlight touch, she ran a finger over Gabriela's bottom lip and said, "Let's not talk ourselves out of it." When she didn't get a response, she lifted her gaze, afraid that maybe one kiss was all she'd get when she wanted so much more.

Gabriela gave an almost imperceptible shake of her head and said, "No, let's not."

CHAPTER TWO

A hand was on her ass. Or maybe a foot. Whitney wasn't awake enough to know for sure. She cracked an eye. Good. The sun wasn't all the way up yet. She had time to order coffee before she had to shower and meet Liz for breakfast. Speaking of Liz, Whit made a mental note to send a bottle of champagne as a thank-you for her excellent work on the wingwoman front. Not that she wanted Liz-as-pimp to ever happen again, but in this one instance, it turned out an all-nighter with a beautiful woman was exactly what she needed.

Her body felt sore in all the right places. She felt satiated. Calm. It was a delicious sort of fatigue that only happened after sex. The kind where you're dead tired but ready to do it all again. The kind of all-consuming sex that was so mind-blowingly good, fatigue couldn't possibly coexist with it. That was just science.

Since they were busy doing other things, they hadn't talked much the night before, but Whitney found herself longing to know more about Gabriela. Where was she from? Where did she grow up? What did she do for a living? All the things you'd find out on a first date were still unknown to her. But they didn't have to be.

She felt a light squeeze on her backside and then soft strokes from the small of her back down to her thigh and back up again. Gabriela's touch was sensual. She didn't hesitate to let her fingers roam close to sensitive parts. Whitney hummed her approval, the lazy smile on her face hidden behind mussed hair.

"Oh, good. You're awake," Gabriela said in between the soft

kisses she'd been peppering Whitney's shoulder with. "Turns out I'm not done with your incredibly sexy body."

Whitney stayed on her stomach and leaned up on her elbows. She ran her fingers through her disastrous hair and pushed it behind her ears. Their eyes met, and big grins ensued, followed by giggles because yes, last night really did happen. Whitney rolled onto her back and threw her hands over her head. "I need some coffee if I'm ever going to function again."

"Does that mean we're done?" Gabriela's hand worked its way back up and circled Whitney's breast. "Because if I hadn't made myself clear, I want you again."

Whitney turned her head toward Gabriela. God, she was so beautiful lying there on her side with that mischievous grin on her face. Her eyes were a light hazel color Whitney hadn't noticed the night before. Not brown but not quite green either. If she wasn't careful, she'd fall madly in love with those eyes. That mouth. That voice. She told herself to go slow because the truth was, her heart was still healing, and she knew nothing of this woman. Nothing at all. "I hate what I'm about to say."

"Then don't say it." Gabriela leaned over and took a hardened nipple into her mouth.

Whitney groaned. "Not helping." She put her hand on Gabriela's head, keeping her there. "Seriously not helping."

Gabriela stopped sucking and placed a few gentle kisses on Whitney's breast. "Sorry. What were you going to say?"

Whitney let her eyes graze the parts of Gabriela's body that weren't covered by the sheet. She ran her finger around Gabriela's nipple, causing it to harden. It would be so easy to make love to her. Not just have sex but really get to know her, mind, body, and soul? It was a very tempting thought, but again, she told herself to go slow. Get to know her outside of the bedroom. Fully clothed and in public where they'd be forced to do nothing but talk. She sighed and said, "I have to meet Liz for breakfast, and then I have a thing to prepare for."

Gabriela took Whitney's hand and intertwined their fingers. "I know," she said. "I guess I was hoping you'd wake up and we'd have time to snuggle while we watched the sunrise."

Whitney smiled. "You're a romantic."

"Hopeless."

So that was two things she knew about Gabriela. Not only was she passionate, she was a romantic too. She brought their hands to her lips and kissed Gabriela's fingers. "How about a raincheck?"

"Hmm," Gabriela said with a tap of her chin. "Order that coffee while I rinse off in your shower, and I'll consider it."

"Can I watch?" Whitney sat up and leaned against the headboard. She grabbed the phone and pushed the button for room service.

"Whitney Ainsworth wants to watch me shower? It would seem I've died and gone to heaven." Gabriela sauntered over to the bathroom, then stopped at the door. "But don't worry. I'll leave that little request out of the interview." She made the motion of locking her mouth and throwing away the key. "Call me selfish, but I'm keeping this part all to myself." She let out a little giggle and shut the door behind her.

Whitney stared at the bathroom door, not sure what she'd just heard. The gentleman on the other end of the line raised his voice and said, "Ms. Ainsworth, are you there?"

"Yes. Sorry. Coffee for two, please." She put the phone back in its cradle and replayed Gabriela's words over in her head. She'd leave this part out of the interview? What the hell was she talking about?

A feeling of dread started to form in the pit of Whitney's stomach. She put on a robe and went to the bathroom door. "Gabriela?" She could hear the shower running, so she opened the door.

Gabriela had her head under the showerhead, her hands in her hair. Water streamed down her chest over her hardened nipples. The sight took Whitney's breath away for a moment. She watched until Gabriela opened her eyes, but then she lowered her gaze. The smart move would be to leave the bathroom until she got some clarification. She turned to go.

"You don't have to leave." Gabriela opened the shower door. "I'd love some company."

Memories of the previous night flashed through Whitney's mind. She heard their moans. She felt Gabriela's hand gripping her wrist while an orgasm ripped through her body. She felt Gabriela's tongue on her clit, circling it with a painful, excruciatingly slow pace. She let her eyes graze Gabriela's wet body before she asked, "What was that thing you said about an interview?"

Gabriela froze. "Oh. Um…"

Whitney grabbed a towel and tossed it to her. "You have five seconds to tell me who you are."

Gabriela turned off the shower and wrapped the towel around herself. "Okay, slow down. Your agent told me you wanted to meet with me. I thought that meant you wanted to do an interview."

"An interview for who? For what purpose?" Whitney felt the first signs of panic. Her face heated up. Her mouth went dry. The hair on the back of her neck stood up, and a shot of adrenaline raced through her veins. She should run. As fast as her legs would take her, she should run from whoever this woman was. "Answer me," she said with a shaky breath.

Gabriela shook her head. "I won't write it. I don't have to write anything about this. I mean, of course I wouldn't write about this," she stammered. "I just mean, I don't have to write about you, you know, the interview."

Hot tears welled in Whitney's eyes. How could she have been so stupid? She never should've opened her door to a total stranger. Even worse than that, she'd given herself to this woman in the most intimate way, and for all she knew, Gabriela wasn't even gay. She blinked away the tears, hardened her glare, and said, "I never consented to any kind of an interview."

"You're absolutely right," Gabriela said. "End of story. I mean, there isn't even a story to write because we never discussed it." She stepped out of the shower. "Any idea where my clothes ended up? I feel kind of vulnerable right now with the way you're looking at me like you want to kill me."

She felt vulnerable? Whitney didn't believe it for a second. It was obvious that Gabriela was one of those journalists who'd do anything for a story. Even sleep with Reece's ex-wife to get some gossipy dirt on her. That had to be what this was about. Whitney's anger flared at the thought. "Your clothes are probably by the door where you stripped them off last night."

Gabriela smirked as she passed by. "Not how it happened."

Maybe it wasn't, but Whitney was determined to make Gabriela feel as badly about the whole thing as she did. She would not let her walk out that door feeling like she'd accomplished something by playing gay for a day. "Who do you write for?"

Gabriela found her panties and slid them on under the towel. "No one," she said. "I mean, just my own blog." She looked around the suite. "Any idea where my bra ended up?"

"You weren't wearing one." Whitney folded her arms. "So last night you were in the hotel bar hoping to get an interview with me for your stupid little blog that only three or four people read? Is that the story you're sticking to?"

"Okay, just to be clear, I didn't actually say that my blog is stupid."

"No, I guess you didn't. That was just me making an educated guess."

Gabriela stopped looking and put her hands on her hips. "Okay, FYI, I don't leave the house without a bra, but sure, make me sound slutty if it makes you feel better, but I wasn't the only one in that bed last night."

"You were the only one who had all the facts. I was blindsided. Where's your damned dress?"

"That's what I'd like to know." They both turned over sofa cushions and looked under furniture.

"I took it off you right by the door," Whitney said. "How far could it have gone?"

Gabriela got up off her knees and pointed. "Aha. So you *do* admit you took it off me." Her towel dropped from her body. She didn't bother to pick it up.

Whitney had to tear her eyes away so she could feign annoyance. "Oh God, would you please cover up?"

"I would, but you obviously hid my clothes while I was in the shower. Is this some kind of weird fetish where you have a box full of keepsakes like a serial killer?"

Whitney was done with this shit. The cute pink dress had apparently vanished into thin air, so she went to her suitcase and pulled out an old T-shirt and some workout shorts. She threw them at Gabriela. "Don't bother returning them."

Gabriela shot her a glare. "I'll sleep with them under my pillow."

Whitney's eyes shuddered closed. There was absolutely no way that the previous night wouldn't become this woman's claim to fame. Her B-list star fuck. It would be the story she'd tell her friends once they were all tipsy on cheap wine. She'd have them salivating until she revealed who the semi-famous person was that she'd slept with. And then she'd reveal every sordid detail in a post for her obscure little blog. But what could Whitney do about it now? Nothing. She could do nothing but hope for the best. She went to the door and picked up Gabriela's purse. She held it out with one finger. "I'd like you to leave now."

Gabriela took her purse and stood face-to-face with Whitney. Her expression turned from anger to what, remorse? Regret? "I didn't—" She lowered her gaze and shook her head.

"You're right," Whitney said. "You didn't." She opened the door and waited, even though what she wanted to do was shove her out into the hallway.

Gabriela stepped out and turned around, looking like she had more to say. Whitney shook her head. "Don't. This was regrettable, to say the least. Let's just leave it at that, okay?"

Was it remorse she saw in Gabriela's eyes? Even if it was, she couldn't trust that it was sincere. Even still, she chose to shut the door like a normal person instead of slamming it as hard as she could. She headed for the bathroom and stopped short in front of the fireplace. How apropos that she'd tossed Gabriela's dress behind her the night before only to have it land on top of the logs in the fireplace. She had half a mind to light that fire and watch the dress burn, but she didn't have time for that. She had to pull herself together and give a talk in less than two hours.

Whitney scanned the lobby. Liz had made herself comfortable on one of the sofas, her phone in one hand and a cup of coffee in the other. She looked up and gave Whitney a mischievous grin. "Was I right, or was I right?" She put up a hand. "No, I don't even have to ask. It's a hundred and two degrees outside, so the only reason you'd be wearing that scarf wrapped so tightly around your neck is because you got yourself some Gabriela with a capital *G*."

Whitney was furious when she'd noticed the small yet obvious mark on her neck that would scream to the entire world that she'd just slept with an overeager college freshman who thought hickeys were a badge of honor. She adjusted the silk scarf and folded her arms so Liz would know she meant business. "Did you by any chance vet her, like *at fucking all*, before you sent her up to my room?"

"Was I supposed to?" Liz raised an eyebrow. "She was gorgeous and interested. I thought you wanted sex, not to fill a cabinet position."

Whitney glanced around. Liz had a naturally loud voice, and subtlety wasn't one of her strong suits. She sat down and leaned in. "I didn't say I wanted sex, you wanted to hook me up, remember? And guess who I just slept with."

"Oh God." Liz's smile faded. "Incest? Please tell me it was just a cousin or something. Preferably a second cousin. Okay. It's okay. Even if it's worse. We can manage this." She picked up her phone and started scrolling through her contacts.

Whitney wondered who the hell Liz thought she was going to call. Was there some kind of sex emergency hotline at the agency? To be fair, considering who else was repped by Creative Talent International—better known as CTI—she could easily imagine the demand.

"Put your phone down." Whitney sat next to her. "Really, Liz? That's the first thing you think of? That she's my long-lost sister? Sometimes I worry about your sanity. I mean, seriously. Who goes there?"

"Oh, you wouldn't believe how many lives have been upended by this easy DNA testing. Secrets are being spilled left and right. We're this close to backstage passes sponsored by 23 and Me. I just thank God my daughter hasn't noticed her strong resemblance to a certain drummer, if you know what I mean."

"You don't have a daughter, Liz. And again, the sanity thing." Whitney tapped her own temple for effect.

"*Hmpf.* You used to laugh at my jokes. I guess the honeymoon is over. Next thing you know, you'll make excuses for why we can't sit together on the plane. And don't think it doesn't happen with some couples. Two hours of not having to hear your spouse drone on about everything they see on Facebook is sometimes worth the questioning look they give you on their way to the back of the plane."

"Okay, number one, we drove here. Number two, we're not a couple. And number three, neither of us would ever sit in the back of the plane."

Liz raised her chin. "Right. We're too uppity for that."

Whitney let out a heavy sigh. Uppity wasn't how she'd describe herself, but she didn't have the energy to argue the point. "Could we please focus on me for a moment? Because that woman was here to write a piece about me. She thought she was getting an interview, not a one-night stand."

The smirk on Liz's face morphed into a look of shock. "Well, that's unfortunate. She didn't mention anything about that to me."

"Nor to me. Not until this morning, *after* we had sex." Whitney covered her eyes. Just thinking about it made her want to hide under a bed for, like, three months. "I really don't need more bad press right now, Liz. My last book bombing was enough, don't you think?"

"Maybe it wasn't about you at all."

"I thought about that too," Whitney said. "But did she really think that if she slept with me, I'd give her some dirt on my ex-wife?"

Liz picked up her phone. "Who does she work for? I'll make a call."

"No one. She said she has a blog. What if she's an entertainment blogger and was here to get some dirt on Reece? Maybe some sordid details about our divorce. God, what was I thinking?"

"Oh, that wouldn't be so bad, would it? Any Reece-related publicity keeps you relevant and in the public eye."

As much as Whitney wanted to disagree, she knew there was some truth to that statement. Most authors at her level of success could walk down the street unnoticed, but everyone knew who Reece Ainsworth was married to. "I guess you're right," she said. "I mean, worst-case scenario would be if I'd slept with that book blogger who went viral with that terrible review. What was her name again?"

"Ha. The one with the silly cheese logo?" Liz's smile disappeared. "Oh God, no."

"What?"

"Okay, don't panic."

Whitney stood. "You're the one who has panic written all over their face. Oh, God. I'm going to have to kill myself, aren't I?"

Liz held her phone up. "It's quite possible that *Brie on Books* is also a hot chick named Gabriela."

Chapter Three

Whitney stood backstage in the Siesta Ballroom. That couldn't be right. Could it? Was it really named after a nap? As appropriate as it seemed, she was sure she had it wrong.

"Welcome to the Fiesta Ballroom, where the fun never stops." A baby-faced tech wearing suspenders with a button that said "They/Them" double-checked her mic pack.

"Thanks," Whitney said. "I could use some never-ending fun right about now."

"Everything okay? You're not nervous, are you?"

Whitney took a deep breath and shook out her hands. "I'm just a little worked up. I'll be fine."

A little worked up? Whitney was fit to be tied. She and Liz hadn't been able to confirm Gabriela's identity yet since the *Brie on Books* website didn't have a photo of Brie, but Whitney didn't need a photo. She knew in her gut that she'd just spent the night with the person who'd given her the worst review she'd ever had in her entire writing career. It was a biting, mean-spirited rebuke of the third book in the otherwise very successful Piper Kane series. And yes, that review had gone viral at the worst possible time. Any excitement she'd felt after having signed one of the most lucrative movie deals of any female author in history had been overshadowed by the suggestion that if the third book were ever made into a movie, it should be called "Piper Bomb 3."

And then there were the hashtags. Discussions focused on #PiperBomb and #WhitneyAinsworthThatMuch. The absolute worst was #SaveHerReece, inspired by the cheese blogger suggesting that the only way Piper's memory could be restored for the whole of humanity would be if Reece played the title character in the movie adaptation.

Whitney hoped the Xanax she'd taken would kick in soon. She glanced at the person's nametag and put out her hand. "Glad to meet you, Chase. I'm Whitney."

The introduction was purely a way to grab on to something or someone so she could feel grounded before she had to walk onstage. She didn't let go but held on to Chase's warm hand and glanced over their shoulder at the crowd that awaited her. Her hope that no one would show up was dashed when she could see it was a full house.

Chase moved in closer and said, "Between you and me, the medical types like to come off as sort of superior, but really, they're just a bunch of overworked folks looking to let loose on their employer's dime for a few days."

"Thank you," Whitney said. "I'm not usually like this. It's been a weird twenty-four hours is all. And I still have a death grip on your hand. Sorry about that."

"No problem." Chase took a step back and looked Whitney up and down. "Okay, so no strings hanging from awkward places. No toilet paper stuck to your feet. No guacamole stains. I think you're good to go."

Whitney raised an eyebrow. "Oh God. You saw that?"

Chase grinned. "I may have seen you leave the bar last night. It's cool. I'm just trying to loosen you up."

"Did you happen to also see the woman sitting at the bar? Long brown hair. Pink dress."

Chase's eyes lit up. "Was she hot or what? I was trying to get up the nerve to introduce myself, but then she left in a hurry."

Whitney grabbed their arm. "Please. If you happen to see her in the crowd, will you kick her out for me? She doesn't belong here. She's…an intruder. A hostile, violent intruder."

"Really? Violent? Let me call security."

While it would've been satisfying to watch Gabriela get kicked out on her conniving ass, Whitney thought better of it and shook her head. "No, don't do that. I'm overstating it. But if you happen to see her—"

"Hey, if she's not an invited guest, I'll escort her to the door." Chase gave her a quizzical look. "Just out of curiosity, did I dodge a bullet last night?"

Whitney huffed. "Yeah, but I got shot right in the gut."

"Understood." Chase went onstage and scanned the crowd. They came back and said, "I think you're good. It's all khakis and polo shirts out there." They glanced at their watch. "You're on in five. Let me know if you need anything else."

She gave Chase a nod and an appreciative smile. Five minutes were usually enough to get herself centered and focused. Problem was, she felt like a fraud. After last night, how could she possibly stand in front of a group of people and pretend she had anything of value to offer them?

While she was growing up, Whitney's father had loved to remind her how easy it was to get by on humor. A well-timed turn of phrase. A touch of sarcastic nuance. And to conquer the world? "Just a bit of wit, Whit." It was his favorite made-up saying.

Her mother, on the other hand, was happy to point out that looks, charm, and intellect—in that order—were what sealed the deal. Whitney had come to find they were both right. Except for the intellect ranking last thing. Looks hadn't gotten her through college, after all. Looks never wrote a best-selling book either.

Some might wonder why a well-known writer of suspense thrillers would be invited to speak at a medical technology conference. Sure, authors gave speeches, but they were usually authors of self-help books or those business titles seen on the desks of CEOs. Books about building inspired companies or creating successful teams and whatnot. These were things Whitney knew nothing about. But, as Liz happily told anyone with a checkbook, Whitney had another kind of gift: she could connect with people and help them turn their dreams into goals and their imagination into action.

Achievement was achievement, no matter what the field, and people seemed to love hearing about how she'd made it, the secrets to her success. At conferences like this one, people wanted to know about ideas and the creative process. "How do you create something out of nothing?" was literally the first "question to cover" in the briefing document the organizers had given her.

Writers often had a reputation for being introverts who rarely saw the light of day. Unless she was hunkered down in her writing cabin, that wasn't Whitney. She looked forward to a good party and loved to work a room. If the tables were turned and she was one of the "medovators" waiting in the audience, she'd probably be the type who looked forward to industry events like this one.

That was the old Whitney anyway. Pre-divorce Whitney. Pre-brokenhearted Whitney.

Being on the speaking circuit wasn't what she'd ever envisioned for herself. She certainly hadn't spent all of her eighth grade Creative Writing class staring longingly at Mrs. Rappaport while she'd dreamed of becoming the next big thing at corporate events.

Just like all the other girls her age, she'd dreamed of becoming the next Raymond Chandler. Okay, so maybe she was the only thirteen-year-old girl in the entire state of Rhode Island who'd imagined becoming a dead detective novelist. To be fair, he did transform the genre, and none of this had anything to do with the fact that he was Mrs. Rappaport's favorite author in the whole wide world too. Nothing at all. Pure coincidence. And since Whitney had Creative Writing first period, Chandler's books and movies were something she and Mrs. Rappaport could talk about before class from time to time. Even as an adult pushing forty, Whitney could feel the heat that rose up in her cheeks when she remembered being given an award for arriving early to school every single day of eighth grade.

She pulled her phone out of her pocket. She figured she had time to stalk Mrs. Rappaport on social media while they introduced her. The desire to know if her stunning middle school teacher still had that long, brown hair that would tickle Whitney's shoulder when she leaned over her desk to check her work suddenly seemed like need-to-know information. If nothing else, it would take her mind off that colossal mistake she'd made the night before. "Excellent work, Whitney," she whispered to herself, mimicking Mrs. Rappaport's sexy voice.

"Please welcome Whitney Ainsworth."

Damn. She'd have to continue her social media stalking later.

Maybe while sipping on a self-congratulatory glass of red for keeping a roof over her head with this lecture circuit nonsense since she hadn't been able to write a single word in over a year. She took a deep breath, turned on her microphone and her winning smile and strutted onto the stage. "Hello, everyone. I'm Whitney Ainsworth, and I'm here to talk about loving yourself."

There were a few snickers, but most of the audience didn't react at all. It was just crickets and a bit of awkward shuffling. God, how she hoped Regret Sex wasn't in the audience. That was what she'd call Gabriela from now on. That particular moniker had previously been reserved for one of the few men she'd ever slept with. She couldn't remember his name now, but she'd slept with him just to make sure she preferred women. Needless to say, he was the last man who'd ever slip between her sheets again.

Whitney needed to focus. It didn't matter if Regret Sex was in the audience, she still had to get through the next hour. But the way everyone was looking at her—their eyes full of skepticism, or boredom, or sheer disdain that they had to sit through yet another presentation when all they really wanted to do was go back to that little bar and get drunk—somehow, that gave her the courage to throw her hands in the air and say, "What? You didn't expect that from a fiction writer whose super famous wife recently left her? But wait, that's not all," she said with the mock enthusiasm of an infomercial host. "The critics hate me too. Some blogger actually said my last book made her regret her career choice. I mean, come on. She's a blogger, which is barely even a thing anymore, but sure, blame my book."

She paused for a moment, stunned that she'd said it. Sure, she'd talk about the lessons learned from her divorce, but talking about her last book wasn't part of her normal presentation for many reasons. One, no one except Liz knew that she couldn't write anymore. And two, the first book in the series was about to be made into a movie, so talking about the failed third book wasn't good from a promotional standpoint. With her writing career in limbo, this speaking thing was all she had left, or at least, that was how it felt. Was she really going to set a match to this too?

She willed herself to get her shit together and get back on

script before everyone got up and walked out. A quick glance around made it clear that no one was leaving. Not just yet, anyway. And on some cringeworthy level, she was curious how they'd react to brutal honesty. Or maybe after last night, she felt like she'd sunk so low, she might as well go out in a ball of flames. "Let me guess," she said. "Most of you didn't know until you just looked me up on your phones that I've authored several best-selling novels and that I am indeed gay. And I bet some of you actually have read the Piper Kane books, but you thought the author, Whitney Ainsworth, was a man."

A few chuckles from the audience confirmed her guess. "I also know that some of you are only here because you thought you could get a little nap in after the long lecture you attended this morning, and I can definitely appreciate that. We have a somewhat darkened room with fairly comfortable seats you can slouch down in. So go ahead and take that nap if you want."

Only one guy took her seriously and pulled his baseball cap over his eyes. A few people seemed to perk up, and even more set their phones down. As she paced back and forth across the stage, she briefly considered whether or not she'd been doing this all wrong before today. Maybe all people ever really wanted was a shitshow. Watching someone else crash and burn had to be better than looking at yourself in the mirror. Whitney had been avoiding that herself for quite some time. And after last night's huge mistake, it would be harder than ever.

"I have another option for you," Whitney said. "You could stay awake, and we can talk about whatever you want to talk about. I mean, I'd love to dole out personalized advice based on the proven life success model I developed while working on my PhD in psychology and refined over years of living an enviable life, but you already know that's bullshit. There's no life success model. No PhD. And besides, I already told you who I really am, a burned-out fiction writer whose wife recently packed up all her stuff and left while I was off trying to finish a book which, by the way, if I haven't mentioned it enough, got some really…bad…reviews.

"Also," Whitney said, "if you're under the impression that being married to an actress is somehow a good thing, keep in mind that I found out she left me because some paparazzi website posted photos on Twitter."

Someone from the audience shouted, "You're better off without her."

Whitney hadn't expected that. Her audiences usually tried to at least feign professionalism, but this seemed to be a younger crowd. She put her hand above her eyes as if she was shielding them from the overhead lights and scanned the audience. "Mom? Is that you?"

Yep. For better or worse, she was all in. But she'd be damned if she'd truly crash and burn while that horrible excuse for a human being looked on. The next half hour would not be *Brie on Books'* next blog post, titled, "Now It's Really Over for Whitney Ainsworth."

"We still love you, Whitney," someone shouted from the back.

She smiled and waved a hand in front of her face as if she was blushing. "Thanks. I'm flattered. I'd say I love you too, but look how much trouble I got into the last time I said that."

More laughs and a few more seconds to think. Whitney had never gone totally off script before, which meant Liz was probably out in the audience experiencing a mild panic attack. Whitney tried not to feel a sense of satisfaction in that, even though everything about the last twenty-four hours was Liz's fault. She was the one who'd accepted this last-minute gig. Not to mention the fucking-her-enemy part.

"Look, I get it," Whitney said. "What do I know, right? I couldn't keep my own shit together, so for me to get up here and preach anything about life or turning your passion into a career or love and relationships would seem fraudulent. Besides, we all know I was a last-minute replacement for a certain cabinet member I promised not to name. How's that for perspective? Getting indicted sounds a heck of a lot worse than finding out about your wife's affair on Twitter."

Surely, Liz had experienced a few heart palpitations by now. But Whitney had a feeling of calm wash over her. Maybe because even the guy who'd pulled his hat over his eyes was laughing along with everyone else. Or maybe it was God intervening on Whitney's behalf. *You know, if there is a God.*

She stepped closer to the crowd and said, "Wanna know what's great about being a last-minute stand-in? They don't have time to give you a bunch of rules. So that means we can have some real fun. What do you say?"

The audience clapped, and a few people whistled. Whitney pointed at a guy in the front row. "You. What's your name?"

The man glanced around and said, "Me? Um, John McGee."

"Of course your name is John," Whitney said. "You want to know why? Because your parents didn't love you enough to give you an awesome name like Jet Fighter McGee. John, let me ask you something. Would you be sitting in the front row listening to some random author if your name was Jet Fighter McGee?"

John frowned. "No."

"And would you be wearing a Hawaiian shirt?"

"Probably not. I wouldn't be wearing khakis either. Oh, and I'd definitely be dating your ex-wife." He laughed at his own joke, along with some of the audience. Others gave a sympathetic headshake with "Ouch" or "Damn."

Anyone in the room who didn't know Reece Ainsworth was Whitney's ex had already googled the information. They seemed to be all in, waiting for her reply. "And I'd wish you the best of luck getting out of that unscathed, John." She stepped even closer to the edge of the stage. "John, what else would be different if your name was Jet Fighter McGee?"

"My head would be shaved. But not like Jeff Bezos shaved. More like the Rock."

"Right. Shaved head, no khakis. A little less Jake from State Farm, a little more Dwayne Johnson from *Fast & Furious*. How about the Rock's muscles and tats? Would Jet Fighter McGee have those?"

"Jet Fighter McGee would have whatever he wanted, wouldn't he?"

"Tell me one thing Jet Fighter would do differently tomorrow that doesn't take a personal trainer or a ton of money."

"He'd ask out the woman he sees in the coffee shop every morning."

The crowd of mostly men started to cheer and egg John on. "Ask her out, Jet Fighter," they shouted. John stood and turned to them. He lifted his arms in the air, making his Hawaiian shirt rise up a bit to reveal his pleated khakis to the entire room.

Whitney laughed to herself. Of course they were pleated. "Anyone else need a better name? Come on up," she said with a wave of her hand.

A young woman jogged down the aisle, her lanyard swaying from side to side. The crowd cheered. She stopped just short of the stage and turned to quiet the crowd. Once they'd calmed down, she shouted, "From now on, everyone in this room will refer to John as Jet Fighter because that's cool as shit." She turned back to Whitney.

"Okay." Whitney laughed and looked down at the woman's lanyard, but it had flipped around during the *Price Is Right* run she'd had just made. "Tell me why you need a new name."

"Look around," the woman said. "It's mostly guys here, right? I'm one of only five women at the medical device company where I work, and I'm the only one in R and D. If anyone needs a badass name, it's me. Because I have to deal with all of this masculinity every day." She stood there with her hands on her hips, staring Whitney down. "So what's my badass name, Whit?"

Whit? Yeah, *Whit* had managed to blow up her gig in the first minute, and now some members of the audience thought they were in charge. But hey, she could play along. "If I give you a badass name, what would you do with it?"

"I'd rule all these guys behind me. I'd set their salaries. I'd rate their performances. And every year at Christmas, they'd all get a fleece vest with *my* company name embroidered on the chest. Oh, and I wouldn't be dating that dumb woman who left you. I'd be dating *you*, Whitney Ainsworth." She threw up her arms in triumph, causing the lanyard to flip back over.

Before the woman turned to the crowd and did a move like she was Rocky Balboa at the top of the museum steps, Whitney squinted at her nametag. *Well, that's unfortunate.* The name she saw had gotten a bad rap, possibly thanks to Beyoncé, or maybe it was just thanks to the thousands of Beckys who'd come before her. Did Whitney have the power to switch that around? Probably not, but she pointed at the woman and said, "Becky doesn't need a badass name to be badass because she already is. So from now on, she'll be known as Becky AF because what she just did was awesome as fuck."

The guy sitting next to Jet Fighter McGee stood and said, "I want an awesome name too. Something better than Jim Smythe."

Whitney grinned. Maybe there really was a God. And maybe, just maybe, she'd leave there with her pride intact. "Okay, Jim Smythe. Let's do this."

CHAPTER FOUR

B rie jumped when her phone shattered the silence in her apartment and woke her out of a dead sleep. It vibrated across her desk, simultaneously buzzing while a computer-generated voice repeated, "Your mother is trying to reach you on your cellular device."

"Hi, Mom."

"Are you ill? You better be on your deathbed."

"Does dead tired count?" Brie grimaced as she tried to loosen up her neck. She didn't make a habit of falling asleep at her desk, but then again, she didn't make a habit of staying up most of the night either. "Oh, crap. I missed our coffee date."

"No worries. We can still have coffee. Just open your door."

"You're here?" Brie went to the door and opened it. "Sorry, Mom. I should've called."

Her mom nudged her oversized sunglasses down her nose and gave Brie a once-over, then leaned in for a cheek kiss. "I'm glad you're okay." She took off her floppy hat and threw it on the sofa like a frisbee. "I'll make the coffee."

It always amazed Brie that her mother, Jade Talbot, regularly dressed as if she was heading to the beach. She had hats of every kind, a large collection of sunglasses, leather sandals in every color. Even her accessories screamed Bohemian Surfer Lady, her favorite piece being a turquoise and silver belt she wore loosely on her hips. It made all of her linen maxi dresses look a little less like the bathing suit covers they really were. They were usually three-hundred-dollar cover-ups from little spendy-trendy shops like Fred Segal, but they were still cover-ups.

Brie, on the other hand, felt naked standing there in Whitney's workout clothes. She would have changed into leggings and a not-quite-so-tight T-shirt by then, had it not been for the desk nap. At least that was what she tried to tell herself, but she knew there was more to it than that. Although she'd been kicked out on her ass, she wasn't ready to let go of her night with Whitney. It seemed silly to think that an old T-shirt and shorts would keep them connected, but that was how it felt to Brie. She had something tangible. Something to prove to herself that it had actually happened. She could still feel the softness of Whitney's lips. They'd kissed gently and forcefully and everything in between. Whitney's kiss had sent Brie to places she'd never been before. Euphoric places. The first kiss came as a shock, but even that kiss was amazing.

Brie wished she could take back the flippant joke she'd made about leaving sex out of her interview. Where would she be right now if she hadn't said it? Would she have Whitney's phone number? Would they have made future plans to meet for lunch? Her heart ached from the loss of not ever knowing if there could've been more between them.

"Gabriela, you're a million miles away."

Brie took in a deep breath to perk herself up and forced a smile. "Sorry. I think I need that coffee more than you do." She sat at her kitchen table.

Her mom looked over her shoulder and narrowed her eyes. "Since when do you wear Adidas? I thought you and your brother were both skater brand kids."

"That was back when I idolized my older brother and wanted to do everything he did, including but not limited to kissing all of his girlfriends."

Her mom laughed. "I remember. But I'll never understand why you both make that big brother, little sister distinction when you were delivered by C-section."

Relieved that she'd successfully changed the subject, Brie waved the comment off. "Oh, you know how Dad claims the doctor pulled Adam out first, so of course he uses that information to try to rule my life and pretend he's wiser than me."

"Five minutes wiser?"

"Right? Tell Adam that, please."

Her mom pushed the start button on the coffee maker and turned. She leaned against the counter with her arms folded and eyebrows raised. She looked Brie up and down and said, "Well?"

Okay. Apparently, the subject of Brie's outfit had not been forgotten. Brie blushed under her scrutiny. She felt like she was back in her childhood home on a Saturday morning after she'd broken curfew the night before. But she wasn't sixteen anymore, and it was her kitchen, and her apartment, and so what if she *wasn't* wearing her own clothes? She reminded herself that her sex life wasn't anyone else's business. And then, in keeping with their longstanding tradition, she crumbled under the weight of the mom look that was being levied upon her. Brie threw her hands in the air. "Okay, fine. These aren't my clothes."

"Of course not. I knew that the second you opened the door because you never wear purple. And now that we've gotten the obvious out of the way, who is she, and how long have you been seeing her without telling me?"

"Not long." Brie leaned over and let her forehead hit the table with a thud. It was moments like these that she wished her parents were still married. Her dad would've said something like, "Jade, stop harassing our children. They're old enough to make their own decisions and suffer the consequences if need be." He was the kind of father who would let his five-year-old twins roam the beach while he surfed, and when something bad happened, like one of them getting stung by a jellyfish, he'd say, "Now you know not to touch a jellyfish." The fact that they might not have made it to an old enough age to make relationship mistakes was beside the point.

Her parents were two young beach bums when a surprise pregnancy threw them into a quickie marriage that left them raising twins when they were still kids themselves. It was only thanks to their mother's trust fund that they had food on the table when they were young. Brie loved her dad, but she knew which one of her parents had been a parent 24/7. For that, she not only loved her mom, she also admired her and tried to show her the respect she deserved. Which meant telling her the truth. Most of the time.

This was not one of those times. "It was nothing. It meant

nothing. It's not a big deal, okay?" Oh God. Did she just tell her mother she had meaningless sex? How was that better than saying it actually meant something but wouldn't go anywhere?

Her mom poured the coffee and sat at the table. She stared at Brie with her suspicious brown eyes. Studied her. The teenager in Brie wanted to get up in a huff and storm off to her bedroom while yelling down the hall to be left alone. But that being-an-adult thing kept her in her chair. Also, she knew it wouldn't work. She took a sip of coffee and changed the subject. "The new girl Adam's seeing seems nice. I bet her prom is going to be a blast."

"Who hooks up on a Tuesday night?"

Usually jokes about Adam's barely twenty-something girlfriend got a bit more mileage, but it seemed that her mom's supernatural gift for knowing the truth before Brie could even tell it hadn't changed. "Someone who wasn't there to hook up." She cringed at her own response. "I was there for work."

Her mom leaned in and said, "Okay, *Brie on Books*. I'm all ears."

Brie shook her head. "Mom, I can't."

"Gabriela, I'm your mother. I know when you're distraught, and I'm not leaving here until I know that you'll be okay. Just give me the short version. The before and after. Lord knows I don't want to know about the during."

Brie's emotions welled up. She was distraught. *Because you don't just have sex with Whitney Ainsworth and get kicked out afterward and come out unscathed.* And then there was the book review, which she knew she shouldn't feel guilty about, but it killed her to think about Whitney reading it. She took a breath and said, "I didn't realize that the person I slept with didn't know who I was, and once she figured it out…well, I'm pretty sure she'll hate me forever."

Much to Brie's surprise, her mom had to suppress a giggle. "Mom, it's not funny."

Her mom cleared her throat. "Sorry, but the way you said it in such a foreboding tone made me feel like we should go to a commercial. You were really channeling your inner Lacey Matthews there."

Brie huffed. "My life is not one of your soap operas, Mom."

"No, it's the lesbian version where there are no unwanted pregnancies but apparently lots of sleeping with the enemy. So spill."

"Well, I'm glad you find it entertaining. I just feel humiliated and lovesick."

Her mom's expression turned back to one of concern. "Lovesick? Tell me about her."

Brie sighed and picked up her phone. A picture could speak a thousand words, as they said, so she googled Whitney and handed the phone to her mom. "She's one of my favorite authors. When I saw that she was giving a talk at a conference near LA, I thought maybe I could get an interview. But then, things went south."

Her mom snorted. "I'll say."

Brie covered her eyes with her hands. "Oh my God, Mom. Please don't make sex jokes."

Her mom kept scrolling, most likely looking at images of Whitney with her ex-wife on the red carpet. Whitney sailing a boat. Whitney and Reece on the cover of *People*, pre-breakup. A fuzzy photo of Reece kissing her new girlfriend in the grocery store. It was all there for everyone to gossip about over their morning coffee.

"Honey, why do you think this woman hates you?"

"I gave her last book a bad review a while ago, and it went viral. But I guess Whitney didn't know who I was before we, you know."

Her mom put her hands up. "Oh, I know."

"I'd posted the review right before Whitney's marriage blew up, and now she's doing these dumb speaking engagements, which made me think she's not writing anymore, and I can't help but think my review played a part in that."

Her mom set the phone down and said, "Honey, I hate to burst your bubble, but someone this famous isn't going to blink at a review from you, no matter how viral it went. I think it's far more likely that losing her wife to a high-powered Hollywood jackass like Kat Blumenthal would give her a bad case of writer's block."

Brie furrowed her brow. "Do you know Kat Blumenthal?"

"Her parents were in my parents' group of friends. They had a lot of barbecues at their house. She had more than a few girlfriends. She even chased after me for a few weeks."

Brie gasped. "What the hell, Mom? You aren't even gay."

"Not to mention I was seventeen to her twelve." Her mom shrugged. "Whether someone was gay or not never stopped Kat. She liked the chase. Sounds like she still does. And trust me when I tell you that having another notch in her belt named Reece Ainsworth is something she'll crow about for years. The woman is insufferable."

Brie leaned back in her chair and folded her arms. The more she thought about it, the more she realized her mom was probably right. "I don't know what I was thinking. Whitney probably never gave my review a second thought."

"But that still doesn't explain this." Her mom waved her hand up and down Brie's body. "And if I'm reading the tea leaves right, which I always do, this famous author gave my beautiful daughter a lot more than an interview last night. Is that what you're telling me?"

Brie slapped her hands over her eyes again. Why hadn't she changed clothes the second she'd walked in the door? "No. Uh-uh. Not talking about that part."

"Take your hands from your eyes. You know you can't hide from me. I'm the one who brought up the L-word, remember?"

Brie lowered her hands. "Most humiliating day of my life, up until now."

"Oh, come on. You were such a cute little lesbian, crushing on all those cheerleaders and soccer players."

"Let's not forget the tuba player."

Her mom burst out laughing. "Oh, I forgot about her. What was she, six-foot-five in bare feet?"

"She was one tall drink of water," Brie said with a nod. "And as straight as she was tall."

Her mom's expression sobered. She moved her coffee to the side and leaned in closer. "Let's cut to the chase. You had shallow, superficial sex with Whitney Ainsworth last night, didn't you?"

Brie cringed on the inside. She almost thanked her mom for saying it out loud so she wouldn't have to. "Yes," she admitted. "But it felt neither shallow nor superficial. At least to me, anyway."

"I see." Her mom drummed her fingernails on the table, a sure sign that she was trying to maintain her composure. "Will anything come of it?" she asked.

"I'm not sure…" Brie stopped herself and shook her head. The cold hard truth was that last night would be nothing but a horrible, regretful blip in Whitney's life that she'd try hard to forget. "No," she said. "But it still wasn't superficial."

"Right. An intense, profound one-night stand with some famous author who has a very famous wife."

"Ex-wife," Brie corrected.

Her mom paused for a moment. Long enough for Brie's emotions to get the better of her again. She blinked back a few tears. Maybe the whole thing was something she should try to forget about too. Just wipe it from her mind. Easier said than done when she could still hear Whitney's voice in her head and see her smile. Brie had seen some happiness there before things turned ugly. That, she wanted to hang on to forever. She wiped her eyes and said, "Sorry. I'm just feeling a bit tired and overwhelmed right now."

Her mom's expression darkened. "You need to understand that these people are nothing but shallow and superficial. Their whole job is to make you think they're something they're not." Her mom reached for her hand. "Baby, I've fought hard to keep you and Adam away from that scene. It's like a vampire that sucks you dry before you even know you've been bitten. Trust me, I know."

"Whitney isn't Hollywood. Her ex-wife was. Is. But Whitney is just an author who spends her time in a writing cabin back east somewhere."

"Which is exactly what you should be doing instead of barely making a living off that blog. When was the last time you worked on your manuscript? Oh, and remind me, what was that degree we paid for?"

Brie sighed. She should've known this was coming. "An MFA. You know that, Mom."

"An MFA? What does that stand for again?"

"Master of Fine Arts." Brie said it as if she'd said it a thousand times before. Because she had.

"In what again?"

"Literary Arts."

"From where?"

"Brown, Mom. How many times do we have to do this?"

"As many times as it takes. We didn't pay for an MFA so *Brie* could review other people's books. We did it for Gabriela. Because we could see potential in all of those short stories she used to write, which leads me to what I wanted to discuss with you over coffee. I've reserved the beach house for one month. Some of the family might complain, but tough for them. I only let them use it out of the goodness of my heart anyway." She reached across the table for Brie's hand. "Consider it your own writing cabin and finish that book you've been working on."

Brie sat a little bit straighter. "Like, all by myself? Just me? For a whole month?"

"I'll make sure your brother stays away, if that's what you're worried about."

It was unheard of. The beach house in Malibu her mother had inherited was strictly for family gatherings. The only person who ever stayed there all alone was Jade Talbot. Brie wanted to burst into tears and jump with joy at the same time. It was exactly what she needed, right when she needed it. "Mom, I don't know what to say."

Her mom got up and pulled Brie into one of those hugs she could never break free from. "Say you'll make the best of it, honey. Tell me you'll find inspiration in the ocean, the sand, the salty air, the magnificent sunsets."

"Have you seen my apartment?" Brie said with a giggle.

"Yes. We're standing in it. Enough said."

Her mom let go and emptied her coffee cup in the sink. "Mom," Brie said. "Don't worry about this thing with Whitney Ainsworth. I'm sure she's forgotten all about me by now."

Her mom stepped up to her and placed her hands on her cheeks. "You're a beautiful, smart woman who I refuse to believe is so easily forgotten. But if that has happened, if she is that shallow, please don't take it personally. Consider it a bullet dodged."

"Right," Brie said through mom-created fish lips. "Bullet dodged."

❖

Whitney threw her head back against the seat's headrest. "What the hell was I thinking letting a total stranger into my room?"

"She's nothing." Liz slowed at a red light and grabbed her phone from the cup holder. She brought it to life and tossed it to Whitney. Brie's website was already up in her phone's browser. "I mean, look at that logo. A piece of cheese sitting atop a stack of books?"

"Did you just say 'atop'?" Whitney lifted her head and peered at Liz's phone. "*Brie on Books*, Liz. Don't you get it?"

"She's had this blog since she was sixteen. Let's hope that's when she designed her logo, and like my mother who decorated her bedroom in 1980's Laura Ashley, decided that it would never go out of style."

"Not everyone has a minor in graphic design," Whitney said. "I've seen worse logos." Sure, it was kind of cheesy, but it was sort of quaint too. Quirky was a better word. She wondered if Brie had quirks that she'd find endearing or if they'd drive her crazy. Unfortunately, she'd never know.

"Oh, it's so bad, I want to enter it into a terrible logo contest," Liz snapped "And why are you defending that sneaky little snake? Was the sex really that good?"

"I'm just saying that you don't have to demonize her to make me feel better."

Liz's eyes widened. "Okay, I realize you're still on an emotional high from all the applause and laughter you just received in that room, but you need to understand that you actually did sleep with the devil."

"And you need to understand you actually sent the devil to my room without so much as a two-second Google search."

"Touché. And I am sorry. We didn't exactly have a protocol established for this, you know? Next time—"

"Next time? Are you out of your mind?" Whitney's voice creeped up a good three octaves.

"Relax, Whit. Only dogs can hear you. If I may finish, I was going to say, next time, we'll forgo the pretty ladies and just leave it at margaritas and guacamole."

"Good." Whitney put her head back again and closed her eyes. Last night had been a big, sexual high, only to end up at the emotional equivalent of the bottom of the Grand Canyon, followed by what turned out to be one of her best events to date. She'd never signed so many autographs or posed for so many selfies. She'd try to focus on that instead of the Night of Many Regrets.

Which could also be called the Night of Many Orgasms. *What a way to go.* Because if she stripped everything else away and reminisced on those few hours before she'd known who Gabriela really was, well, that could be some time well spent. Possibly while riding home in Liz's car, if her agent would shut the hell up for five minutes.

"We'll ruin her," Liz said. "She's finished."

Whitney sighed. "Leave it alone, Liz. I don't want to finish anyone. I just want to forget it ever happened and focus on my writing."

Liz gaped at her. "I'm sorry. You want to focus on your what?"

"You heard me." Whitney shrugged as if it was no big deal. "I may have jotted down some thoughts earlier."

Liz took her hands off the wheel and gave a loud yet indecipherable cheer. "Oh, sweet Jesus, I was right. You just needed to get laid."

"Oh, my God. Sleeping with the cheese blogger—no matter how hot she is—is not going to help me write. I just started fleshing out ideas I already had, and watch the road. Your light is green."

"Oh please. What ideas?"

"It's a new book about a literary agent who becomes tortured by her own ego. The ego actually takes on a life of its own and has little ego children that trap her in a town house in the Valley and force her to wear synthetic fibers and eat takeout from chain restaurants. It's horrifying."

Liz gave her a side-eye. "Wow. You're hilarious post sex."

"Just get us home already. I'm going to rest my eyes."

Whitney would never admit it, but Liz was probably right. After the event, she'd gone back to her room with all kinds of thoughts running through her head that she had to get down on paper before she forgot them. That hadn't happened in a long time. In fact, she couldn't remember the last time she'd felt an urgency to open her laptop. Maybe her career wasn't over after all.

CHAPTER FIVE

B rie had nothing to loosen up her dry throat. She clenched her hands into fists to keep them from shaking. Her body sent out warning signals, but she ignored them and stayed right where she was. It would turn out to be a colossal mistake. She knew it before she'd gotten on the plane. She'd known it when she ordered a drink from the flight attendant and had a pleasant chat with the woman sitting next to her, as if being on that plane, headed to this particular city, was the most normal thing in the world.

When she told the cab driver where to take her, she decided it was the kind of mistake that could get her thrown out on her ass by security. She should've worn better clothes for that. Something with a little more padding. The Sears Toughskins the kids in commercials wore back in the day would survive far better than distressed jeans.

There would probably be shouting. And humiliation. Much like the first time she'd met Whitney Ainsworth, sans the hot sex, of course. Oh, and the shouting would be in public this time. So yeah, total humiliation was on the docket. There wasn't really an outfit for that. The only thing she could wear that could silence Whitney long enough for Brie to say what she had to say was nothing. Nudity might stun her into silence. But then it was back to being thrown out on her ass, or more likely, arrested. Nude and handcuffed only worked in the bedroom.

Brie heard the final applause and watched the women's conference attendees file out of the ballroom. She hoped they'd all be well on their way and out of earshot by the time Whitney spotted her, in case there was some of the aforementioned shouting.

Whitney stopped dead in her tracks when their eyes met. Brie's heart took a tumble and rumbled around with the butterflies in her stomach. She couldn't remember where she'd left all of her well-rehearsed words. She felt like an adoring fan waiting for an autograph from her favorite author, which was exactly who she was before that fateful night. Sure, she was disappointed in Whitney's last book, but she was still a fan.

Whitney looked as gorgeous as ever in her navy-blue pants and white silk blouse. Her hair was a bit shorter, hanging just below her shoulders. And much to Brie's relief, Liz wasn't with her. "Whitney, I—" Before she could finish, Whitney made an abrupt turn and walked away.

Should she follow and risk a big scene? She'd come this far. She had to at least try. She caught up and walked beside her. Unfortunately, she got caught up in the scent of her perfume and forgot how to speak. Again. And not just her scent, but also, they'd never walked side by side like this before. Brie imagined herself reaching for Whitney's hand. Placing a hand on her back. Whispering something in her ear that would make her smile.

"You're stalking me now?"

"No," Brie said. "Not stalking."

"We're in fucking Cincinnati," Whitney snapped back. "That's a long way from LA, which means you're either a stalker or a really big Bengals fan." She hit the elevator button several times.

"Honestly, I'd rather you think I was a stalker than a Bengals fan." Brie's smile wasn't returned. In fact, Whitney's expression seemed to harden even more. "All joking aside—"

Whitney put up a hand. "Stop. Just tell me what you're doing here. And don't tell me you just happened to be in the area, because like I said—"

"Fucking Cincinnati. Got it." This was going about as well as Brie thought it would. Why did she have to get so tongue-tied and make stupid jokes? She wished she could just blurt out the truth like they did in all those silly rom-coms. Just pour her heart out right there by the elevators. *I'm just a blogger, standing in front of an author.* Unfortunately, what worked in the movies rarely worked in real life. No, in real life, bystanders didn't swoon at the girl who flew all the way to Cincinnati—uninvited—to explain herself. In real life, they called for backup, hence the need for those Toughskins.

Brie held the elevator door open and said, "Give me five minutes of your time and I promise I'll be out of your life forever."

"Oh, but I've lost my mind, remember? I hate my fans, and I write shitty books."

"I never said it was shitty. I said it was timid."

Whitney stepped into the elevator. "This coming from Cheese Logo Girl. Well, this might surprise you, Brie on Books, but I really don't give a damn what you think of my books or anyone else's, so please just leave me alone."

"Is this what you look like when you don't care?" Brie slid between the doors just before they closed. Whitney's perfume assaulted her senses again and sent her right back to their first kiss.

"No," Whitney said with a firm shake of her head. "This is what I look like when my stalker corners me in an elevator."

The elevator hadn't moved, most likely because no buttons had been pushed. The door opened, and a family barged in. Two beleaguered-looking parents with two toddlers in strollers filled the space. Whitney pushed her way past them and escaped the elevator with ease. Brie had a harder time getting past the group, but she managed to get out and follow her to the lobby.

"Let me buy you a drink, Whit. Please." Brie knew she sounded desperate, but she needed to set the record straight. She needed to explain her review, or more specifically, she needed to explain that she had no part in the review taking on a life of its own. How she'd been horrified when people had started using her words to dump on Whitney. And she needed Whitney to know why she had been in the bar that night.

Whitney turned back and shot her a glare. "I'm not Whit. You're not Brie. And we…" She waved a hand between them. "Are definitely not friends. Or anything else. Got it?" She turned on her heel and carried on down the long hallway.

The words stung. She wanted to shout something like, "Hey, don't be so goddamned rude," but decided to catch up to her instead. "Just five minutes and then I'll leave, I swear."

"Yeah, you keep saying that. It's a shame you didn't have more to say before you decided to seduce me."

"It's a shame your agent wasn't more forthright with me," Brie snapped back. "She could've used words like, she wants to fuck, not talk."

"Oh, would that have changed your decision? Because it sure felt like you were just as into it as I was."

Brie grabbed Whitney's arm and stopped. "Look, we can fight this out and leave each other bloody, or we can have a civilized conversation over a glass of wine where you can admit that you didn't really want to know who I was, and I'll admit that for me, I walked in expecting to get an interview. Instead, I got more than I ever could have imagined, and I'd really like to know if there's anywhere else for us to go." She let go of her arm. "Sorry I grabbed you like that."

Brie should've backed away to give Whitney a little bit of breathing room, but she stayed right there in her personal space. She'd let go of her arm, but it would've been so easy to take her hand and intertwine their fingers. So easy to whisper, "God, you're beautiful. Mind if I stay right here forever?" She tried to hold Whitney's stare, but the need to take everything in and commit it to memory overwhelmed her. She focused on those soft, kissable lips first. Then the neck she'd spent quite a bit of time on. And the jawline she'd run her tongue across until she'd found a sensitive ear. Given the chance, she'd whisper all kinds of sweet nothings, except they'd mean everything. She'd apologize and compliment and of course, try to seduce.

Her eyes met Whitney's again, and the hard glare brought her firmly back to the present. "I'm already bloody," she said before she walked away.

Despite the fact that Whitney went into the hotel bar, Brie felt increasingly sure that they would not share a bottle of wine or anything else. Ever. Her brisk saunter, and Brie had to admit, she had a great saunter, was saying "Fuck the fuck right off, you fucking fucker." Or something along those lines.

The prickly heat of shame worked its way up Brie's neck. How could she have possibly thought this was a good idea? She didn't. She'd known it was a terrible plan, and she'd gotten on that plane anyway. Her throat tightened, adding to her urge to walk away before she broke down in tears and made a bigger ass out of herself than she already had. But she hadn't been kicked out yet, and until she was, she'd keep trying.

She followed until the two of them stood at the bar. That meant there would be plenty of witnesses for whatever happened next. *Great, Brie. Just great.*

She decided to leave a little space between them. Maybe stay out of punching range. Not that she thought Whitney was the violent type. Far from it. Her touch was tender. Her fingers soft and nimble. Still, she sat two stools away.

Whitney did a double take and said, "Jesus Christ, you don't give up. Are you going to become my own personal groupie and follow me from city to city? Wait. Is there a tattoo I should know about?"

Brie didn't have any tattoos, but she considered the many options. She could put the cover of the first Piper Kane book on her shoulder. Or just the initials PK on her arm, maybe etched into the side of a smoking gun. How funny would it be if she were able to pull up her sleeve and reveal a super-fan tattoo? Not funny at all under the current circumstances, she decided.

The bartender set a napkin in front of each of them and said, "Hi, I'm Ian. What can I get for you ladies?"

"It's only me," Whitney said. "She was just leaving." She pointed behind him at a bottle of wine. "I'll have a glass of the pinot."

"Any appetizers?"

"No thanks," she said.

"Are you sure? The brie is especially good today. Nice and mellow. Melts in your mouth."

Brie suppressed a grin. Whitney remained perfectly still. Her gaze never left Ian. "Of course it is."

"It'd go great with that pinot, and we serve it with rustic bread and dried fruit. I promise you can't go wrong with the brie."

Whitney sighed and shook her head. "Sure, why not." Her eyes lit up, and she turned to Brie. "That's it, isn't it? You had your cheesy logo tattooed on your ass, and that's why you haven't updated it."

Another comment about her logo? Brie had no idea where

this was coming from, but there was no way she'd leave the ass comment unaddressed. "If I'm remembering correctly, you've seen my ass up close and personal."

"Can't say I remember a thing about it."

Brie wasn't buying it. Whitney continued to hold her stare. One of them would have to break first. In the meantime, she'd take in Whitney's scent for a few more seconds. She'd imagine herself leaning in for a kiss. She'd feel those soft lips on hers again and rest her hand on the bar to steady herself because that kiss would surely make her lose her balance.

Brie swallowed hard and said, "Are you saying you'd like a refresher, Whitney? It's not what I came here for, but that's never stopped you."

When Whitney replied, "Not even if you were the last person on earth and your ass was made of candy," Brie's heart felt the blow.

She felt it best to not say another word. What she needed to do was tuck her tail between her legs and leave. Just walk out and never, ever lay eyes on Whitney Ainsworth again. Before she made it to the door, she heard Whitney say, "See you in San Francisco." She turned back around but Whitney wasn't looking at her. Had she said it to her or someone else? Brie decided to let it go and walked out.

❖

Brie slammed her laptop shut when her dad walked into the office. She knew Whitney's speaking schedule by heart, but she wanted to check it one more time. San Francisco was next, and she was sure it was Whitney who had shouted, "See you in San Francisco," in the bar in Cincinnati. But what had she meant when she'd said it? Was she implying that Brie would stalk her at her next event too, or did she actually want her to be there? If she was honest with herself, she'd realize the latter option was true and drop it. She conjured up a smile and said, "Hey, Dad."

He raised an eyebrow. "I thought only your brother watched porn during working hours."

"Dad, that's disgusting." Brie wrinkled her nose. "He doesn't, does he?"

"I certainly hope not." Her dad chuckled at his own joke. "Have you seen him? I have the new artwork."

"I haven't," Brie said. "But I actually wanted to talk to you about artwork, logos, specifically. Mine is kind of outdated." She could tell by her dad's stunned expression that he wasn't sure what to say. She sighed. "Go ahead and say it. It's cheesy."

"Pun intended?"

"Yeah, yeah."

"I remember how proud you were when you presented it to me and your mom."

"You laughed behind my back, didn't you?"

"Honey, we were mostly proud of your initiative. Any laughter was short-lived." He set the portfolio he was carrying on her desk and sat in the chair across from her. "You were sixteen, and you wanted to start a book blog before anyone knew what that was. The fact that you were worried about how it looked told me I had raised a savvy entrepreneur. None of your friends had logos in high school, did they?"

Brie tapped her chin while she thought back on her high school years. "I don't think so, but one of them created a special little marking to add to her tattoo for each guy she slept with. Does that count?"

"Have I ever told you how thrilled I am that you're a lesbian?"

Brie swooned. "More times than I can count, Dad. And I love you for it."

All those years in the sun had caught up with him, so his laugh lines jumped out when he smiled. She'd always loved that he was so quick with a smile or a laugh. "The friend with the tattoo thing. You just made that up on the fly, right?"

Brie flashed a mischievous grin and shrugged. It was her dad's turn to think back fifteen years. With sudden force, he slapped his knee and said, "Cyndi. It was your friend, Cyndi, wasn't it?"

"You know I can't tell on my friends. Now, can we get back to the point?"

"Of course, baby." He paused. "What was the point?"

In addition to all of his years spent in the sun and surf, he'd smoked more than his share of weed. It often showed. "We were talking about my logo."

"Right. Brie on Cheese." He gave her a wink, letting her know he was just messing with her. "I could have the agency take a whack at it. It's the least they can do."

"I don't know. That might be a little more involved than I'm looking for."

For the most part, Brie had kept quiet about her blog. Her family knew it was out there, but they never pressed her about it, and it was rare for them to discuss its contents. Her parents knew she didn't necessarily want them reading it since she posted her personal thoughts there in the form of short stories and, every once in a while, a journal entry or two.

She'd stayed fairly anonymous to her followers as well. She never posted photos of herself, and people knew Brie but not Gabriela Talbot. What her parents definitely did not know was that her revenue from the site had grown quite a bit. Enough that she'd been able to support herself and save a bit each month too.

After Whitney's comment about her logo, Brie hadn't stopped thinking about it. As low-key as she liked to keep *Brie on Books*, she knew a new look was in order. It was time to up her game with a redesign.

"Speaking of logos, check these out." Her dad opened a folder, revealing several new design samples for his brand. "This one would look great on a snapback, don't you think?"

"Wow. These are dope, Dad."

Her dad's custom surf shop, Ratty Boards, had been a small, one-man enterprise up until the early 2000s. Jake Talbot had started by working out of their garage making custom surfboards. After he'd opened a surf shop on the beach, he'd eventually made a small profit on snacks, beach towels, and sunblock for ill-prepared beachgoers. The tourists loved his Ratty Boards T-shirts and hats too. By the time the store became a recurring location for the supremely cheesy yet long-running lifeguard drama *Guard Hard*, Ratty Boards had developed a solid reputation. All of that changed when his landlord sold out, and their section of beach was developed into the oceanside equivalent of a strip mall.

The loss of the store had been hard on Brie and her brother. They loved being beach babies, as her mom liked to call them. And having the store right there on the beach made it feel almost like they lived there. When she was quite young, Brie's big aspiration in life was to one day work behind the register. Once she realized she was gay, she figured her desire to work there had everything to do with all the bikini-clad women who frequented the store and nothing to do with what her dad called her "great work ethic."

Although it didn't seem like it at the time, losing the store was actually a blessing in disguise because it forced her dad to go completely online. He'd put almost no effort into his online presence up to that point, but the show and his "killer merch," as he called it, had created some pent-up demand. Fast-forward ten years and his custom boards were sold all over the world now. Along with branded surf and skate gear.

The name came from a guy Brie would never forget. She and Adam must have been about eight or nine when her dad epically failed at getting them to school one day. They'd made it all the way to the drop-off line when he'd said, "Hey kids, wanna get out of here? What do you say we go have some fun?"

Brie remembered Adam cheering from the back seat while she'd informed him that it was a school day, and she was pretty sure it was the law for her to be there, and also, she had a report due on James Buchanan.

He was already turning the wheel to ease the car out of line when he said, "It's only a school day if you're in school. Also, it's one hundred percent legal to play hooky if you're with your pops, and I promise you, James Buchanan will still be dead tomorrow."

And that was how they'd ended up at the beach together, getting ready to test out one of his early prototypes. The guy who'd named the company was just some tourist who'd felt the need to comment on the board. Comment wasn't really the right word. The guy had totally insulted and disparaged her dad by telling him his board looked like a ratty piece of shit. Brie had tried to kick sand in the asshole's face, but her dad had held her back and said, "That's a sick name for a surfboard." And Ratty Boards was born.

Even now, Brie liked to imagine that guy sitting in his mediocre house in some nondescript suburb nowhere near the beach. His wife had left him, and he was drinking cheap beer while he watched *Guard Hard* to ogle the women. She pictured a wave of recognition cross his face when Ratty Boards showed up in that same stretch of beach in the title sequence. In Brie's fantasy, Tourist Tom felt jealous and defeated but didn't know exactly why. She knew how unlikely it was that he'd pieced it all together, but she'd bet money on the lonely guy with cheap beer part of the story.

Although Brie's interest in surfing had waned years ago, she still liked working for her dad part-time in the office, even if it was nowhere near the beach. When she'd been fresh out of college, she'd needed the income. She'd stayed because, well, she still needed the income, and it broke up the solitude of writing about books and not finishing her own manuscript. It helped that she genuinely liked being around her dad and brother.

"Put a mark by the designs you like best," her dad said. "We all get a say in this, including your mother."

"Because she knows what surfer dudes like in their board art?"

"Because she's still a silent partner. And because I value her opinion when it comes to design."

Brie smirked. "Wow, Dad. Did it hurt to say that?"

"More than you'll ever know," he said with a wrinkle-eyed wink.

He looked older than his fifty years. His straw-colored hair had some gray mixed in with it now, but it was his tanned skin that aged him. Thousands of hours on a surfboard would do that to a body.

He leaned back and put his feet up on Brie's desk. Back in the day, he'd let his flip-flops wear down to almost nothing before he'd buy a new pair. Now that he had his own line of them, he wanted to have "good sales feet," as he called it.

Brie leaned forward and took a closer look. "Oh my God, Dad, did you get a pedi?"

"I've been getting them for over a year now. You just haven't noticed. If you're wondering if that hurt my feelings, yeah, maybe a little."

"You're full of shit."

"Are you just noticing that now too?"

Brie sat up straight and eyed him. Something about his appearance seemed different. Tidier, maybe? Not that her dad was a slob, just casual. Board shorts, T-shirts, flip-flops, and a Hawaiian shirt for dressier events. That was the extent of his wardrobe. Oh, and zip-up hoodies and Vans if it was cold outside.

She noticed that the little tuft of hair that usually peeked out from under his shirt collar wasn't there. Was he—*sweet Jesus, don't let it be so*—shaving his body? "Oh, dear God, you're manscaping." Brie slapped her hands over her eyes. "If you're dating someone, please don't tell me. I can't deal with that right now."

"I know the feeling. It's certainly the last thing I want to know about you," he said. "But because I'm your father, here goes. Jade called me. She said I should talk to you."

Brie uncovered her eyes. "About what?"

"She said you'd tell me."

This was getting way out of both of their comfort zones. They didn't talk about heavy stuff. She had her mom for that. Her mom, who had to know everything about everything. She wouldn't be able to deal if her dad suddenly, without any warning, decided to follow suit due to a mid-life crisis or something. And why couldn't her mom keep her mouth shut? It was humiliating on so many levels, including the *Dad doesn't need to know about my sex life* level.

"Why do you and Mom still have to talk to each other?" she asked, her voice raised an octave. "And why is everyone in this family up in everyone else's business? It's fine if we're not all that close. Lots of families do it. I think we should look into it."

"Ha ha. Very funny. Look, you and Adam are adults. You're way more grown-up than I was at thirty, so I'm not going to tell you how to live your life, but maybe hooking up with someone you don't know isn't the best idea."

Brie wanted to slide off her chair and disappear under the desk. She wanted to stomp off to her bedroom and slam the door shut and shout, "I knew I couldn't trust you, Mom."

She hated it when her mom tried to force her dad to be a more serious father. It had all felt so disingenuous when she was a kid, and it didn't feel that much different now. He was the fun one. The one who let her avoid serious stuff like feelings. And school. "I can't believe she told you."

"Honey, you know your mom is hell-bent on keeping you and Adam away from the Hollywood life she grew up in"

"Whitney is an author. She's not a fake Hollywood type like some of Mom's friends." As much as Brie's mom loathed the industry scene, she still had plenty of acquaintances who air-kissed and casually referred to celebrities by their first names in everyday conversation. With rare exceptions, Brie had always felt like the only thing that mattered to these people was what their "friends" could do for them at any given moment. Loyalty was fleeting, to say the least.

He put up his hands. "You know I don't want in on any part of this, but I also don't want to see my baby hurting. And I certainly don't want your mother thinking I'm a bad father."

"You're not a bad father." Brie smirked. "But you did surprise the hell out of me with that Cyndi reference. I had no idea you even knew who my friends were back in the day."

"I knew who they were. I just get a bad rap because your mom had full dossiers on your entire class and couldn't understand why I didn't need to know who Cyndi's father dated before he married her mother." He sighed. "Just tell your old dad that everything is okay, and I'll drop it."

"I'm fine," Brie said. "Mom should worry about Adam, not me. He's the one with the rugged movie star profile and the bleached white teeth."

"Oh geez, don't say that too loud, or I'll lose my best spokesmodel."

"Heard it." Adam poked his head in the office. "And for the hundredth time, I am a spokesperson who happens to be a model." He pointed at Brie. "Breezy, my office. Now."

Brie did her best to look aghast. "I don't take orders from you." She turned back to her dad. "I don't take orders from him. Never have, never will. We're clear on that, right?"

Her dad motioned with his head. "Go talk to your brother. Tell him he looks handsome today. He loves that crap."

Brie rolled her eyes. "Somehow, you managed to spawn a metrosexual and a homosexual. You must be so proud."

"Who knew my Ridgemont High sperm were such over-achievers."

"Dad! Ew. Enough with the porn and sperm talk." She got up and started down the hall toward Adam's office. She smiled when she heard her dad chuckle behind her. He might not have been the perfect father, but he'd always been honest with them. And he was probably the kindest man Brie had ever known. Kind, gentle, nonjudgmental. She paused at Adam's door and glanced back down the hall. She wasn't wrong in her assessment. Her dad had upped his grooming game. Her first instinct was to figure out why. Would she have to watch her dad canoodle with his new lady? Would she eventually have a stepmom to contend with? That felt weird.

He got up and stopped short when he saw her still standing there. "Everything okay?"

She gave him a nod. She'd also have to give him the same respect he'd just given her by not digging into his private life before he was ready to talk about it. "Love you, Dad." She blew him a kiss. He caught it and put it in his pocket like he'd done a thousand times before.

She turned her attention to Adam and plopped down in a chair. "You look like shit. Rough night?"

Of course, Adam never looked like shit. While Brie's dad lived in shorts and flip-flops, Adam was Mr. Banana Republic in his slim-fit gray trousers and suede loafers. The baby blue glasses complemented his eyes, but no way would she ever tell him that. He had enough women fawning over him. He certainly didn't need Brie's help.

"It's amazing how you just went from sugar sweet daughter to mean little sister in under a second," he said. "It must be a new record."

"You'd be surprised how quickly I can get up and leave too."

"Fine. I'll be quick. She's ten years older than you."

Brie tilted her head. "Who?"

"And that's not even the worst thing, according to Mom."

Was somebody joking? Did Brie's mom spend all day on the phone? Or maybe she conferenced both Brie's dad and brother in so she could share the sordid details more efficiently. Good thing Brie's grandma had passed, or she'd hear about it too, no doubt.

"Well, thank God you never get laid, Adam. I don't have time for the mandatory family meetings. Also, who cut your hair? She missed a spot."

Adam glanced at his watch. That was another thing about him, he always had an exquisite watch on his wrist. Today it was the Tag Heuer Formula One with the navy-blue wristband. Also, his haircut was perfect, and he knew it.

He leaned forward, and in an ardent tone, he said, "Do you want to know what the worst thing is?"

"Maybe that my family has been discussing my love life behind my back?"

Adam leaned back and laughed. "I'm just messing with you, Breezy. But it did occur to me that I haven't been the best older brother to you." He put up a finger. "And before you decide to declare today a national holiday, let me teach you something, even though it's kinda too late." He cleared his throat. "Okay, here goes." He covered his mouth in an obvious attempt to suppress his laughter.

Brie rolled her eyes. "Okay, just say it already."

"When you hook up with someone...don't run home and tell your mother about it." He barely got the words out before he burst into laughter.

Brie shot out of the chair. "Okay, smartass, but just so we're clear, I didn't tell Mom. She guessed."

Adam wiped his eyes dry. "You post songs when you meet someone new. I'll be on the edge of my seat waiting for a Tiffany classic to drop."

He held it together for about two-point-five seconds before he flung his upper body on the desk and did that high-pitched, wheezing giggle that drove Brie crazy. She was about to walk out when she realized what he'd just said. "Wait. You never told me you read my blog."

Adam sat back up and paused before he waved it off with his hand and said, "That cheesy thing? Of course not. I just happened by it last night on my way to something else."

"That's not how the internet works. Like, at all. You have to click a button. You know, the one labelled *it's time to spy on my sister today?*" Brie tilted her head and furrowed her brow at him. "Is your nose getting bigger?"

Brie cringed at the thought of her family reading her blog. It felt intrusive somehow. Besides, she was the only book lover in the family. It wasn't as if they were going there to see her latest review or recommendation. No, Adam's only reason for going there was to spy on her, and that ticked her off.

"Look, Mom is just a little bit concerned about you," Adam said. "Your taste in women has always been questionable."

"My taste in—" Brie stopped. "Wait. You're jealous, aren't you?"

He shook his head. "Brie."

"No, you're jealous that I had mind-blowing sex with someone as beautiful and successful and mature as Whitney Ainsworth, so here's a suggestion, try dating someone over the age of eighteen if you really want to know what that feels like." She got up and pretended to drop the mic before turning and walking out of his office.

"She's twenty-one," Adam shouted. "Skylar is twenty-one."

"Same difference," Brie shouted back. She went back to her desk where she could think about all of this humiliation in peace. All her mother's fretting over it and discussing it with the family was for nothing anyway. Whitney had made it very clear in Cincinnati that she wanted absolutely nothing to do with Brie. Just thinking about Cincinnati made Brie cover her eyes in embarrassment, even though she was alone in the room. Thank God her family would never know about Cincinnati.

CHAPTER SIX

I s someone tailing us?"
Whitney looked over her shoulder. "What are you talking about?"

Liz leaned closer and mumbled out the side of her mouth. "You've been scanning our surroundings ever since we stepped off the elevator. It's probably best if we split up. I'll just duck into that cute little store over there and act like I'm browsing handbags when really, I'll be sizing up the situation and working out an escape route. If the shit hits the fan, I'll pull the car out by the loading dock. Right after I take a gander at that fabulous Balenciaga." She started to veer off toward the bag she had her eye on when Whitney grabbed the strap of her current handbag and pulled her back.

"Liz, your handbag obsession verges on addiction. You know that, right?"

"I've been addicted to worse things in my life. So what gives, Ainsworth? Why the sudden interest in your surroundings?"

Whitney let out a big sigh. Probably too big if she didn't want a lot of questions. "Cheese Wedge."

Liz blinked. "I don't know this code word. Does it mean they've spotted us, so I should kick off my heels and run like hell?"

"Brie. The woman who seduced me."

Liz laughed. "I love the nickname, but honey, she did not seduce you."

"Whatever. Could you please just scan the conference room when we go in and somehow let me know if she's there?"

"Wait." Liz grabbed her arm and stopped. "Are you serious? Why would Cheese Wedge be in San Francisco?"

"I played reverse psychology on her in Cincinnati, but I'm not sure she understood that."

"Okay, back up. She was in fucking Cincinnati?" Liz put her hands out as if she needed to steady herself because the news caused a minor earthquake. Normally, Whitney would consider it an overly dramatic response, but in this case, not so much.

"That's what I said."

"Why the hell was she in fucking Cincinnati?"

"I have no idea. She said she wanted to explain. But I didn't give her a chance. But then, I thought it would be a great idea to shout 'See you in San Francisco' just when I'd finally gotten her to leave fucking Cincinnati."

They'd given the city that thoughtful nickname when they'd discovered they couldn't get a direct flight from LAX at the time they'd needed it and that the conference had been booked at an airport hotel. In their texts, they'd shortened the name to FCOH, adding in the state's abbreviation for no reason whatsoever.

Eventually, Liz pointed out that, given the extracurricular activity that had taken place, the city that really deserved a special name was Fucking Palm Springs, but by then, it was too late. They'd already been to Fucking Cincinnati by way of Charlotte, which, for anyone not keeping track, was not on the way to Cincinnati at all. It was also on that trip that they'd discovered Charlotte's airport code was CLT, which led to such thoughtful texts as, "You know I love some CLT," and, "It's CLT, Whit. They're practically begging you to come."

"Fucking Cincinnati," Liz said in a wistful tone. "The town where we learned that you, Whitney Ainsworth, should never party with members of your audience after a conference."

Whitney shrugged. "I'll admit, getting up on the bar was a bit much."

"You *Coyote Ugly*'d that place. But it was understandable, given that you'd just signed the divorce papers that morning."

Whitney glanced around one more time. "Let me know if you see her."

"Are you joking? I'll call the cops if I see her."

"No, just, you know, lick your lips like a crazy person or something."

Liz stifled a giggle. "Now I really hope she's here."

Whitney wasn't sure what she was hoping for. Was it the sick pleasure she'd derive from rebuffing Brie again that had a small part of her hoping Brie would show up? Or was it something else? Either way, she didn't want Liz to question her motives, so she took her by the arm. "Come on. Let's go so you can buy a handbag for what most of the world pays for a new car."

"Aw, Whit. Thank you for understanding my love language."

Whitney searched her favorite playlists and tapped the play button on the one titled Decompress. She set her phone on the nightstand and picked up the glass of wine she'd poured before her shower. Normally, she would use her post-appearance time to jot down notes about what had gone well and what hadn't, but her notebook sat on the bed next to her, open to an empty page.

It also wasn't like her to let a trip to San Francisco go to waste. Most of her trips to the city could be done in a day, but she almost always scheduled an overnight stay so she and Liz could hit some fabulous restaurant they'd never been to before.

They'd talked about trying to grab seats at the counter at Petit Crenn, but Whitney wasn't up for it. She'd told Liz she was tired and possibly coming down with something. Liz didn't seem to buy it, but she went with it anyway. For an impeccably dressed, image-conscious power agent, Liz was uncommonly willing to go with the flow.

At that particular moment, that probably meant striking up a conversation with an attractive man at the hotel bar. At least this time she wouldn't be sending the stranger up to Whitney's suite like she'd done with Cheese Wedge.

Brie. Again. Whitney couldn't seem to get her out of her mind. She spent entirely too much time thinking about her. Had she been too hard on her? Too rude? Too accusatory? Too unforgiving? Hell, no. Brie was the one who'd written that scathing review on her silly little blog. She knew perfectly well what she'd written before she'd knocked on Whitney's hotel room door that night. How could she have even remotely thought that Whitney would want to sleep with someone who'd ripped her work apart? It made no sense.

Was Brie really that arrogant? Was having a review picked up by *HuffPost* really that good for a blogger's ego? Did she think inspiring a few mean-spirited hashtags meant she had power? Or was she just a garden-variety form of delusional? Maybe she thought they'd have some kind of stimulating discussion about books. Maybe debate the symbolism in *Lord of the Flies* and wax dreamily about Jane Austen characters? But most of all, Brie surely thought Whitney would want to experience some unique insights about the Piper Kane series from the woman who gave the world the genius known as *Brie on Books*.

Confident as Whitney was in her assessment of the situation, she couldn't seem to keep herself from reliving their night together. Flashes of Brie's body would pop into her head at the most random times. Like yesterday, when she'd pushed the button on her coffee maker, and the small freckle on Brie's inner thigh popped into her head. She'd ended up standing there with her eyes closed while the coffee brewed, trying to remember every inch of Brie's body. Every word she'd either whispered, whimpered, or groaned. Every gasp for air.

Though it wasn't easy, Whitney had to admit that she was somewhat disappointed Brie hadn't shown up at the conference, if only so they could spar for a few minutes before Whitney blew her off like she'd done in fucking Cincinnati. Though brief, it had been a satisfying moment of retribution. And damn if Brie didn't look just as sexy in jeans as she had in that cute summer dress. Her blog might have the world's most ridiculous design, but the woman could wear clothes. Whitney had held that discarded dress up to breathe in the scent of her accidental lover before folding it up and tucking it into the front of her roller suitcase.

She knew she'd made a habit of objectifying Brie, but wasn't that what one did with a stranger? Because Whitney knew Brie's body fairly well, but her heart and mind were still a mystery.

Probably a mystery best left unsolved. No, not probably. Definitely. Or at least most likely. For sure. Absolutely. She was glad that was settled.

That didn't mean Whitney couldn't spend a little more time with Brie, if only in her head. Take Cincinnati. During their brief encounter, Whitney had learned that Brie had a quick tongue. Okay, so that one she already knew. A sharp tongue. Quick with the sassy replies. Gutsy. Courageous. Determined. Or she was an emotionally unstable stalker, depending on the point of view. Whitney didn't want to believe it was the latter. She wanted to believe—at least for the next half hour or so—that Brie was as smart as she was sexy. As witty as she was passionate. As loving and kind as her touch felt.

They could've had sex again in Cincinnati, had Whitney been up for it. When they were sitting at the bar, Whitney had lied. She had vivid memories of Brie's ass. There was no tattoo, just silky softness she'd made a point to knead when Brie was on top of her. The memory of it made Whitney want to experience it again, so she set the glass of wine down and opened her robe. Her nipples were already taut. She licked her finger and circled her nipple while she envisioned Brie's warm wet tongue doing the same.

Brie's tongue had been magical. Skilled. Adept at taking Whitney to the edge but not letting her tumble over too quickly. She remembered a moment when Brie had teased her nipple with her teeth. It had felt so good, Whitney had opened her eyes so she could see exactly what Brie was doing with her mouth. Their eyes had locked because Brie had already been looking at her. It was such a turn-on. Whitney had felt an overwhelming desire to devour her unexpected lover, so she'd urged Brie to scoot up, and she'd delved deep into her mouth.

Brie had moaned and gasped for air and rocked her hips. They'd kissed for minutes, not seconds. They'd explored with their tongues. They'd searched with their eyes, communicating without words. Whitney didn't have to wonder what Brie was thinking. In that moment, she knew that nothing else existed for either of them. Only each other. Whitney couldn't remember a time it had felt like that with Reece. Their beginning was a bit more traditional, with actual dates and get-to-know-you questions. Not that she meant to compare, but it was hard not to.

Whitney moved her hand lower and sank a finger between her wet folds. She was so wet, it wouldn't take much for her to come. She jerked when her finger found her swollen clit. A light touch was all she'd need.

Her clit ached as she circled it. Her stomach clenched. Her back arched. She wanted to say her name as she came. "Brie," she whispered.

Her legs clenched shut, and she cried out as the orgasm ripped through her body. Her breaths were shallow, her clit throbbed, and all she wanted to do was say the name again. "Brie."

Whitney grinned and let out a light chuckle because there was no denying that Brie, queen of the cheeses and writer of terrible reviews, was really good in bed, even when she wasn't in the bed. Whitney hadn't been with many women, but she knew being with Brie—the real version or the imagined one—was different. She felt freer, more alive. Then again, that was probably just because she didn't know the woman.

Fantasies were fine, but once her breathing evened out, Whitney came back to her senses. She would not—in real life—ever do something as stupid as that again. Period.

❖

It had been two months since Brie had made the rational decision to not have a replay of Cincinnati in San Francisco. Why Vegas was different she wasn't sure. Maybe it was the fact that she could drive there from LA with only a two-hour traffic delay instead of an eight-hour one. Maybe it was because she wouldn't be able to go back to her normal life until she had closure. Normal being the life where she could get lost in a book instead of thinking about Whitney. The life where she could write a thoughtful, helpful review of that book and then discuss it online with her followers. The life where her mom stopped asking her why she seemed preoccupied and distant. Brie needed to try one more time. And then, one way or another, she'd find a way to let go.

She'd arrived too late to catch any of Whitney's speaking engagement, not that the overzealous security guard standing by the door would've let her in anyway. She mapped the way to the nearest coffee shop and found the banks of elevators that went to the hotel rooms. She stood where the two paths crossed and waited.

Partygoers and gamblers filled the hotel. So did miserable-looking parents with small children in strollers. A woman in a veil, tiara, and a T-shirt that said "Bride" was flanked by four women whose shirts said "Bitch." They drunkenly sashayed by with their arms interlocked, loudly singing "Friends in low places." Not the song. They just sang the phrase over and over. Once they passed, Brie could see a group of middle-aged men with golf bags who probably didn't plan to golf at all once they'd said good-bye to their wives for the weekend. Teenage soccer players in uniforms and cleats pushed their way to the front of the elevators.

Brie clocked a bar directly across the lobby. If she could convince Whitney to have a drink with her, maybe she'd have enough time to set things right between them. That was, if she could even spot her in the large crowd.

She decided to stand on a wooden bench for a better view and noticed several groups of men with corporate lanyards around their necks. They were probably members of Whitney's latest audience, which meant she wouldn't be far behind. That sent Brie's stomach into free fall. She should've had a drink to stave off the nerves. But that meant she'd have to eat something to stave off getting drunk, and she was way too nervous for that.

She'd decided to go with a "smart casual" look, just in case by some miracle they ended up having that drink together. Her well-starched pink button-up and cropped khaki chinos probably screamed preppy, but at least they didn't scream "I'm trying way too hard." After a couple of kids walked up to her and asked her if she was one of their "leaders," she decided her outfit screamed camp counselor. Not the look she was going for at all.

She'd stood on the bench for a good twenty minutes before she decided to step down and sit. She leaned back against the wall and closed her eyes. What was she even doing there? And when had she become an actual, card-carrying stalker? Oh, not to mention that glutton for punishment thing she'd become so good at since she'd met Whitney.

She realized that absolutely nothing about this was right. Maybe she could salvage the evening with some video poker and a stiff drink at another hotel's bar. There were certainly plenty to choose from on the Strip. It might even be fun. At least then she could convince herself that the trip wasn't a complete waste of time.

The good news was, she hadn't run into Whitney. It was also the bad news, but at least she hadn't humiliated herself again. The thought made her double over and cover her eyes because just thinking about how embarrassing she'd become made her want to cry or scream or throw up.

She heard someone clear their throat and opened her eyes to find two sets of feet right in front of her. A set of nice heels and some red suede loafers. Her eyes worked their way up and found Whitney and that Liz woman standing there with smug looks on their faces. Again, she didn't know whether to cry, scream, or throw up. Maybe all three. If she did vomit, the heels would recover. The suede loafers were iffy. And Brie's heart? Also iffy because just the mere sight of Whitney made it ache in a way Brie didn't think was possible.

"We wondered how long you planned to stand on that bench," Whitney said.

"Actually, we placed bets, and I won." Liz put out her hand. "Pay up, Ainsworth. There's a blackjack table with my name on it."

Whitney opened her wallet and pulled out a hundred. "Impress me by doubling it at the tables, and I'll buy dinner."

"Whatever happens, you're still buying. Don't you know you're my meal ticket?" Liz slapped Whitney's ass and walked away. Brie wasn't sure she liked Liz very much. She was the one who'd gotten them into this whole mess. Then again, maybe Brie should send her a big bouquet of flowers. Either way, she was having way too much fun at Brie's expense.

"She'll lose it all, and then I really will have to buy dinner," Whitney said with a sigh.

Brie couldn't bring herself to stand yet. Not when tears threatened to make themselves known. She didn't want Whitney's sympathy. She wanted a conversation. And that would require her to stand eye to eye with her and not fall apart, or worse, fall into her arms. With the steadiest voice she could muster, she said, "Hey, at least you put some real money on me. I'd be offended if you'd only bet five bucks."

"I despise small bets. Put your money where your mouth is, or don't waste my time."

"What was the bet exactly?" Brie immediately regretted the question. "Wait. I don't really want to know."

Whitney stood with her hands in her pockets, not even trying to pretend she obviously found this hilarious beyond words. And Brie sat there wishing she could die. Just keel over right then and there. She'd always be known as the woman who'd died in the lobby of Caesar's Palace. Maybe they'd put a plaque on the bench that said something like, *In memory of Gabriela Talbot. Not the first to leave her dignity on a bench in Vegas and certainly not the last.*

"I bet Liz that you'd shout my name across the lobby like Rachel did with…"

Brie lifted her gaze. "Ross?" She couldn't begin to imagine where this was going.

"No, from that movie," Whitney said. "The one where the soccer player is a wanker. Damnit, I can't remember the name of it."

Brie racked her brain too. Her eyes shuddered closed when she realized it was from the movie *Imagine Me and You*. It was getting worse with every second that ticked by. Where was that heart attack when she needed it? The comparison wasn't funny, even if it was sort of accurate. Or maybe that was exactly why it wasn't funny. She feigned a scoff and said, "For that to happen, I'd have to one, be in love with you and two, lack even a shred of dignity."

"So…" Whitney pursed her lips in what was an obvious attempt to suppress a giggle and asked, "What brings you to Vegas?"

Brie had to admit that the only appropriate reply was a simple *touché*, followed by an exit out the loser's door. Then she remembered where she was. Every door in the building was a loser's door. Her next move had to be a strong one. She needed to shut down the mockery and stand up for herself. So she summoned every ounce of bravado in her body, stood, and took a step closer. "Does it matter what I'm here for? Whitney?"

She took in Whitney's scent, her striking features, the panic in her eyes when she lacked a quick comeback. "It's okay," she said. "We'll just pause until you come up with a good reply or even just back away because you can't handle all this heat."

Much to Brie's surprise, Whitney stood her ground and said, "Is it chilly in here? I may need to grab a sweater before dinner."

Brie tried to hide her amusement as she let her eyes wander down to the tiny bit of visible cleavage before she looked her in the eye again. This whole feigning confidence felt kind of good. "Not a bad comeback. It'd rate it a solid eight."

Whitney didn't move, but Brie knew she only had a few seconds before she bolted. Words might hasten the departure, so she kept it short. A simple, affectionate greeting. "Hi," she whispered. She dropped her gaze, afraid of what she might see in Whitney's eyes. Anger. Hatred. Disbelief. Disgust. The options were endless.

She only raised her gaze when Whitney took a step back. Not a huge step, just enough to make Brie feel the loss. "You're stalking me," Whitney said, her tone a bit lighter. More of a statement than an accusation.

Brie finally cracked a smile. "I prefer the term *groupie*. It sounds less serial killer and more sex, drugs, and rock 'n' roll."

"Well, you came to the right town for all three. Also, if you're interested, there's a ventriloquist's convention on the third floor. Seems like it might be right up your alley."

That reply gave Brie a tiny spark of hope. She could work with it and maybe keep Whitney talking for a bit longer. "Damnit, you got me," she joked. "That's what I'm here for. I was just too embarrassed to say it out loud. You know, like this. Hey, Whit. Meet Mrs. Cornflower." Brie closed her lips and mumbled, "Hi, my name is Mrs. Cornflower."

Whitney nearly kept a straight face as she turned and walked away. Nearly but not entirely. She probably thought her abrupt departure would cause Brie to give up. She was wrong. What Brie saw at the tail end of Whitney's turn was the start of a smile. Brie saw the corners of Whitney's mouth curve upward just enough. Just enough for Brie to discover something called hope.

What surprised Brie when she caught up to her was the smile on Whitney's face. An actual, full-blown smile. Brie moved closer and said, "Why do I get the feeling you're happy to see me?"

"Ha. What gave you that idea? I just lost a hundred bucks thanks to your abundant dignity."

"It's your face," Brie said. "It's back to how it was when we woke up that morning, and your hair was all sexy-messy, and neither of us could believe what just happened. Because as you know but aren't fully ready to admit yet, it was an amazing night we spent together."

Whitney kept walking with her eyes straight ahead. "Don't you need to go find your fellow impersonators? I'm sure they're missing you by now."

"Ventriloquists, not impersonators, but that's neither here nor there."

"Ha. No truer words were ever spoken."

Brie hoped they were headed toward the elevators that would lead to Whitney's hotel room. She also hoped it would be a long walk. Worst-case scenario, they'd bump into Liz or a fan or the conference organizer, and the conversation, along with any hope Brie had left, would die. She needed to talk fast. "Believe it or not, I can tell the truth," she said. "I do it all the time. In fact, I'm really not the lying bitch you think I am. People who know me say I'm loyal and trustworthy and kind. Oh, and I make a mean apology burger. Wanna know what my secret ingredient is?"

"Not particularly," Whitney said. "But I'm sure that won't stop you from telling me." She caught a closing elevator door and stepped into a crowd.

Brie managed to squeeze in behind her. Whitney turned, which put them face-to-face and closer than they'd been since they'd slept together. She rolled her eyes and whispered, "Great."

Brie thought so too, but she actually meant it. It hadn't been a very long walk, but this, being crammed into an elevator together was so much better. They were surrounded by huge suitcases and loud people who were probably drunk before their plane landed. When one particularly sloppy man stumbled into Whitney, Brie desperately wanted to wrap her arm around Whitney's waist to steady her and tell the drunk guy to watch himself. But she didn't dare touch her. Not when Whitney's only concern seemed to be not making eye contact. All Brie could do was whisper, "I'm sorry."

She was sorry for so much, but she didn't have time to elaborate before the doors opened, and Whitney brushed past her so fast, she almost knocked Brie over. Brie went far enough onto the fifteenth floor to watch Whitney walk to her room, but that was where she stopped. Enough was enough. She raised her voice and said, "I won't bother you again."

Any hope for reconciliation died with the death glare Whitney shot her before opening her door and slamming it shut. No one could say Brie hadn't tried to make things right. First, flying all the way to Cincinnati and then driving to Vegas. She'd given it her best shot, and surely Whitney could appreciate that on some level. Granted, it might be the *I have a stalker and she scares the hell out of me* level, but there wasn't anything Brie could do about that now. She'd blown her chance. It seemed like it was time to let the tears go. And let Whitney go. For good this time.

She pushed the down button on the elevator and walked over to the window to wait. Not because she thought the view would be nice. All she could see was air-conditioning machinery on top of a parking garage. She just didn't want anyone seeing the tears running down her face and ask if she was okay. She was not okay. She was heartbroken. And possibly in love with a woman she'd slept with only once and barely knew. And yet, she felt like she knew Whitney intimately through her words. Her books. But it was a false intimacy. It was all false. None of it was real, and Brie needed to accept that fact and move on.

She wiped her tears away and took a deep breath. It wasn't too late to drive home. She could get back to LA by midnight if the traffic was light. It sounded better than wallowing in her own misery in an overpriced hotel room.

"Brie?"

Oh God. Had Whitney just said her name out loud for the first time ever? Brie brushed any remaining tears away and went back to the hallway. Whitney stood there by her door. But not for long. She went back into her room before Brie could even acknowledge her. The door didn't slam shut the way only heavy hotel room doors could, so Brie took her time walking down the hallway, unsure of what was going on. She kept to the far wall even as she came up on the room. Whitney was there, leaning against the door.

Was it an unspoken invitation? Was Whitney too proud to say the words out loud? Brie stepped closer and said, "Are you inviting me into your room?"

"Don't read too much into it. There's zero trust here."

Whitney's eyes gave her away. She dropped her guard just long enough for Brie to see the need. The desire. It wasn't for more than a split second, but it told Brie that if she stood in front of Whitney, their lips just inches away from each other, she'd feel that desire too.

"That's okay," Brie said. "It doesn't have to mean anything, the sex we're about to have." It was a bold statement. And also a lie. If it came to that, could she really keep her emotions in check? And after all the travel to multiple cities, would Whitney even believe it if she did control herself? She'd have to, or Whitney might freak and kick her out on her ass again. She made a mental note to keep track of her clothes this time.

Her heart raced as she stepped farther into the room. She only took in a breath when she heard the deadbolt lock. Vegas had its charms, and nice suites with views of the lights on the Strip was one of them. A curved couch faced the floor-to-ceiling windows. She wondered if that was where they'd start, or would they go straight for the bed?

"Would you like to share a bottle of wine?"

Brie hadn't expected that. Not at all. Sharing a bottle of wine usually meant speaking words and expressing feelings and getting to know the other person. Brie assumed Whitney would want to get straight to the sex the way she'd done the first time. As she recalled, Whitney had even said the words, "Don't talk." Or something along those lines.

"Brie?"

"Yes! Yes, I'd love to," Brie blurted. "Sorry, I just assumed we'd…you know."

Whitney twisted one of those impossible lever corkscrews into the cork. Brie hated those damn things. She always managed to get cork in the wine. "Did you come all this way to…you know?" The pop of the cork punctuated her question as Whitney expertly finished her task. It was kind of a turn-on.

"Well, I didn't *not* come all this way for that," Brie said. "What I mean is…never mind."

"You were so brave a moment ago. Why the nerves now?"

"Oh, just having some flashbacks to that morning when I wasn't even given time to find my clothes before I was kicked out." Brie found herself particularly grateful that Whitney was pouring two generous glasses of wine since all her bravado had disappeared into thin air the moment she'd stepped into the room. Her mind flooded with memories of that morning. The yelling, frantically searching for her clothes, the anger in Whitney's eyes. How had it all gone so wrong after such an incredible night? And what would happen next? Brie was pretty sure if Whitney wanted sex, they'd already be ripping each other's clothes off. She realized then that yes, she had hoped it would come to that. She had this unrealistic fantasy in her head that they'd talk and work things out while a sexual tension built between them that neither of them could ignore. It was all very sexy and dramatic in her head.

She also feared that maybe she was only there for Whitney's amusement. A payback of sorts. That thought put her guard up.

"As I recall, you didn't leave naked," Whitney said. "Are my workout clothes still under your pillow?"

A flippant remark that put Brie in the "fan" category? Yes, she should definitely protect her vulnerable heart. "I may be a Whitney Ainsworth fan, but I have my limits. Besides, I hate purple."

"A fan? Am I really supposed to believe that? Fans don't usually eviscerate their favorite author's books." She handed Brie a glass.

"Eviscerate is a strong word." Brie swirled the wine and raised the glass to her mouth. She took a quick sniff and then a sip. "Oh my God. This is sublime."

"Don't change the subject," Whitney said. "Annihilate. Obliterate. Rip to shreds." She took a sip and held the glass up to the light. "Good Lord. That *is* amazing. It's like Jesus himself crushed these grapes." She swirled the wine in her glass and appeared to consider the possibility. "Nah, he doesn't need grapes."

Brie narrowed her eyes, then raised a finger. "Ha. Got it. Water into wine." She took another sip and set her glass on the leather coffee table that was really just the arm of the sofa disguised as a table. She gave herself a mental pat on the back for knowing that was what it was before she said, "Okay, so we really do need to talk before we…you know."

Whitney folded her arms and kept the glass in hand. God, she was sexy. "This might surprise you, Brie…may I call you Brie now that I've seen you naked? Good, because I have a bad taste in my mouth about the Gabriela thing. Anyway, I didn't invite you into my room for sex."

Brie hid her disappointment with a smirk. "Right. Well, just so you know, I wasn't trying to be misleading with my name. I guess it just felt like a work situation where I wanted to sound professional. You know, with a professional name."

"You're here to interview me."

Brie's eyebrows shot up. "I am?"

"That's what you claimed you wanted in the first place, so now's your chance. Besides, *tenacious blogger* has a better ring to it than *sexy stalker*. Ask me anything."

Brie blinked. "You said *sexy*."

"I also said *stalker*. Do you have any questions?"

Brie picked up her glass and followed Whitney to a small dining table where they could sit across from each other. She sat and took a sip of wine while she tried to collect her thoughts, which was an almost impossible task with Sexy Lips sitting across from her. She cleared her throat and said, "Okay. Um, I guess I'll start by saying how amazing it was to be with you."

"That's not a question."

"No, it's not." Brie needed to pull herself together and focus. But Whitney was there. Right there, sitting across from her, chatting over a glass of wine they way they would if they were friends catching up. Or even on a first date. And Brie needed to know. "Was it amazing for you too?"

Whitney let out a quick laugh before she reeled it back in. "I think, if this is going to work, we'll need to pretend that never happened. Go back to before you stepped foot in my room that night."

"It's kinda hard for me to remember anything with you sitting there looking all sexy and smelling so good, and do you always have wine at interviews? And also, that music you just turned on…it was playing that night when…okay, don't kick me out. I can do this. Just give me a second." Brie took a deep breath and tried to focus.

"Maybe I can help you. Why that review?"

Brie closed her eyes. Her shoulders sagged. "Frustration, Whitney. I couldn't believe you'd leave the series there. I'm a reviewer, but I'm also a fan. And as a fan, it felt like a big slap in the face."

Whitney tilted her head. "How so?"

"No happy ending? No medals for Piper's bravery? No love interest? I mean, what the hell?"

Whitney set her glass down and folded her arms. "Ah. So you're upset that I didn't let Piper fall in love with her nemesis. Who happens to be a woman."

"I didn't say that." Brie paused. She needed to calm down so she wouldn't put Whitney on the defensive. "I don't care if it's a man or a woman. Just let her have some happiness if you're actually ending the series. We cared about her. Obviously, she has to struggle as part of her journey, but this is about the end of her journey. After she's already overcome the obstacles. Where's the payoff for the reader?" Relieved that Whitney seemed to consider her point of view, Brie took another sip of wine and waited for a reply.

"I did put her through hell," Whitney said. "And she put me through hell with the last book."

"Piper did? Or are we talking about your ex-wife now?"

"Don't go there," Whitney said. "You do not have permission to say anything about my private life."

Brie put up her hands. "Okay, just so we're clear, this isn't a real interview. I'm not planning to share any of it. Not after, you know, that thing we're not thinking about."

Whitney leaned forward on the table. "But before that thing, you were looking for answers. Surely, that wasn't just for your own satisfaction. You would've posted something, correct?"

"Of course. I wanted to know if there'd be more to Piper's story. A lot of people do. Or at least, we want to know why it ended like that."

"Okay, so you wanted to know if there's more to the story. Is that all?"

Was it getting hot in there? Brie leaned back and ran both hands through her hair. She pulled it back into a ponytail to get if off her hot neck for a moment. She was stalling. She didn't want to bring up her review out of fear that Whitney would explode into a rage and kick her out again. After a deep breath, she let her hair fall back to her shoulders and said, "No. That's not all."

Whitney didn't respond. Or rather, her response was to stare Brie down. There was no getting around it. Brie would have to bring it up. "The timing of my review," she said. "The impact of it. The hashtags. All of it. I never meant for any of that to happen. I wrote a review for people who love to read books. It turned into a review for people who love to bash celebrities. Not intentionally but that's what happened, and I'm so sorry for that. And I can't help but wonder if that sucked some of the joy out of writing for you, because God, if it did…" She trailed off and waited to be escorted to the door. But Whitney turned to look out the window, her expression a pained one.

"Sometimes, as a writer, real life can smack you in the face so hard it takes your words away," Whitney said. "Your creativity. Your passion for the story. Your desire to even open a book, be it yours or someone else's. Piper might have been a victim of that." She shook her head. "Not might. She was."

It took all of Brie's strength to not stand and pull Whitney into a hug and tell her she wasn't alone. She desperately wanted to comfort her, but that might lead them in a different direction, and Brie sensed Whitney wanted to talk about it. She just needed a little nudge. "And now you have writer's block?" she asked. "Is that why you're doing more of this speaker circuit thing?"

Whitney looked her in the eye. "I'll say one thing for you as a therapist. You're cheap."

Brie smiled. "And as your fake therapist, I'll say one thing about you as a patient. You're deflecting."

With a sigh, Whitney said, "Fine. It pays the bills. And keeps my mind off…her."

They were talking about the ex-wife again. Reece. Brie saw that as a good sign. A sign of trust. So she risked asking, "You're still in love with her?" Whitney didn't answer. "Sorry," Brie said. "That's none of my business."

"None of this is any of your business." Whitney leaned back in her chair and folded her arms again. "Why stop there?"

Brie wasn't sure if that comment was an invitation to keep asking questions. She glanced around the spacious suite. They were right above the Strip, where people were celebrating all sorts of occasions. Weddings, birthdays, anniversaries, bachelor and bachelorette parties. One elevator ride and they'd be right in the thick of it. And then she imagined all of the quiet, lonely hotel rooms Whitney had been in lately. Was she avoiding her life? Was the pain of a failed book, quickly followed by a failed marriage, too much to bear? Was a lonely hotel room better than an empty house? Overwhelmed with guilt for the additional pain she'd caused, Brie stood. "I'm sorry. For the book review, for chasing you all over the country, for scaring you." She took a deep breath and tried to hold back the tears. "But I'm not sorry for the night we shared together. It's a beautiful memory, and I won't pretend it was anything different." Their eyes met, but Whitney didn't respond. Before she turned to walk away, Brie said, "You're a brilliant writer. I hope you can find your words again."

Her hand was on the door handle when she heard Whitney say, "I don't regret it either, the night we shared." Brie turned but kept her hand on the handle. Whitney stopped a few feet away. "If you stay, can you promise that you'll never write about me or stalk me or…hurt me?"

Brie let go of the handle. "I can promise all of those things."

The shower had steamed up. Brie stripped and opened the door. Whitney had the bodywash in hand. Brie grabbed the scrubber and said, "Let me." She squirted body wash on it and urged Whitney to turn around. She moved Whitney's hair to the side and kissed her shoulder before she started. She ran the scrubber over her shoulders and down her arms. She paid special attention to her shoulder blades and spine, massaging the soap in, then worked her way around to her stomach, and between her breasts.

Whitney turned in her arms. The expression on her face confused Brie. She wasn't sure if she was enjoying the attention or not. She was about to ask when Whitney grabbed her face and kissed her. Brie dropped the scrubber and gripped Whitney's waist. The kiss was deep, and Brie had to reach to her side and grab the wall for balance. Whitney moved to her neck, and Brie heaved for air. "Your kiss takes my breath away," she whispered.

Whitney moved back to her mouth, and Brie whimpered when

their tongues collided again. She wrapped her arms around Whitney and kneaded her ass while they kissed. She needed a wall to push her up against, so she turned them slightly and made sure Whitney was steady on her feet before she leaned against her and deepened the kiss.

Even though they were in the shower with water running over their bodies, Brie could feel the ache and the moisture building between her legs. She worked her way down to a taut nipple and circled it with her tongue. Whitney rested her hand on Brie's head and whispered, "Yes. I love that."

Brie loved the way Whitney's hand felt on her head. Gentle yet firm. She imagined for a moment that Whitney was holding her close for other reasons than just to keep her nibbling on her breast. Whitney moaned and spread her legs. Brie straightened back up and kissed her, and Whitney deepened the kiss.

She took Brie's lip into her mouth and sucked on it, then bit down, and Brie knew what she was trying to tell her. Whitney wanted it hard. She wanted to be fucked in the shower hard enough to make her cry out. To make her gasp for air. To make her forget.

With their eyes locked, Brie slid her hand down Whitney's stomach and into her creamy folds. Whitney grabbed her shoulders and gasped at the touch. Brie circled her clit a few times before she pushed inside. Whitney did cry out, and Brie held her tightly while she fucked her against the wall.

Whitney dug her fingers into Brie's shoulders and moaned her appreciation. When it started to feel like maybe she couldn't take any more, Brie pressed their foreheads together and moved to Whitney's clit. She massaged it until she felt her body tense up, and then she lightened the pressure so her orgasm would last longer. It seemed like Whitney wanted to say something, but it came out as a squeak, and then an "Oh God." She came hard in Brie's arms, and they both slumped to the floor.

Whitney kept them cheek to cheek while she caught her breath. "Fuck, that was good," she whispered.

Brie rested her hand on Whitney's head and hoped it made her feel safe, and wanted, and...loved.

CHAPTER SEVEN

Whitney groaned when she saw both Liz and her publicist, Josh, on the doorbell camera. She held her phone up to her mouth and said, "What the hell?"

Liz leaned in way closer to the camera than she needed to and said, "Oh, just let us in. We brought doughnuts."

Whitney dragged herself out of bed with her phone in hand. "Get your damn lips off my doorbell, Liz. And what happened to me having a day to myself after you talked my ear off on the way home from Vegas?"

"Did I mention I have doughnuts?"

Whitney squinted at the phone. "That's one giant doughnut, or you got a new handbag. Really with the shocking pink?"

Liz petted her bag the way she would a cat. "I'll have you know it's vintage Chanel."

"Ha. Since when do you buy used?"

"I buy used when the previous owner was Angie Dickenson, aka Police Woman, aka my childhood woman crush."

"Mine too," Josh said. "Whit, would you mind pressing that little button so we can come in?"

Whitney tapped the button on her phone and went into the bathroom. "Make some coffee, would you, Josh? Liz can't make good coffee to save her life."

"Will do, sunshine."

"Bitter coffee, bitter wife," Liz said. "What can you do?"

Whitney sat on the toilet and put the phone up to her mouth. "I am not your…" She paused when she heard Liz's laugh echoing through the house. She tossed her phone on the rug and shouted, "I'm not your—"

"Whitney?"

Josh was in her bedroom? That seemed strange. Good thing she'd closed the bathroom door. "Yeah?"

"I need to ask you to not look at the news until you come downstairs. Can you do that, please?"

Whitney eyed her phone. Josh didn't usually make house calls. Especially not at 7:15 in the morning. "Yeah, okay," she said with hesitance in her voice. "Josh, should I be worried?"

"Just promise me."

"Give me five to get dressed."

This sucked. Up at seven meant she'd only had about six hours of sleep over the past forty-eight hours. She'd tossed and turned most of the night, her thoughts centered on what to do about Brie Talbot.

She'd finally learned her last name when Brie had put her contact information in Whitney's phone. Brie Talbot. Sexy, frustratingly persistent Brie. What the hell was she going to do with her?

Whitney had ducked out early, leaving Brie in the hotel room. She'd claimed she and Liz had a meeting back in LA. The truth was, she could've stayed longer. It was only her own fear that drove her away. Fear of the unknown. Fear of what Brie might expect from her. Fear of falling hard for a woman she barely knew. It was best to leave it the way she had, with the promise of a lunch date sometime soon.

She left her phone where it was while she threw on a pair of joggers and a T-shirt. If Liz had been the one to ask her not to look at her phone, she wouldn't have complied. Liz was prone to overreacting. She once anticipated a meltdown when Whitney's nipples were visibly taut in a photo some magazine had posted. But Whitney had just laughed and reminded Liz it was cold that day.

Josh was another story. It wasn't often that she needed his advice. Hardly ever since she'd divorced her famous wife. Sure, she had her own level of fame, but it was her and Reece as a couple that had put her in the spotlight.

Living in New York, where walking was the main mode of transportation, it was easier for photographers to get shots of them doing everyday things that would end up in the gossip magazines or blogs. Once they'd moved to LA, it was more red-carpet appearances at movie premieres and fashion shows and charity events where they'd be photographed together. That and the occasional "celebrities: they're just like us" snap as they came out of Starbucks. It never bothered Whitney too much. The attention only brought more awareness to her own career, which in turn, meant more book sales.

But why had Josh made a house call? Whitney's heart sank when the thought occurred to her that this could be about Brie. Had she posted something on her blog? Had she taken naked photos of Whitney while she'd slept?

Her hands started to shake just thinking about the possibility, and by the time she got to the kitchen, she was ready to quell her nerves with a shot of anything. Unfortunately, coffee and doughnuts were the only things on the round kitchen table. Josh stood and pulled out a chair for her. "I believe your favorite is a plain cake for dipping?"

Liz rolled her eyes. "Firstly, don't say it like you knew it before today, Josh. And secondly, Whitney's the only weirdo in the world who orders a plain doughnut. And thirdly, don't even try to make me feel guilty about this apple fritter I'm about to stuff in my mouth."

Josh sat in between them. "And fourthly, they wouldn't make plain doughnuts if they didn't sell."

Josh didn't know about Brie. Whitney was dying to know what was going on, but she didn't want to say her name if it wasn't necessary, so she joined in on the silly doughnut banter. "Thank you, Josh. I've been trying to tell Liz that for years. Plain cake doughnut lovers are everywhere. They could be your doctor, your neighbor, your insurance agent."

"They should make a doughnut offenders list so I know where *not* to live," Liz quipped.

Josh laughed, but Whitney wasn't going to give Liz the satisfaction. She broke her doughnut in half and dipped one end into her coffee. "Mmm, coffee cake."

Liz took a big bite of the fritter and slapped the table a few times while she moaned her delight. "Mmm, just taste all that sweet, fried apple goodness."

Josh picked up his chocolate glazed with sprinkles and took a bite. Liz and Whitney stared him down until he reluctantly said, "Mmm, good sprinkles."

"Good try, Josh. Maybe with more feeling next time." Liz furrowed her brow at Whitney. "Your hands are shaking. Why are they shaking?"

"Maybe because I was jolted awake by the ominous twins, and they still haven't told me why." But they didn't need to tell. She knew it had something to do with Brie. Thank God she'd ducked out of that hotel room early. Thank God she had Brie's last name so she could sue her sorry ass for selling whatever it was she'd sold. She was probably flat broke. How much could a person make with a dumb blog anyway?

Liz dusted the crumbs off her fingers. "They broke up. There you have it."

Whitney lifted her gaze. "Wait. What?" How could she and Brie break up when they were never together? Did that conniving woman announce to the world that they'd been a thing, and now they were no longer a thing? *Oh, but here's proof that they were a thing with some naked photos?* Whitney fumed.

Josh set his doughnut down and wiped the sides of his mouth with his napkin. "Your bedside manner is atrocious, Liz." He sighed and said, "We wanted to be the first to tell you that Reece and Kat broke up, but honestly, is it a surprise to any of us?"

Liz huffed. "I should've put money on it."

"Oh," was all Whitney said. On the one hand, it was a relief that they weren't there to warn her about some horrible betrayal on Brie's part. It was more than a relief. In fact, if she'd had her phone, she would've called Brie right then and there and thanked her for not betraying her trust and to set up that lunch date.

This was about a different betrayal. And it made sense that Josh didn't want her to look at her phone. Photos of Reece and Kat would be everywhere. There would be statements from Reece's publicist. Paparazzi chasing her down. They would have called Josh for a statement. They'd need to work out something. A vague acknowledgement of the situation along with best wishes for her ex-wife. Nothing real, of course. She imagined what the real version might look like:

Whitney Ainsworth takes some small pleasure in knowing that her ex-wife's relationship with that horrible Kat woman has come to a swift and inevitable conclusion. As a hopeless romantic and lover of grand gestures, she is also deeply appreciative of being informed of this by her ex-wife's publicist. Lastly, being the complex and layered person that she is, Ms. Ainsworth must admit that she struggles with the idea that her entire marriage ended over a fling that lasted about as long as it takes to make a decent lasagna, and she wonders what it says about the validity of her marriage that her mind is generally consumed by someone else entirely.

"Should I call the caterer and start planning the celebration?"

Leave it to Liz to think this was something worthy of a celebration. "Do you think it feels good knowing that my marriage ended because of a short-lived fling? I'd rather believe Reece is a better person than that. She's someone I once loved, after all."

Liz softened her tone. "I know, sweetie. And we've got your back, but just hear Josh out."

"I got a call from Reece's publicist late last night," he said. "She wants you back. She wants a reconciliation."

"Your first public appearance together should be very special," Liz said. "Don't let the paparazzi get the first shot. Plan it. Dress for it. Wear the right handbag."

"Liz was thinking that perhaps a reconciliation could be good for both of you, career-wise. If that's the case and you decide to get back together, even just for show, we need to make the most of it for both of you."

Whitney couldn't believe what she was hearing. They wanted her to go back to Reece, but do it in an over-the-top way for publicity? Were they fucking kidding? "Liz, if you think for one second that I would get back together with Reece for publicity, you must be as high right now as you were when you bought that handbag."

Liz gaped in silence while Josh tried to play peacemaker by saying, "We understand. All we're asking for is a little heads-up if it does happen. You need some good press for a change. You need to express some happiness that Reece is playing Piper Kane. It's business. We've got a week before shooting starts, so that should be plenty of time."

Whitney folded her arms in defiance. "It is absolutely plenty of time for nothing to happen."

Josh stood. "No comment to the press if they ask me about Reece and Kat?"

Whitney considered it for a moment. Did she owe Reece her condolences? Would a comment from her mean anything to anyone? She waved it off. "I wish her the best and look forward to getting to work on set."

"Got it." Josh pointed at Liz. "That goes for you too. Don't do anything I'm not aware of first."

Liz put up her hands in defense. "I'll just be sitting here, eating my fritter while I relive our special night together, Josh."

He huffed. "It was twenty years ago, and Dustin still hasn't forgiven me for breaking his favorite hammock."

Liz gave him a wink. "Good one. Talk soon."

Once she heard her front door close, Whitney said, "Dustin Hoffman's hammock? Is there anywhere you two have *not* pretended to have sex?"

"I gotta admit, Josh is much better at this game than I am. He beats me every damn time. Wish I could remember how it even started."

"I'm sure you started it by shamelessly flirting with him for real. Lucky for Josh, he knows a self-indulgent ego boost when he sees one."

Liz shrugged. "If I wasn't so self-aware, I'd take offense at that. Now, are we going to continue our discussion about Reece and Kat breaking up? I know you had to put on a tough girl act for Josh, but it's just us now, so lay it on me. I can take it."

"It wasn't an act. I have no comment. I have no opinion on the matter."

"Uh-huh. And no thoughts on her desire to reconcile?"

"I feel nothing."

"Good thing you're better at writing than acting." Liz grabbed Whitney's hand. "I'll be here whenever you want to talk. Or slash her tires. Either one."

Whitney wasn't being entirely disingenuous. Having had all of fifteen minutes to absorb the news, she was still in shock. Once it sunk in, she knew she'd have lots of opinions and feelings. She just didn't want to have them in front of Liz since it might involve the throwing of dishes and possibly some gnashing of teeth followed by desperate wailing to the universe. *Why now, God? Why fucking now?*

"You really don't see the potential?" Liz asked. "Imagine a year from now when you're both promoting the movie. You could do that together. As the 'couple' everyone loves. You could still live separate lives. Who needs love, after all? This is Hollywood. All that glitters is definitely not gold."

"I'd rather have all of the awkward questions like, how was it working with your ex-wife? Or was Piper Kane written with Reece in mind? Was it always the plan to have her play Piper in the movie adaptation? Is it true you tried to get her fired after she cheated on you? Was it a hard separation?"

Liz leaned back in her chair and stared Whitney down. "Why are you pretending that you haven't spent the last year and a half pining over Reece?"

"Still being in love with someone and missing the life you had with them are two different things. I missed our life together. And sure, I wanted it back for a while, but my God, Liz. It was you who had to pick me up off the floor when Reece left me, and now you want me to just forgive and forget? Just jump right back into the thing that almost broke me? I'm over it, and I'm going to stay over it."

"I want you to be happy. Reece made you happy. Sure, she made a mistake, but taking the high road isn't the same as forgiving her. Maybe it's time to start thinking about that."

Whitney eyed Liz. She looked guilty. "What do you know that you're not telling me?"

Liz leaned forward. "I could ask the same question. That excuse you made for missing dinner because you were tired wasn't true, was it? You slept with her, didn't you?" Liz slapped the table. "You fucking did. And now she's taking up room in your head, isn't she?"

Taking up room in her head? Brie Talbot was taking up a whole McMansion in her head. No, not a McMansion. An estate. And also maybe a sliver of her heart. Whitney found herself unable to hide a smile when she said, "Hey, you're the one who *wingwomaned* her into my bed."

"And wow am I paying for it." Liz sighed. "Okay, so maybe I'd heard a few rumors about Reece and Kat. And maybe I wanted you to be on top of your game when the inevitable happened. And when I saw her staring at you in that bar, I jumped on it." Liz reached for her hand and squeezed it. "It's called getting back in the saddle. And if you want to use her to make Reece a little jealous, I'm all for that."

"You hooked me up with her so I could practice?" Whitney pulled her hand away. "I thought you were my friend."

"I am, sweetie. I want you to shine like the star you are. Whitney and Reece Ainsworth, brightest lesbian constellation in the sky."

"Ha. Pretty sure that label belongs to Quinn Kincaid and Lacey Matthews now, and they can have it. Hate to break it to you, but I am not your lesbian romance meal ticket."

"Okay, look. I know I'm laying it on kind of thick here. And I love to hate Reece more than anyone. I just want you to be sure. So maybe hear her out before you have to start working together."

Whitney had heard enough. She got up from the table. "Let yourself out, Liz. And next time, warn me before you decide to double-team me with Josh. I don't work with people who don't have my back." She went to the kitchen sink and wet down a sponge so she could look busy until Liz got a clue and left. She scrubbed the same spot on the counter until she heard the front door close, then tossed the sponge in the sink and leaned against the counter. Eventually, there would be a lot of emotional baggage to unpack, but she couldn't help but smile a little in that moment because the bad news wasn't about Brie.

❖

Brie stepped onto the deck and took in a deep breath of the sea air. Her mom wrapped her arms around her from behind and said, "Everyone has been told to stay away. I'm the only one who will check in on you now and then."

"I'll be fine, Mom. Better than fine. I love this place. Every good memory I have of Grandma happened on this beach. Remember how she used to bury me and Adam up to our necks in the sand? And she'd chase us into the surf, and we'd swallow salt water because we were laughing so hard."

"And then you'd throw it up and come crying to Mommy. Yeah, I remember."

Brie turned and scanned the faded blue clapboards on the house. "She even let us help her pick out the color when it was painted last time. Geez, that was years ago."

"You wanted her to paint it bright turquoise blue with candy pink trim. Thank God she said no."

Brie tilted her head. "Hey, maybe I could paint it while I'm staying here. It wouldn't be that hard."

"A house that sits on pylons? No, that wouldn't be hard at all." Her mom turned Brie back around so they were face-to-face. "Write your book, Gabriela. No painting. No beach parties. No getting on that Ryder dating app. You don't need that kind of distraction."

Brie narrowed her eyes. "What do you know about a lesbian dating app? Is there something you're not telling me? Am I going to have two mommies soon?"

Her mom threw her hands in the air and went back into the house. Brie followed her. "What's her name, Mom? When do we get to meet her? Does she have any kids? What are her parents' names? I need to google them."

Her mom turned and smirked. "You do a better impression of your father than you do me. Come on, let's hear it."

Brie lowered her voice. "You want to go to the Santa Monica Pier? Take Adam with you. No, wait. How old are you again? Hell, I was riding my bike all over LA when I was nine. Go ahead, kid. No, wait. Let me think about this. Hmm."

Her mom shook her head. "See? I have to worry about you kids for both of us."

"And I appreciate it, but you do realize your kids turned thirty this year, right? I mean, Adam is still a little boy in so many ways, but I'm adulting just fine." Brie said it with so much determination, she almost believed it herself. And it was probably even true before a certain author threw her life into a complete tailspin.

Her mom stepped closer and put her arms on Brie's shoulders. "You both are. And I'm so proud. But this mom worrying about her kids thing never goes away." She pulled Brie into a hug. "I love you, sweetie."

"Love you too." Brie held on a little longer than she normally would. In her heart, she was a mama's girl all the way, and while she didn't always love her mom's intrusions into her private life, she appreciated knowing how much she was loved.

Her mom backed away toward the door and blew her a kiss. "Don't forget to set the alarm at night. The code is in the fridge under the butter dish, and the extra key to the side gate is in your grandpa's toolbox."

"I remember all of Grandma's favorite hiding places." Brie shooed her out the door, blew her a kiss, and locked the door behind her. She took a deep breath, spread her arms, and twirled around the room. "You're all mine, house. All mine." Now if she could just stop thinking about Whitney for two seconds, she might even get some actual writing done.

❖

Five times Whitney had to listen to that damned Sam Smith song about cheating, the one she'd changed Reece's ringtone to in a weak moment well over a year ago. And that didn't include the twenty texts her ex had sent begging for a conversation. Said conversation would probably involve a lot of crying on Reece's part. A lot of "I'm sorry" and "I never stopped loving you." It would all fall on deaf ears. Whitney wasn't interested in Reece's apologies. Not anymore.

After a hot shower, she crawled into bed and turned on the TV to find something boring she could fall asleep to. It was a bad habit she'd picked up on the road. Even the nice hotels had that little gap at the bottom of the door that let in the sounds of obnoxious travelers who couldn't give a damn who they woke up at two a.m.

She found an infomercial, turned the volume down a bit and checked her phone one last time. She groaned when she saw she'd missed another text from Reece while she was in the shower. Maybe this would require a phone call with her lawyer to find out what her options were because she'd be damned if she was going to change the phone number she'd had for going on fifteen years.

She shot up off her pillow when she read the message.
Going on Falcon tonight. You don't want to miss it.

Reece didn't have a movie to promote, so why would she go on his show right now? Whitney grabbed the remote and found the right channel. And there she was, sitting across the desk from Johnny Falcon and wearing a skintight, blush-colored miniskirt and matching crop top. Whitney had to admit, she looked beautiful.

She heard Johnny say, "Here's a question for you, Reece. Do you know which clip of the show has gotten the most views on YouTube?"

Reece laughed. "Well, I know which clip I've watched at least a dozen times."

Whitney turned the volume up. "The kiss," she whispered. Not that she'd watched it more than say, twenty times. Hell, every lesbian everywhere had boosted the view count on that clip.

Johnny looked to his audience. "Can anyone beat Reece's view count of the Quinn and Lacey kiss?"

The audience roared, and Whitney had to smile because that hot kiss turned into a marriage that she hoped would last longer than her own.

Once the audience calmed down, Johnny said, "Now, you've had a recent breakup, correct?"

"Correct," Reece said.

"I guess that blows our chances for a Reece and Kat kiss."

The audience showed their disappointment with a collective groan. Whitney said, "Thank fucking God."

"I have something pretty good, though," Reece said. "It might not top a kiss between those two hotties, but I'm hoping it'll impress a certain someone."

"Oh God." Whitney covered both eyes and watched through her fingers. "No, Reece. Whatever it is, just no."

"You see, Johnny, I made a huge mistake and hurt the person I love most in this world, and I'm not talking about this recent breakup. I'm talking about the one before that."

Johnny turned to the audience. "For those of you who have been living under a rock, Reece is talking about her ex-wife. The beautiful and talented writer of the Piper Kane series, Whitney Ainsworth."

The crowd applauded. Whitney dropped her hands from her face. "Okay, that's nice, I guess." But as much as she enjoyed receiving a compliment from Johnny Falcon, she knew this wasn't going anywhere good.

Reece clapped with the audience and said, "I'm going to get her back, Johnny. I just have to prove to her how committed I am, and nothing screams commitment like a tattoo, am I right?"

Whitney's jaw dropped. She jumped out of bed and stood in front of the TV with her hands on her hips. "What the hell did you do?"

With the audience chanting, "Show us," Reece stood and pushed her skirt down below her belly button.

The camera focused in on a fresh tattoo, and Whitney's eyes shuddered closed as she whispered, "Oh my God."

"Interesting location," Johnny said.

Reece sat back down and flashed a grin. "She'll see it every day."

The crowd cheered and whistled, and Whitney screamed, "*Fuck*."

She grabbed the remote, turned off the TV, then threw it at the screen. Her phone rang. She picked it up and yelled, "A tattoo? Are you fucking kidding me?"

"I was as surprised as you," Josh said. "I have Liz on the line with us."

"Oh, good. So tell me, Liz. Were you surprised? Because if you knew that Reece had my name tattooed on her body and didn't warn me—"

"I swear, I didn't know anything, but wow, does that woman have nerve. It's kind of a turn-on, and I'm not even gay."

"Shut up, Liz. It wasn't brave. It was a cheap stunt," Whitney said. "A cheap stunt that's going to make my life more difficult than it already is."

"A very permanent stunt, wouldn't you say? And when are you going to wake up to the opportunity she just placed at your feet? This is gold, Whitney, and I'm sure Josh would tell you the same because God knows you could use some gold publicity dust after your last book. Not that it's a bad book, but that Cheese Whiz bitch—"

Whitney cut them off and tossed her phone on the bed. It was hard for her to remember a time when she would have swooned at such a public declaration of love from Reece. She knew those feelings had existed at some point, but they felt so far away now, in another past on some parallel universe. In this universe, she was just pissed at the audacity and tackiness of it all. She was also frustrated. She wondered if the day would ever come that Reece would stop screwing up her life. She'd started to think it might not.

CHAPTER EIGHT

B rie opened the front door and grinned from ear to ear. "I'm so glad you called."

After Vegas, she'd decided to let Whitney make the next move with the hope that she could lose the stalker moniker before it stopped being funny. So to have Whitney standing on *her* doorstep instead of the other way around felt so good, she hadn't stopped smiling since Whitney's name lit up her phone.

"I'm in need," Whitney said.

Brie felt the statement in her core. Three words out of that sexy mouth and she was already ripping their clothes off in her mind. Whitney's would be easy. One quick move and she'd have her hoodie unzipped and hanging off her shoulders. She couldn't see what was underneath it, but she hoped it was thin and see-through. Not that it would last long on her body, but hard nipples poking through a white tee was such a turn-on. She liked to bite on them through the material before she removed it from her lover's body. Same with sexy panties.

She stepped back and said, "You came to the right place."

Whitney walked in. Brie stared at her jeans-clad ass until she turned around and said, "I'm in need of a friend who isn't Liz."

Brie tried to pull her mind out of the gutter while at the same trying to hide her disappointment. "Right," she said. "Right. That calls for a cold one, don't you think?"

She turned and went to the kitchen. Her face felt hot, along with other parts of her body. She seriously needed to get control of her thoughts. "Two beers coming right up. Hope you like IPAs. That's all I have right now."

She pulled two frozen mugs out of the freezer and held them against her hot cheeks for a moment, then got two cans from the fridge. When she turned, she saw Whitney's handbag sitting on the kitchen island but no Whitney. "Where'd you go?"

"I'm out here," Whitney shouted from the back deck.

Brie stepped outside. Whitney was leaning on the balcony, her ass on full display again. Brie took a deep breath and said, "Beautiful night, isn't it?" She set the mugs and cans on the balcony ledge. "I wasn't sure if you'd want to drink out of the can."

"The can is fine." Whitney picked it up and read the label. "Ploughed Under. That sounds about right. Mind if I get drunk? I took an Uber here."

"Um…yeah, knock yourself out." That was when Brie noticed just how distraught Whitney looked. She chided herself for focusing on other body parts first, but what a body it was. Okay, she really did need to focus here because if she'd heard right, Whitney was there because she needed a friend. A friend. As in, a trustworthy confidant. The realization made her want to jump for joy and pull Whitney into her arms, but she managed to keep her cool. "Can I ask what happened?"

Whitney seemed surprised by the question. "You must not be a Johnny Falcon fan."

"I am, it's just that I'm kind of on a TV and social media break."

"How nice for you. Wish I could do the same." Whitney took the can and moved to the first step that led down to the Malibu shoreline. "Nice digs, by the way."

Brie sat next to her. "It's my grandparents' place. Well, my mom's now, but this is where we came for family get-togethers and holidays. I've never stayed here alone until now."

"Why is this different?"

"I'm here to write. Hence, the TV ban. But I keep looking around the place, and I'm noticing things I've never noticed before. Things I could repair or paint or refinish. All of the mission furniture in the living room is so cool, but it needs some TLC. The leather cushions on the sofa…" Brie stopped when Whitney put a hand on her leg. "Sorry, I could go on and on about this place."

Whitney shook her head. "No, it's not that, but can you back up to that thing you said about being a writer? How did I not know this?"

"Because I haven't published anything yet. I mean, I write a blog, but there's a book I've been working on, and my mom thought if I had this place to myself for a month, maybe I'd find some inspiration here." Brie took in a deep breath of the ocean air. "I hope she's right because that English degree I have hanging on my wall is starting to feel like something I bought online, and those four years are just a lesbian-sex-filled dream."

Whitney gave her a nudge. "Don't sell yourself short. On either front."

Brie tilted her head. "I'm not sure what you mean."

Whitney held up her can. "It'll take a few more of these before I'll admit that a certain book review, while completely off base and slightly cruel, was well executed. What I will admit, having only had half of a beer, is that you are an amazing lover. Something you learned during your college years, perhaps?"

Something felt off to Brie. It was possible that Whitney had started drinking before she even got there, and that was why she'd taken an Uber. By someone drunk or not, Brie liked being told she was a good lover. Especially by someone as incredible as Whitney.

"You're not so bad yourself," she said. "But that's not why you're here."

"That's true," Whitney said. "But I didn't realize it would be a beautiful moonlit night, and no doubt, there's a master bedroom with its own balcony where we could make love to the sound of waves crashing on the shore. I mean, come on. This is not something to be squandered."

"You probably didn't realize that I make a mean breakfast quiche either. Not to mention my cinnamon French toast."

Whitney smiled. "Isn't it funny that after the two nights we spent together, we didn't have breakfast together?"

"Well, that was just unexpectedly hot sex. The kind where you go home in someone else's workout clothes."

"And what would this be?"

Whitney was close enough to kiss. Her eyes were daring Brie to make the first move. Could it be that she'd gone there for a friend, but when she saw Brie, she also had the desire for more? It would be so easy to grab her hand and lead her to the bedroom, but Brie could smell something other than beer on her breath. Something that smelled a lot like whiskey. It wasn't the time to admit that it had always been more than just sex for her. So she put her arm around Whitney's shoulder and said, "You need a friend right now, and I want to be that person for you. So I'm going to give you a nice side hug and stop thinking about what's under that hoodie of yours, okay?"

Whitney's smile faded. "As much as I want to show you what's under this hoodie, I really do need a friend right now."

There was so much for Brie to be thankful for. She and Whitney were breathing the same air again. There was no hostility. No raised voices or harsh words. In fact, this was exactly what she'd longed for—time to talk. Time to just be together. She just needed to get the words "We could make love to the sound of waves crashing on the shore" out of her head. And she needed to not wrap her other arm around Whitney and kiss her shoulder and tell her how much she'd missed her. She stood and offered her hand. "Let's go for a walk."

They took their shoes off, and she led Whitney down to the surf. A cool breeze blew through their hair, and even in just the moonlight, Whitney looked beautiful. Sad but beautiful. And she hadn't let go of Brie's hand. In fact, her grip had only tightened.

They stopped before the water hit their feet. Whitney seemed to want to just stand there with her eyes closed and let the breeze blow on her face. After a moment or two, she opened her eyes and said, "My life is about to become a circus for all to watch. Oh, and there are several ringleaders trying to run the show."

"Is there a clown? I love a good clown," Brie quipped.

"Then you'd love Liz right now. She's making a total ass of herself in front of my house, trying to get me to answer the damn door."

"How do you know?"

Whitney smiled and pulled out her phone. She tapped on the app for the doorbell camera, and there was Liz, about two inches from the doorbell announcing that she'd wait as long as it took for Whitney to answer the door. "Your car's in the driveway, Whit. I know you're here."

Brie giggled. "How long are you going to let this go on?"

"I figure another hour or so ought to do it."

"Well, she'll never find you here. So back to the circus. Who's on the flying trapeze?"

"That would be Reece, and boy, did she get some applause."

"Is this where Johnny Falcon comes in?"

Whitney nodded. "Yeah. It's a shitshow. I mean, Johnny's show isn't shit, just…my life right now."

Whitney describing her life as being a shitshow when she wasn't referring to Brie was yet another thing to be grateful for. She led Whitney back to the dry sand where they could sit and talk. She snuggled in close and held Whitney's arm. "Tell me," she said.

Whitney shook her head. "Last night, Reece went on Falcon to show off her new tattoo."

"I didn't realize she was into tattoos. She must hide them well for photo shoots." Brie froze for a second. "Wait. I mean, not that I check out your wife's photos online. Shit." She slapped a hand over her eyes. "Okay, but it was just the one time."

Whitney gave her a side-eye and giggled. "It's okay. I think there might a tribe in the Amazon rainforest that hasn't been bombarded with photos of my ex-wife, but that's about it. The rest of us don't have a choice."

Brie realized what this was. And it was understandable that Whitney's feelings would be hurt by it. Especially since Reece went on TV to show it off to the whole world. Talk about a slap in the face. Of course she'd be upset by it. "Did she go for something cute like a pussycat or just something super on the nose like, I heart Kat?"

"She went for a name. My name. Right here."

Brie gasped when Whitney pointed at her lower abdomen. "Wha…I don't…she put your…isn't she with Kat?"

"You really did go dark, didn't you? God, I wish I could do that. I wish I could just sit here on this beach and let the world figure its fucking self out." She sighed and said, "They broke up. And now Reece thinks she can pull a stunt like that, and I'll just fall back into her arms, I guess."

Whitney finished the beer while Brie sat there in disbelief. How could she have missed all this? And who in their right mind would tattoo their ex's name on their body? And what did this mean for her and Whitney? Maybe this was the reason they were in the friend zone. "Who does that?" Brie blurted.

"That's the thing that gets me," Whitney said. "Reece isn't usually an impulsive person. I could never have imagined her doing something like that."

"You probably never imagined she'd cheat on you, either. People surprise us sometimes."

"That is so true," Whitney said. "Take Liz. Even after everything she saw me go through with the breakup, she had the nerve to push me to take Reece back."

"She pushed me to your hotel room too. What is it with that woman?"

"Oh, she explained that part," Whitney said. "You were only a means to get me back in the so-called saddle again. I guess you were supposed to remind me what sex feels like. As if I'd forgotten."

Brie gaped. "Wow. I don't feel used at all. Not that I regret any of it at this point." The truth was, she wanted to kiss Liz right on the lips for being a bad friend to Whitney so she could be there for her instead. She'd have to send her a bouquet with a card that said something like *Keep on being you, Liz. Love, the Saddle.*

Whitney rested her head on Brie's shoulder. "That's sweet of you to say. I don't regret it either."

Brie kissed her forehead like a good friend would do. "Can I ask how long it had been?"

Whitney sat up again. "Since I'd had sex? Gosh, I don't know. Reece and I separated about eighteen months ago. So not since before that. I was at my writing cabin in upstate New York, trying hard to meet my deadline on the last book and failing miserably. Reece was here in LA working on some low-budget indie film. Anyway, I had to drive down the mountain every few days to pick up phone service. I guess I should've suspected something was wrong when I didn't have any texts from her. What I did have was a voice mail from Liz telling me to call her back before I did anything else."

"Oh God," Brie said.

"Yeah. A big oh God. Liz is the one who told me that Reece had been spotted kissing another woman and that Josh, my publicist, was fielding calls for me. Everyone wanted to know if we'd broken up, and all I could think about was the reunion trip I'd planned for us. A romantic getaway to the south of France. Silly me."

Brie wrapped both arms around her. "I'm so sorry for what you've been through. I can't even imagine." The part she really couldn't imagine was the celebrity aspect where a person's every move was photographed and analyzed and discussed over coffee by total strangers. It made her feel dirty for ever picking up a gossip rag in the grocery store and thumbing through it.

Whitney patted Brie's arm and held it. "Thank you for saying that. It feels good to have someone say they care and really mean it."

With her whole heart, Brie meant it. And thinking she'd played a part in the pain Whitney had suffered made her want to cry. "I felt bad about the book review before," she said. "But now that I realize I added to all the heavy shit in your life, all I want to do is figure out how I can make it up to you."

Whitney nudged her. "Hey, you were the bomb in bed. I'm definitely back in the old saddle, galloping my way back to lesbian land or whatever."

"Glad I could help. And to be honest, I'm kind of proud to have fucked you back to 1996 when people actually said something was the bomb." They put their heads together and giggled. It felt so good to have Whitney back in her arms again. It felt right to Brie in every way. So right, she wished it was their house. Their beach. Their moon. God, how she wanted to take Whitney to the bedroom and make love to her. Wake up with her. Make breakfast for her and then make love to her again. But now wasn't the time.

So just like Brie had done before, she took in the moment, the sounds, the smells, the feel of Whitney's warmth. Her smile, her shampoo that smelled like strawberries. She also took some solace in the fact that this was where Whitney came for comfort. Not Liz. Not Reece. It was Brie. And that had to mean something.

"Thank you for listening to me," Whitney said. "I obviously needed to vent."

Brie turned Whitney so they were eye to eye. "I want you to look at me when I say this. I've got your back, okay? Anything you need. Anything at all, just ask."

Whitney's eyes filled with tears. She buried her face in Brie's neck and cried. And Brie was there for it. No matter what. She was there for it.

❖

A group of fifty female CEOs gathered together for talks on self-empowerment, spiritual growth, and how to escape from the stresses of life wouldn't give a crap about Whitney's love life. Would they? God, she hoped not.

After Reece's stunt on Falcon, she wanted to cancel everything and stay out of the public eye, but before she could do that, she had to fulfill the commitments she'd made. Leaving people in the lurch wasn't her style. So there she was, standing backstage in a very high-end resort in Marin County, hoping she had something, anything, relevant to say to these women. And also hoping none of them watched Johnny Falcon. Or read the news. Or looked at Twitter. It was all wishful thinking.

She'd chosen to wear a thin turtleneck sweater instead of a blouse and jacket. That particular audience wore enough power suits in real life. They didn't need to scrutinize Whitney's and wonder where she shopped. A white turtleneck with navy blue pegged trousers and a new pair of white Burberry sneakers seemed like the right choice. Casual but still refined.

She'd come alone. Liz was not out of the doghouse yet. Not by a long shot. She'd driven the seven hours alone the night before, needing the silence and lack of attention she'd surely get if she flew because now everyone with a phone knew what Reece's ex-wife looked like.

Her phone vibrated in her pocket. She'd declined so many calls already from Liz, Josh, Reece, journalists, her friends back in New York. Even her mom had reached out, but her mom loved Reece, so she knew how that conversation would go. She checked her phone and decided it was a call she'd gladly take. "Hey, you," she whispered. "What's up?"

"Glad I caught you before you went onstage," Brie said.

"Oh God. What now?"

"No, it's not like that. I just wanted to say good luck. You got this. Just be your charming, funny self, okay?"

Whitney breathed a sigh of relief. "I thought you were going to tell me Reece had bought a billboard or something equally embarrassing."

"Oh. Well, she did buy off the Department of Transportation. Yeah, every digital sign on the freeway has a sappy poem about love and forgiveness, and knowing LA drivers, they're all flipping it off as they go by anyway."

"Very funny."

"Hey. Don't put anything past a woman on a mission. I mean, look at me. I went to fucking Cincinnati for you, remember?"

"Yeah, that was a missed opportunity on my part. We should've—"

"Had sex in Cincinnati. I know, right? Hey. Bucket list." Brie stammered, "I mean, not now, you've got other things on your mind. Obvi."

Whitney smiled. "Obvi." She gave the stage manager a nod. "Hey, Brie, I just got the one-minute warning."

"Go get 'em, Whit. And let me know how it goes, okay?"

"I will. And thanks for calling."

Whitney took a few deep breaths while they announced her, then walked onstage to applause. She gave them all a wave and said, "Hello, everyone. Given the state of my life right now, I feel like I'm probably here for everyone's comic relief."

Enough women in the room laughed that she knew she couldn't pretend everything was fine. "Let's just get it all out on the table," she said. "My life is a mess. Messy, messy, messy. Anyone else feel that way? No? Okay, good. This would be a good time to whisper to the person next to you that you feel so sorry for me, and honestly, I would appreciate that sentiment because what. The. Fuck. With that tattoo?"

The audience roared with laughter and applause. Whitney sat in the wingback chair they'd put on stage, something she'd never had onstage before. She noticed several phones staying up in the air for longer than it would take to snap a photo, so she asked, "I wonder how many of you are hoping for some kind of shitshow today? An emotional breakdown on stage or a violent rant of some sort. Don't worry, I already did that in the hotel room. And in the car on the way here. And in the shower before I left. Maybe in the bathtub the night before that. But that's okay, right? Because letting it out is how we get through it. At least, I hope it is, or I'm screwed."

She had them, all of them, in the palm of her hand. She stood and went to the edge of the stage. "You all are some of the smartest, most successful women I will ever meet. So let's talk about your messed-up lives instead of mine. Female CEOs? Are you kidding me? The shit you must have to deal with."

The audience roared and whistled before someone yelled, "I can top the tattoo."

Whitney grinned. "That's a tall order. So let's hear it."

She'd make it through this one just fine. And then, maybe it was time for her to get back to what she was really good at. Maybe it was time to give Piper Kane the ending she deserved. And maybe, as a thank you gift to Brie, she'd make Piper gay. After all, there wasn't anything better than watching, or reading about, two women falling madly in love.

❖

Brie had spent way too much time wandering around with her headphones on. Her dad had been kind enough to let her work remotely while she stayed in the beach house, but it wouldn't last long if she didn't get her work done.

She probably shouldn't have called Whitney to wish her luck. Objectively, it was a good thing for a friend to do, but hearing that sexy phone voice took Brie back to hotel rooms and heavy breathing, and fuck, why did she call her? It would be far more appropriate to think about their conversation on the beach since it involved non-sexual hugs that were meant to comfort, not titillate. But having her lips on Whitney's temple and breathing her in while she cried felt very intimate to Brie. That made her wonder if Whitney felt it too, the bond that was forming between them. She loved that she could be there for Whitney, but it was more than that. Whitney had asked about her family, her blog, her past, her writing. Especially her writing. That was one thing that came up again and again. Brie's support system consisted mostly of family and a few college friends back east. The connection with Whitney felt right even if it was mixed with a bit of lustfulness from time to time.

Hard as she tried to just be the supportive friend, her thoughts kept going back to what Whitney had said to her a few days before. "You are an amazing lover," she'd said. And oh, how Brie wanted to give her more of that amazing love. Maybe on the two-person lounger on the deck after dark. That would be romantic and unforgettable.

She went outside and stretched out on the blue and white striped lounger. She ran her fingers over the fabric and imagined Whitney lying next to her, wrapped in a blanket, her hair messy from the breeze. She'd be naked under that blanket. Brie set her phone down and closed her eyes so she could really envision it.

It would be just after dusk. The backrest of the lounger set to almost flat. They'd have their bathing suits on and beach towels wrapped around their bodies. An empty bottle of wine sitting on the side table. It would've cooled down enough to need a blanket. Brie would get a big one from the closet instead of two smaller ones.

When Whitney removed her damp towel, Brie would stand there for a few seconds and admire that body the way she'd done all afternoon. When Whitney asked if something was wrong, Brie would cover it up by saying, "It looks like you got some color."

Whitney would pull her bikini top to the side and say, "Yeah, I guess I did."

Brie would lie back down and wish she could point out some stars, but in LA, they were hard to find, so she would put the blanket over them and lie on her side, facing Whitney. That was a much better view anyway.

"Look, it's a full moon," Whitney would say.

Brie would reach over and run the back of her finger across Whitney's cheek. "I just want to look at you," she'd say.

Whitney would roll onto her side as well, and they'd gaze at each other. Brie's eyes would wander down to that tan line and back up again. "I want you," she'd whisper.

Whitney wouldn't hesitate. "What are you waiting for?"

Brie would get on top of her, their almost naked bodies melding together the way they'd done before. Whitney would open her legs and wrap them around Brie's hips. They'd move as one, grinding into each other, breathing harder, eyes locked on each other. Whitney would make that little moaning sound, and Brie would muffle it with a kiss. Their tongues would explore, and that breathing would get real shallow.

Whitney would pull that bikini top to the side again. All the way this time because she loved it when attention was paid to her breasts. And Brie was more than happy to nip and suck until she felt Whitney urge her over to the other one.

Whitney would push her hips up hard to create more pressure, but it wouldn't be enough. She would push her bikini bottoms down and whisper, "Fuck me." And when Brie slid her hand between them, she'd feel just how turned on Whitney was.

Brie wouldn't have to go slow. She'd push in with two fingers, and Whitney would cry out. She'd dig her nails into Brie's shoulders and buck her hips, and that was when Brie would also have to cry out because nothing she'd ever experienced could compare to being inside the woman she loved.

Brie's eyes popped open. She'd just used the L-word. Only in her head but still. If she went there in her head, she was bound to say it out loud at some point, and it would be so bad if Whitney didn't return the sentiment. Not really bad so much as heartbreaking. And she knew it wasn't what Whitney needed right now. She needed space. She needed to get over her ex. To keep her public image intact. To write a book. She needed a friend. And maybe that would have some occasional benefits. And why was Brie obsessing about everything they weren't? She decided to set those thoughts aside and closed her eyes again. Because the deck was very private, she decided to slip her hand into her shorts. "Now, then. Where was I?"

She was inside Whitney. Curling her fingers inside her. That was when Whitney would need Brie's tongue in her mouth too. And a thumb on her clit. And the words "Fuck, you're so sexy." And Whitney's entire body would tense up because she was close. So close. And then she'd say it out loud. "Fuck, I'm close."

Brie jumped when her phone rang. She took her hand out of her shorts and sat up. "Hello! I mean, hi. How did it go?"

"Everything okay? You sound…"

Turned on? Flustered? Like I was just about to come?
"Nothing's wrong. I'm good. I was just…um, nothing. What's up?"

Whitney laughed. "You wanted to know how it went, remember?"

"Right." Brie put a hand between her legs and squeezed them together. "How did it go?"

"Did I interrupt something? I can call back."

Brie wanted so badly to tell Whitney exactly what she'd been thinking. And doing. But that wasn't going to happen. Kindness and support were her focus right now. A shoulder when needed. Possibly a lunch date or two. Whatever it took to keep Whitney in her life was what she'd do because losing her now, right when they were really getting to know each other? No. Brie wouldn't let that happen. "You didn't interrupt anything. Tell me how it went."

"I'd rather get on the road and tell you tonight when I get back. I'm really calling to ask if I can stay the night with you. I won't get any sleep knowing there are paparazzi parked on my street. Reece's stunt on Falcon has them clamoring for some kind of money shot."

"Isn't your house gated?"

"It is, but the street isn't private. Also, I made the mistake of giving Liz my gate code, but it's okay if that doesn't work for you. I can check into a hotel for a night or two. I'm sure this will die down as long as Reece behaves herself."

"Okay, stop, Whit. Of course, you can stay here. There's an extra spot in the garage. I'll send the code, okay?"

"I really appreciate it," Whitney said. "And I promise, I won't be a bother. Oh, and Brie? This means a lot to me. Thank you for being a great friend."

"Of course. See you soon." Brie set her phone down. Whitney wouldn't be a bother, but she'd sure as hell get Brie *hot* and bothered. She looked at her watch and figured she had six to seven hours to get her libido under control. She got up and went back into the house. "Cold shower, here I come."

CHAPTER NINE

TV wasn't the sound Brie expected to hear through the master bedroom door. Whitney had gotten in so late, she was sure she'd hear a steady snore. She knocked gently. "Whitney? Are you up? I have coffee."

Whitney opened the door. "I couldn't sleep. And I'm pretty sure I'm having a breakdown, so enter at your own risk."

Brie had no idea that Whitney slept in actual pajamas. In fact, she thought the long-sleeved button-up with matching bottoms was something they only wore in old movies. It was quite possibly the cutest thing she'd ever seen. "I'm digging the pj's. Very hip in a Dick Van Dyke sort of way."

Whitney got back under the covers and leaned against the headboard. "I wear them when I travel alone in case there's a fire and I have to run out into the street or something. Also, I get cold sleeping alone."

Yep, the cutest thing she'd ever seen. Brie gave her a cup of coffee and set a muffin on the nightstand. "Like I said, I'm digging it." She sat on the edge of the bed with one leg up. "So a breakdown, huh?"

"Not because of the conference. It went fine. It was the ride home. All that alone time had me thinking long and hard about my life and wondering how I got so sidetracked. I wish I could just go back east and hide out in my cabin and write book four."

Brie perked up. "Book four? There's going to be a book four?"

"Well, I can't let that damned *Brie on Books* be right, can I?"

"*No.* She's a terrible person with a terrible logo. She needs to be put in her place ASAP."

"Oh, I put her in her place all right. Right up my…"

She giggled, which made Brie giggle. "Yes. Yes, you did."

Whitney slapped her hands over her face. "God, I'm a mess."

Brie put a hand on Whitney's leg and gave it a comforting rub. "You're not doing so bad, considering. And the cabin sounds like a great idea."

"I can't leave LA right now. I'm a consultant on the movie, and they start shooting in a few days."

Was there a movie god? Or gods? If so, Brie wanted to thank them for keeping Whitney in LA. Hell, she'd worship them. Offer up a human sacrifice. Build them a temple. She kept those thoughts to herself and asked, "What else is bothering you?"

Whitney took a sip of coffee and held it on her lap. "Isn't that enough?"

Brie figured there was more, but she didn't want to push it. "If you say it is, then it is." Brie pointed at the plate she'd set on the nightstand "Hey, I made that muffin with my own hands, so I expect you to at least take a bite."

Whitney didn't move. She kept her eyes firmly locked on Brie. Her nose was red, and her eyes were swollen, and that pajama top was buttoned crookedly, but she still had a sexiness about her that made Brie feel all kinds of warm inside, and steady eye contact only made it worse. She was about to stand when Whitney cleared her throat and said, "I need someone in my life to tell me I'm not insane if I don't run back into Reece's arms."

Brie gave her a wry smile. "I can see why you picked me, then. Now, about that muffin."

Whitney pulled the paper wrapper back and took a bite. "Mmm, tasty muffin."

"That's what *she* said."

Whitney narrowed her eyes. "You were waiting for an opening, weren't you?"

"A muffin opening? I have no idea what you're talking about."

"Uh-huh." Whitney set it back down and dusted the crumbs from her fingers. Her smile faded before she said, "Listen. I know we had a rough start."

Was that what they were calling it? Because Brie had come to think of it as the best thing that had ever happened to her. Sure, it was a complete disaster, and in the moments after getting thrown out on her ass, it had felt like the most tragic event to ever occur. But still. She liked where they were, and she hoped that wasn't all. The morning buzz Brie had going wasn't just from her first cup of coffee. She'd been hyped up and happy because in the next room, Whitney was sleeping. Whitney was in her house. Not in Brie's bed, which would've been so much better. One thing Brie knew for sure, she wasn't ready for the whole *we started off rough so let's forget about that hot sex we had and be friends* speech. "Maybe I like it rough," she said with a shrug. "Wanna find out?"

"Really? I'm trying to apologize here, and you're making sex jokes."

"Oh," Brie said. "Well, in that case, I'll bite my own tongue for an apology, although you do it better than anyone." She put up her hands. "Sorry. Zipping my lips now."

Whitney smirked. "How could you possibly think about sex when I'm wearing these not very sexy pajamas?"

"*Au contraire, mi amore.* They bring back my preteen Laura Petrie fantasies. We just need some twin beds—" Brie jumped up. "Oh, my God. All of the DVDs my grandma had of that show are probably in this house somewhere. I remember watching them with her here." She sat back down. "Okay, I have to find them."

"Maybe I can come back some night for pizza and Laura Petrie," Whitney said.

"And muffins. Don't forget the tasty muffin." Brie gave her a suggestive wink.

Whitney rolled her eyes. "Do you want an apology or not?"

"More than anything. Even better if you're naked while expressing your regrets. Okay, fine. Keep the pajamas on. I'm good with that too." Brie crossed her legs and clasped her hands together. "Okay, go. I'm ready."

"If I wasn't such a mess right now, I'd shut you up with a kiss."

Starting on her shin, Brie slowly walked her fingers up Whitney's leg. "Have I told you what a terrible friend I am? Amazing lover. The opposite of amazing friend."

Whitney grabbed her fingers before she could go past mid-thigh and held on. "I doubt that. I bet you're a really great friend. And I really want you to be my friend."

Brie forced a smile. "I want you to be mine too." She kept the "with benefits" part to herself.

Whitney took a deep breath. "Okay, coming in hot with an apology. I'm really sorry I was so rude to you the night we met."

Brie tilted her head. "Actually, you were rude the following morning. That night you were anything but rude."

Whitney leaned forward and took Brie's hand in both of hers. "Can you start over with me? I mean, I don't want to erase the good parts, just the bad parts."

"Will there be flirting and innuendo and Laura Petrie roleplay? You know what her signature phrase was, right? Well, it just so happens that I can do a mean impression."

"I have to hear it." Brie tried to pull her hand away, but Whitney held on tight. "I'm serious. I have to hear your Laura Petrie impression."

Brie stood. "Maybe one day, if you're lucky. In the meantime, your purple workout clothes are on a shelf in the bathroom. I'll meet you on the deck in five."

"What are we doing on the deck?"

"Yoga," Brie said. "It might make me a glutton for punishment, but I'm going to get your ass in the air." She closed the door behind her and took a deep breath. Not only would this friend thing not be easy, it would be damn hard.

Whitney slapped Brie's butt on the way back into the house. "I had no idea you were so limber. That thing where you put your leg over your head and—" She stopped when she saw a stranger in the house.

"Mom," Brie said. "What are you doing here?"

That was Brie's mother? Whitney thought she looked too young to have a thirty-year-old child. And she certainly didn't seem happy that her daughter had a friend in the house. She looked like a mama grizzly ready to stand up for her cubs.

"What did I say about Tinder, Gabriela?"

Brie spun around and whispered to Whitney, "I don't use Tinder." She spun back around and said, "Mom, this is Whitney. I told you about her, remember?"

"Yes, I recognize the purple clothes." Her mom reached into a bag and pulled out what looked like the ingredients for chicken salad. Whitney realized how hungry she was when she caught a whiff of the whole chicken that had clearly just come off the rotisserie at the grocery store. "I didn't realize you had company." her mom said without looking up.

It was apparent to Whitney that Brie's mother was being less than gracious. In fact, the Tinder comment must've been meant as some kind of insult. She wasn't sure what the purple clothes comment was about. But then she remembered that Brie had to wear them home after their first night together. Which probably meant Mama knew. Which was only slightly more horrifying than two creepy twins standing at the end of the hallway in an abandoned hotel.

The way Whitney saw it, she had two choices. She could cower behind Brie, or she could walk right up to the woman and offer her hand. She chose the latter. "Whitney Ainsworth. Brie was kind enough to let me stay the night when I was too tired to drive home last night."

Her mom was polite enough to give her hand a quick shake. "Jade Talbot."

She went back to sorting out her groceries, so Whitney backed away. "I'll get out of your way since it looks like you have lunch plans with your daughter, who's a really lovely person, by the way."

Jade stopped what she was doing and scrutinized Whitney from head to toe. "She is a lovely person, which is why I encouraged her to stay away from Hollywood types. And then I saw your wife showing off that tattoo with your name on it, and I breathed a sigh of relief that I'd given Gabriela that advice, assuming she'd chosen to follow it. So imagine my dismay when I walk into my own house, and here you are."

"Mom."

Jade put up her hand. "I'm talking, baby. Don't interrupt me. Now, I've tried my damnedest to keep my kids away from the atmosphere I grew up in. I want something better for them. I know

I can't save them from heartache, but I can be damn sure they won't need a publicist to manage it when they do."

Whitney cringed. *Touché.* "Ma'am, I understand why you don't want them to be a part of this."

"I'm not sure you do. Thirty plus years ago, when I was a teenager, do you know what it was like to exist in a world full of men who believed they were entitled to everything? Their power and wealth bought them whatever they wanted. My parents were powerful enough that those men knew to keep their distance from me. I had a few friends who weren't so lucky."

"Mom," Brie's voice registered just above a whisper. "Why didn't you tell us this before?"

"I've tried my hardest to keep you from it. All of it." Mama Bear looked at Whitney and continued. "I want them to find loyal partners who won't cheat on them with the likes of Kat Blumenthal and then come running back when they realize who she really is."

How did this woman know who Kat Blumenthal "really is"? Whitney looked to Brie for an explanation.

"My mom grew up with Kat. Old Hollywood families."

Jade continued. "Kat's sense of entitlement isn't so far off from those men I was talking about."

"Ah," Whitney said. She didn't know Kat well. Barely at all, really. She couldn't blame her for wanting to keep Brie away from that. But she guessed Jade's ire toward her was about more than her association with Kat or even Hollywood in general. "I take it you saw Reece on Falcon?"

"The whole world saw her on Falcon." Jade stepped closer to Whitney and folded her arms. "I can't account for Gabriela's taste in women, and I can't tell her who she can and can't spend time with. What I can do, if I ever see a photo of her so much as walking down the street with you, is reach out to people I know in the industry."

Brie moved between them. "Okay, enough, Mom. Stop playing mob boss. Whitney isn't who you're making her out to be. She isn't going to hurt me, okay?"

"I want to hear it from her, Gabriela."

Brie stepped out of the way again, her face bright red with embarrassment. "I'm so sorry about this."

Whitney gave her a reassuring smile. "It's okay. Your mom is a fierce woman who loves her kids. I'm not offended by that. In fact, I admire it." She turned to Jade. "My life is messy right now, and unfortunately, the whole world gets to witness it. And believe me, I'm embarrassed about that. In fact, I'd like to run away from all of it. But I can't. I have to stay in LA because they'll be shooting a movie adaptation of my first book soon. So I'm stuck here, in the middle of the mess that my ex-wife created. And to top it all off, she has the lead role in the film, obviously not my choice at this point. So, yeah, it's a circus, but I can assure you that I'm not the clown or the ringmaster or the lion tamer. Unlike the rest of the world, I don't even want to be in the audience for this particular show. I'm just so grateful your daughter extended me kindness last night when I knew she was taking time for herself to write. I needed a friend, and she was there for me."

She said it all so fast, she wasn't sure if it even made any sense. Jade's silence was deafening. "I'll get my things," Whitney said.

"You'll stay for lunch." Jade went back to her groceries. "If you just did yoga with Gabriela, then you'll need sustenance before you leave. I'll never understand how she turns serenity into an aerobic activity." She looked Whitney in the eye. "Sorry about the Tinder comment. I knew who you were the second I saw you, and not just because of the clothes. It's nice to meet you."

Brie's sigh of relief made Whitney smile. She gave her a wink and said, "Nice to meet you too, Jade."

Brie opened Whitney's car door for her and stood behind it. "Who knew you had such a way with parents?"

Whitney put up her little finger. "I have Jade right here."

"Yeah, once she got off her high horse, I could tell she really liked you."

Whitney tossed her purse in the car. "Well, I am a celebrated author and public speaker. Having a way with words should definitely be in my wheelhouse."

"Can I be in your wheelhouse? Sorry. My bad." Brie backed

away from the car. Why couldn't she just shut up and accept what she had with Whitney right now? Hell, she was hanging out with her favorite author. That didn't happen every day.

Whitney closed the car door and took a step closer. "I don't want you to think you're the only one this is hard for."

Brie glanced at the garage door and hoped her mom would stay in the damn house. "Are you saying you're having to stop yourself from kissing me good-bye too?"

"I'm saying that even if I wanted to, I'm in no condition to start anything with anybody."

"Right. Reece."

"Yes, but not because I have feelings for her. I'm just dealing with a lot. She's a lot. My team is a bunch of traitors, or at least it feels that way, and I have a movie that's about to start. Oh, and a book I want to write. And I know it's not where we naturally go, but I really need you as a friend right now."

She looked so weary, Brie wanted to pull her into her arms, but she kept her hands by her sides. "I understand. The important thing is that I don't lose you. I kinda like having you in my life now, you know?"

"Yeah. I do know. It feels pretty good to me too." Whitney opened her arms. "How about a hug good-bye?"

Brie held her close. "You're welcome here anytime. I know because my mom said so."

"Call me. Or I'll call you. One of us should call."

"One of us will." Brie said the words as she let go, but she knew it wouldn't be her who called next time. She'd done enough chasing. She knew Whitney needed some control in her own life for the first time in a long time. Brie had made it clear what she wanted, but whatever happened next would have to be up to Whitney.

"Good luck with your writing," Whitney said. "If you need any tips, I just happen to be a—"

"Celebrated author," Brie said. "I kinda already knew that about you, Whitney Ainsworth. You see, I have this little blog that you've probably never heard of."

Whitney got in her car and leaned out the window. "See you later, Cheese Wedge."

"Hey, I've got my people working on that logo. Just sayin'."

Whitney rolled her window up and backed out of the driveway. She gave Brie a wave before she drove off. "See you later," Brie whispered. "Sooner rather than later, I hope."

Her mom turned off the kitchen faucet and dried her hands with a dish towel when Brie walked back inside. Brie sat at the table and covered her eyes with her hands. "Don't ask."

"I have to, honey. How deep in are you?"

Brie clasped her hands in front of her mouth. "Seriously. Don't ask."

"Oh, Gabriela. What am I going to do with you?"

"I'll be okay. I just have to figure out how to let friendship be enough for now."

Her mom sat next to her. "One would think you'd be an expert by now. Remember my friend Joy? I had to convince you that you couldn't marry a married woman three times your age."

Embarrassed, Brie shook her head. "I remember feeling so sure that she loved me too."

That was pretty much the story of Brie's dating life. She had such a knack for falling too hard too fast for women who were either unavailable or totally wrong for her. It was possible Whitney fell into both of those categories. It was also possible she wasn't falling for Brie at all. She turned to her mom. "What did you see? I mean, do you think Whitney could ever love me?"

"Oh, I think she'd be crazy not to, but if you're asking me if I saw that look in her eyes when she looked at you...I can't be sure. But I know for sure that she cares about you, and I believe her when she says she wouldn't hurt you."

Brie huffed. "Great. So I'm firmly planted in the friend zone now. She told me she needs that more than she needs a relationship."

"That's smart on her part. I'm not much for TMZ, but if you watch it for five minutes, you can see why Whitney needs a break. Besides, maybe she's trying to protect that tender heart of yours. Not to mention hers." Her mom stood and pulled Brie up. She took her into her arms and kissed her cheek. "Use the pain, honey. Write your way through it. I'm sure Whitney would tell you to do the same."

❖

Brie closed her laptop and finished her glass of wine while she watched the sun disappear into the ocean. It was a completely different experience having the beach house all to herself. Normally, there would be laughter coming from both the house and the water. The sounds and scents of dinner being made would waft out the sliding glass door. A football or basketball game on the TV. All of that was special, but this was special in a different way.

It was a soul thing. A stillness that allowed her to experience nature in a way she'd never had before. She closed her eyes and took in a deep breath of the salty air.

"Breezy?"

She opened her eyes and turned around. "And here I was just thinking about how much I was enjoying the silence."

Adam plopped down on the lounger and patted the spot next to him. Her dad had texted her earlier to see if she wanted to go surfing with them, so it wasn't a surprise that his hair was a mess, and his board shorts looked like they were still damp.

Brie liked this version of her brother more than the slick businessman look he sported during the day. It wasn't like him to not grab a beer before going outside to chill on the deck. Brie narrowed her eyes. "Oh God. Mom told you. That's why you're here, isn't it?"

He put out his arms. "Come let your big brother hug your boo-boo away." He pushed out his bottom lip for effect.

Brie let out a dramatic huff, but she got up from the table and cuddled in next to him. "If this ends in a tickle fest, I will seriously punch you right in the balls."

"You always miss, Breezy. It must be a lesbian thing."

The truth was, Brie had only hit her target once. Unfortunately, Adam had cried like a little baby, so her dad had taken her aside and explained just how much it hurt if you hit a boy there. That was why she continually made the threat but purposely missed. "It must be," she said with a shrug. "But at least I can find a woman's—" She screamed when he found her underarm but managed to wriggle away and jump off the lounger.

He chased her down the stairs, through the deep sand. She threw off her bathing suit cover and tossed it behind her in the hope he'd trip over it, but he caught her just as she jumped through the waves and lost her balance. She came up out of the water sputtering, and he came up laughing his ass off. She jumped on his back, and he spun around a few times before throwing her into the water again. They both crawled up to dry sand and collapsed in a fit of laughter.

Once they'd caught their breath, Adam rolled onto his side. Brie could see it in his eyes, so she said it for him. "Love you, stupid big brother."

Adam laughed. "Love you too, dumb little sis." He got up and pulled her up. "Got any chips and salsa? I'm starving."

"Oh," Brie said. "Let's roast marshmallows and make s'mores. Want to?"

"Hell, yes, I want to." He grabbed her bathing suit cover and draped it over her shoulders.

❖

Brie wasn't angry Adam had invaded her special time at the beach house. It was kind of nice to have him all to herself outside of work and parent stuff. They teased the hell out of each other, but the bond between them ran deep.

He came out of the house with a fishing pole and sat on the lounger next to her. "What the hell are you going to do with that?" she asked.

"Roast my marshmallow while I gaze at the stars."

Brie watched him attach the marshmallow to the hook, knowing he hadn't really thought it through. "Just be a normal person and sit up while roasting your marshmallow." She set a plate in between them. "I've got your graham crackers and chocolate right here."

He slowly leaned back and let the marshmallow dangle over the flames. "Shh," he whispered. "There's a genius at work."

Brie snorted. "This is why you can't get women. They see you do stuff like this and they're like, he hasn't got any brains in that pretty little head of his."

The fishing line melted, and the marshmallow fell into the flames. Adam stared at it for a few seconds, then tossed the fishing pole to the side and said, "How is it that you manage to snag better-looking women than me?"

Brie stifled her laughter and pointed at the fishing pole. "Need I say more?"

"I'm being serious. Whitney Ainsworth wouldn't give me a second look."

"That's because she likes pu…the fairer sex. Besides, I haven't managed to snag anyone. Or are you just referring to getting a pretty woman in bed? Because, yeah, that isn't a problem for me." She flicked an imaginary piece of dust off her shoulder and cleared her throat.

Adam unsuccessfully tried to hide a grin. "We haven't talked much about personal stuff lately."

Brie's expression sobered. It wasn't like Adam to initiate a serious conversation that wasn't about work or their parents. When it came to the two of them, he never showed his vulnerable side, if he even had one. And getting girls wasn't the least bit difficult for him, which made Brie wonder what this was all about. "You want personal? Well, as you already know, I fell for a pretty girl again. An unavailable pretty girl, which is not news to anyone. Seems to be my modus operandi. What about you?"

Adam lay his head back. "Believe it or not, I want to settle down and have some little ones running around. Try to be a bit more present as a dad than ours was, you know?"

"You're ten years older than Dad was when he had us. You'll do just fine, bro."

He ran his fingers through his messy hair and hemmed and hawed for a minute. Brie put a hand on his shoulder. "What are you worried about? I'm sure there are lots of women out there who would love to make babies with you. And you'd make Mom and Dad the happiest grandparents on earth. I think they consider me a lost cause at this point."

"Yeah, there's just one little problem I have."

Brie scrunched her nose. "Ew. Personal is one thing, but talking about your low sperm count?"

"I don't have a low sperm count, Breezy. It's much worse than that." He let out a big sigh and groaned. "I have this problem where I always compare the women I date to you, and they never stack up."

"Dude, that's gross. Seriously. So not funny."

"I'm being serious, Breeze. I don't mean in, like, a pervy way. I mean like I want a girl who's smart and kind and talented and funny. A girl who'd go to the ends of the earth for the one she loves. And who wants me to do the same."

Brie's jaw dropped. "Are you punking me? You are so punking me right now. You want me to buy into that, and then you'll say, ha ha, just kidding, you're a hot mess."

Adam shook his head. "Not this time. And it's so fucked-up. I mean, who wants to marry their sister? Not literally, but God, I'm not explaining myself well."

He was serious? Brie wanted to laugh out loud, but he seemed so pained by it, she didn't dare. Why would he want to find someone like her? He needed a woman who would appreciate his fine taste in clothing, shoes, and haircuts. Someone who worried as much about her appearance as he did. Someone with collagen injections, not someone who wore sneakers with oversized sweaters and ate cake whenever she wanted. That reminded her that she needed to definitely not mention the slice of chocolate cake with double fudge frosting waiting for her in the fridge.

Although the thought was a really difficult one to wrap her head around, maybe what Adam was really trying to say was that he wanted more than just a pretty face. Maybe he wanted his future wife to be a talkative, opinionated lesbian with a bad logo. No, that wasn't it. He wanted someone real. Someone down to earth. That kind of woman she could get behind. Not literally because she'd be Adam's wife but figuratively for sure.

"Okay," she said. "So maybe it's a twin thing. But here's what I know, bro. You will be a great dad and a fantastic husband, and you'll have it all way before me, so I'll have to dote on your kids and of course be their favorite aunt, and most importantly, I'm going to love who you choose to marry because she'll look and sound just like me, and that isn't weird at all. Are you kidding? I'll fucking love it. I might even develop a crush on your wife, so watch out. Wait." She tried to protect her underarms, but he was too quick for her. "Stop. Adam, stop."

Once he'd tickled her to the point of making her scream at the top of her lungs, he lay back again and put his hands behind his head.

"Ew," she said. "I thought metrosexuals shaved their hairy armpits. Get that shit away from me."

Any other time, he might torture her by forcing her to smell those pits, but he surprised her when he put his arms down and said, "Thanks for the talk, sis. I'm going to start dating blondes with short hair and big boobs." He jumped up and was about to walk away, but he stopped. "Also, you're going to find the one, sis. Someone with as big a heart as yours."

Brie smiled, but what she really wanted to do was cry because who knew if he was right about that? "Promise?" she asked.

"Promise. Gotta go. Tinder's waiting." He grabbed some chocolate and graham crackers and went back in the house.

Brie pulled a big beach towel over herself and watched the flames dance in the firepit. She touched the empty spot next to her where Whitney would be lying if they were together. She imagined Adam's kids, along with her own, chasing each other around the deck and begging for another marshmallow. They'd have a daughter that looked just like Whitney with blond hair and big brown eyes. She'd have her mom's laugh too. When she tired from playing with her cousins, Brie would wrap her in a towel and hold her while they talked about how hot fire is and how big the sky was and why sand felt so funny between her toes. And when she finally fell asleep, Brie would reach for Whitney's hand and whisper, *I love you.*

Maybe it wasn't meant to be, but she could still dream.

CHAPTER TEN

A public lunch wasn't a good idea, but Whitney didn't love the idea of letting Reece back into the home they'd once shared, either, and she knew their first meeting since their divorce couldn't be when they both walked onto the Piper Kane set. Not in front of the entire crew and definitely not right before the first table-read.

Whitney pushed the button to open the gate. It was early. Too early for a night owl like Reece, but that was their best chance for privacy. She opened the front door a crack and went into the kitchen to pour herself a cup of coffee.

"Whit?"

"In here."

Reece rounded the corner and stopped. "Hi."

There was hesitation in her voice. Whitney could appreciate that. She was hesitant too but probably for different reasons. She stayed on the other side of the island and tried not to make eye contact just yet. "Coffee?"

"God, yes." Reece set her purse on the table and pulled out a chair. "Should I sit here?"

"Sit wherever you like." Whitney poured another cup and took them both over to the table. She chose not to sit directly across from Reece but one chair to the left. A strategy based on nothing except her petty desire to inflame the permanent kink in Reece's neck.

Her blond hair was piled on top of her head the way she usually wore it on the weekends. Her jeans were also of the weekend variety, distressed and sitting low on her hips. All of this was good as far as

Whitney was concerned. It meant Reece wasn't trying too hard. She was being her normal self, not the Hollywood version.

Whitney leaned back in her chair and folded her arms before she looked Reece in the eye. "That was quite a stunt you pulled on Falcon. I don't suppose you really thought through how it would affect my life. All the unwanted attention, all the speculation. We are long over, and you know it. No amount of ink is going to change that."

"Okay, so I guess we're going to be all formal like we're in the lawyer's office." Reece dropped her gaze and sipped her coffee. "I've missed my favorite cup."

"Take it."

"Ouch."

Whitney raised an eyebrow. "Ouch? Really, Reece?"

"Okay, I know. I get it."

Whitney wasn't sure Reece got anything. Did she have any idea of the damage she'd done? The pain she'd caused? Probably not. She did seem a bit shaky, though. "Are you nervous?"

"Terrified," Reece said. "So I'll just come right out and say it. I miss us, and I want you back."

"How convenient since you just got dumped." Whitney made sure she sounded confident and unshaken. She had to if she was going to have any control over the conversation.

"Actually, I did the dumping," Reece said. "I should've done it sooner, but Kat is a strong personality. Way stronger than me."

"She forced you to have sex with her? Maybe you should've called the police instead of moving in with her."

"That's not what I mean. I mean, I was a fool, Whit. Start to finish, I was a damned fool. She sucked me into her world and made me think it was where I belonged, but I hate her world. I hate how fake it is. I hate how I couldn't trust anyone, including her. And I hate that I believed all her promises for way longer than I should have.

"Yeah. It's rough when you can't trust the person you're sleeping with."

Reece winced. "I deserve that and any other references to infidelity you want throw my way."

"How big of you to admit that. I wish you'd shown that kind of maturity before you decided it would be a swell idea to have an affair with another woman."

Reece lowered her gaze. "Why am I here, Whit?"

"Two things. I want you to change your name back. It isn't fair to keep mine, so change it now, before you become Piper Kane."

"I won't ever go back to that name. Ever."

Whitney couldn't blame her. Reece Wiener didn't have the same ring to it. It wasn't Hollywood enough. There were other reasons too. Her dad was the epitome of an obnoxious car salesman, famous throughout the state of Nebraska for his TV commercials. *Test drive a car at a Wiener's and get a free pack of wieners. Buy a car and we'll give you a year's supply!*

"Then change it to something else," Whitney said. "It doesn't belong to you."

Her eyes filled with tears. Whitney had to look away. Reece crying was something she never could take. It melted her convictions and made her forget why she was ever mad in the first place, and Reece knew it. She had to stay strong.

"I guess I could do that," Reece whispered. She wiped her tears away and let out a short laugh. "Sorry. I'm really not doing this to break you down."

"You already took care of that," Whitney said. "For a long time, all I could think about was how a rug had been pulled out from under me, and I couldn't get back up off the floor. But you, Reece, you were out there having the time of your life, weren't you? Laughing and drinking too much wine before you two fucked each other silly in a hotel in Paris or Rome or wherever the hell it was. Yeah, I saw the photos."

Reece covered her eyes and shook while she cried. Once she got her emotions under control, she asked, "What's the other thing you wanted to talk about?"

Whitney wasn't surprised she didn't want to address the truth. Moving on to the next thing was much easier than admitting that was exactly how it happened. "We're going to have to work together on the set. How do you see that going?"

"After this conversation, not so well."

"Yeah, me neither." Whitney leaned forward in her chair. "But we both have the same goal. We both need it to be a box office hit so they'll want to make the next movie and the next."

Reece nodded. "I want that for both of us."

"Good. Then here's the plan. You stop it with the media stunts. No more grand gestures on national television. In fact, don't ever mention me again in the media. If someone brings it up, deflect. And in turn, I'll give you the respect you deserve as the lead in this movie. No one will see anything but professionalism from both of us. If we both do that, we'll get through it and then get back to getting on with our own lives."

"Okay," Reece said. "But aren't you even a little bit curious?"

Whitney leaned back again. "About what?"

"My tattoo. Don't you want to see it up close?"

Whitney stared at Reece and wondered if she was really looking at the woman she'd married seven years ago. She knew her face. Her lips. Her body. She knew what made her laugh and what made her sad. She knew how to turn her on and how to boost her confidence when she felt insecure. But the woman who'd done something so manipulative, so insincere, so downright asinine…that woman was foreign to her. "Your tattoo is just proof that you're still willing to bulldoze right over me if it suits your needs. So, no. I have no desire to see it up close. Seeing it on Falcon with the rest of civilization was enough for me."

"Okay. Wow, it's getting chilly in here."

Whitney wanted to pound the table and scream and throw things and say *fuck you* over and over. But showing rage would mean showing emotion. So she simply tilted her head and said, "What did you expect? Did you think that because there was a time when I was so proud and so happy to be your wife that I'd welcome you back with open arms? You killed that, Reece."

She didn't answer right away. Then she got up and emptied her cup in the sink. She stood there with her back to Whitney for a moment before she turned around and leaned against the sink. "Why did you serve me coffee in that cup?"

The cup was a gift she'd given Reece. Just something she'd seen in a hotel gift shop in Montreal. The saying on it was in French, so Whitney had to google it.

Sans toi tout est absurd.

Translation: Without you, it's absurd.

Why had she pulled that particular cup out of the cupboard? There was only one answer. "It's just another thing you left behind."

Reece picked up the cup and dried it off with a dish towel. She walked back over to the table and put her purse on her shoulder. "I'd like to have it, if that's okay." Whitney gave her a nod. Reece took in a deep breath of air. "I'm trying so hard to be mature right now, but what I really want to do is get on my knees and beg for your forgiveness because I really am so sorry for the pain I've caused you, and I appreciate your willingness to talk to me at all."

"It's not willingness so much as professional necessity." Whitney got up to walk her to the front door. "And I appreciate your restraint because God knows I'm using mine."

Reece paused at the door. "See you on the set. Can't wait for Piper to kick some ass."

Whitney decided now was a good a time as any to start with the promised professionalism. "At least we can agree on that."

❖

Brie hit the Post button on her blog and pulled her mom's desk light to her mouth as if it was a microphone. In her best DJ voice, she said, "Good evening, LA. Take a listen to Bazzi singing one of my faves. It's dedicated to a very sexy woman who will probably never be mine. But hey, a girl can dream."

She pushed the lamp away and leaned back in her chair. No doubt she'd get a text from her nosy brother after he listened to the song. Needless to say, he was not happy that Brie had been given sole access to the beach house for a solid month, so he'd most likely consider it his prerogative to harass her for posting a song.

The sun was setting on a breezy Friday night. Brie had most of the windows open that faced the ocean. Other than a few pelicans diving into the surf, the beach was empty. It was a perfect night for sitting by the firepit with a beer and some good music.

When she was young, the fire had to be built with paper and kindling. Now it just took a turn of the gas key, and she could have three-foot-high flames if she wanted. She opted for a low burn so she could put her feet up and not toast them like marshmallows.

Her hair was still wet from her post-dinner shower, so she took it out of the bun she'd thrown it up in and let it dry on her shoulders. One beer probably wouldn't be enough to take her mind off Whitney, so she'd brought three out.

Whitney would be on the movie set with Reece soon, and Brie just needed to get over it. Just move on. Write her damn manuscript. Write book reviews. Read books to review. Write in her journal. Get on Tinder and have sex in her mom's bed.

That last one was the worst idea imaginable. No doubt she'd compare Ms. Tinder to Whitney and end up sexually frustrated. Meanwhile, all she had to do was close her eyes, and there was Whitney in all her naked glory.

"God, she's so beautiful," she whispered. "So. Fucking. Beautiful."

So was Piper Kane. Even Piper made it into her dreams sometimes. Why Whitney hadn't given Piper a love interest was a mystery. With each new book, Brie was sure someone, man or woman, would catch Piper's eye. She'd always hoped it would be a woman, of course. Lesbians everywhere would go nuts if that happened.

She looked at her watch. It was going on six hours since she'd typed, *Busy tonight? Pizza and Laura Petrie?* She knew what a six-hour delay meant. Whitney was ghosting her. Plain and simple. A classic ghosting. She finished off her second beer and let the bottle roll across the deck and come to a stop in the lowest corner, right behind her first bottle. Who needed a recycling can when you had a low spot on the deck? This was the first time she'd seen it so empty. When the family was around, the bottles piled up fast in that little corner.

Was someone knocking on the front door? Brie stilled herself and listened closer. There it was again. She got up and shouted, "Be right there."

The antique front door had one of those sliding panels at eye level instead of a peephole. When she was little, Brie would beg her dad to lift her up when someone knocked on the door so she could slide it open and say, "Hello, who's there?" It was also a great place for a game of peek-a-boo, so that was what they called it, the peek-a-boo window.

She slid it open and was pretty sure her eyes lit right up. "Hi."

Whitney held up her phone. "It lost the will to live before I could reply."

"I'll open the garage door so you can park." Brie closed the window and whispered, "Get your shit together." But her heart was pounding, and her stomach was doing flip-flops because she was here. Whitney was here.

Whitney got out of the car and handed Brie a pizza box. "I had no idea what kind you like, so I played it safe and got half-cheese and half-anchovies. Do you have beer?"

"I'm two beers ahead of you, so you'll have to catch up. And anchovies are safe?"

"Just kidding. The other half is veggie." Whitney wrapped her arms around Brie's waist and gave her a hug. "Hi, Cheesy." She let go and headed straight for the fridge.

Brie raised an eyebrow. "You're cheery tonight. And can we stop with the cheese nicknames? I'd prefer something a little more awesome."

"What's up, Blogalicious?" Whitney twisted the cap off a long neck, gulped a surprising amount of it down, and said, "Are you saying being cheesy ain't easy?"

They had a staring contest until Whitney busted out laughing at her own joke. Brie furrowed her brow. "Did you just win the lottery or something?"

"Can't I be glad to see you?"

Whitney flashed her a smile so big, it caused Brie's tummy to do a flip-flop. In a failed attempt to act casual, she shrugged and said, "Yeah, I guess it's okay that you're here." She received another gorgeous smile before she got two plates out of the cupboard and grabbed some napkins. "Bring as many beers as you plan to drink and follow me."

Brie pulled another Adirondack chair closer to the fire. She considered settling in on the double lounger, but did she really want to put herself through the torture it would surely end up being? How could she possibly lie next to Whitney and not want to kiss and cuddle?

"Cute pants," Whitney said. "Perfect for the beach."

Brie had forgotten she was wearing a rather worn-out pair of white linen pants that were mostly see-through and had exceeded their lifespan by a few years. Luckily, the cardigan she'd thrown on earlier covered up the fact that she wasn't wearing any panties.

"You're looking rather beachy yourself." Brie tried not to stare at the cut-off jean shorts and the gorgeous thighs she remembered so well. The white T-shirt wasn't a V-neck. That was for the best.

"I thought maybe we could go for a walk again," Whitney said. "I loved that the other night."

Now that their hands were empty, Brie took the opportunity to return the earlier hug. "I'm so glad you're here. Sitting by the fire alone isn't nearly as much fun." She held on a little longer than she should have. Were her thoughts, wishes, and desires written all over her face? Worried she'd reveal too much and make things awkward, she backed away and pointed at the house with her thumb. "Those beers I drank are…I'm just going to go use the little girl's room."

"Brie."

She turned back around. "Need something while I'm in there?"

"Just hurry back."

Brie's heart skipped a beat. "I will."

She desperately wanted to ask what had happened with Reece. Whitney had said she was over her, but if Reece Ainsworth meant to get Whitney back, she would. Brie needed to accept that fact. All of the talk show hosts seemed to love her. She had a good sense of humor and could be self-deprecating.

Granted, there was the cheating thing. And the divorce. But sometimes, couples could work through that stuff. And marrying the same person twice happened all the time, right? Brie shook her hands dry and looked in the mirror. Her eyes welled with tears. "Don't," she whispered. "Don't make a fool of yourself." It didn't help that she felt slightly tipsy. All the joy mixed with all the sadness was right there, waiting to burst out in a hot, blubbering mess.

Water. She needed to drink nothing but water for the rest of the night. She blinked the tears away and opened the door but stopped short when she saw Whitney standing there, waiting for her. "Oh! What are you doing here? I mean, do you need the bathroom? Sorry if I kept you waiting." She needed to stop talking and go get that water, but Whitney was blocking her way.

"Are you okay?" Whitney asked.

Brie folded her arms across her body. "I'm fine. Why? Don't I look okay?"

"Maybe I shouldn't have come over unannounced."

"No, it's fine. I'm glad you're here." Whitney moved aside, so Brie went into the kitchen and opened the fridge. She stared at the bottle of water but didn't grab it. The cool air felt nice on her blushed face. Would it be weird if she stayed there for a while? She could kill two birds with one stone and make a mental grocery list while she settled down, if she could settle down. She could use more coffee creamer. Cheese and fruit. Sandwich stuff.

"Brie, talk to me."

She shut the fridge but didn't let go of the handle. Would it ruin everything if she told the truth? Would she get through the night without crying if she didn't? "I just find myself missing things I haven't even had."

"What things?"

Brie's head was telling her to shut the hell up before she ruined everything. "Never mind. It's stupid."

"Brie, what things?"

She couldn't turn around. She'd cry if she had to say it to Whitney's face. "Sundays," she whispered.

"Brie, turn around."

Whitney was on the other side of the island. She looked as distraught as Brie felt. She lowered her gaze and said it again. "I miss Sundays. I miss breakfast in bed. Arguing over books and movies and who gets to control the remote. Walks on the beach after making love. Hearing the sound of a book being written in the other room while I make dinner." She raised her head and met Whitney's gaze. "I could list a thousand things I'm going to miss that I never even had."

Whitney rounded the island and pulled her into her arms. The tears Brie could feel on her cheek weren't her own. Did that mean Whitney would miss those things too? Of course not. She wasn't thinking in those terms. The prospect of dating Brie probably hadn't even crossed her mind. The tears were most likely stress-related, and there Brie was, adding to it with her over-the-top feelings.

She was about to let go and apologize when she felt a gentle kiss on her cheek. And then another closer to her jawline. Brie closed her eyes and tilted her head so Whitney could go lower and find that sweet spot on her neck that always sent shivers through her body. Hot breaths against her ear sent her head spinning. This was what she wanted, to get lost in everything Whitney. Her touch, her scent, her lips, her soft skin, and that sexy voice. But she wanted Whitney to want it to.

She opened her eyes and took Whitney's face into her hands. "You don't have to do this," she whispered.

Whitney slid her hands into Brie's sweater and held on to her waist. "We don't have to feel this way tonight. Tomorrow's another day, but tonight—"

Brie's lips collided with Whitney's. She'd heard enough, and she'd had enough of pining for what was right in front of her. Even if this was all she could have, she'd take it. But she wanted it on soft sheets like they were used to. Because if she had any say in it, this was not going to be a quickie up against the fridge.

The bedroom was lit only by the moonlight shining off the ocean. Whitney took her time undressing Brie. She moved behind her and took the cardigan off. She gave each shoulder some attention with little nips and kisses that caused a wave of goose bumps.

Brie raised her arms and moaned under her breath as the tank top slid across her hardened nipples. Her hair was moved to the side and an arm snaked around her waist. Whitney kissed her ear, then whispered, "I'm in charge, okay?"

Brie nodded as hands reached around and untied the drawstring on her pants. They fell to the floor, and Whitney gripped her hips. "You're mine tonight, Brie. And I want us to do something I've been thinking about. Something special."

Brie had no words. She was already so turned on, just about anything would take her over the top without too much effort. "Okay," she whispered.

"Turn around and watch me undress."

Fuck, yes, she would turn around. Her eyes had adjusted enough to the darkness that she could clearly see Whitney pull her shirt over her head and take off her bra. Her nipples were also hard, and Brie so badly wanted to take one into her mouth. But this was Whitney's dance, and she needed to follow her lead.

The sneakers came off next, then the cute shorts fell to the floor. Skimpy panties were the only thing left, but Whitney stopped. Her eyes grazed over Brie's body, down to her pussy and back up again. "Not fair," Brie said.

Whitney stepped closer. "Take them off me."

Brie got on her knees and placed a gentle kiss above the panties and then several right on them. She slid her fingers under the band and slowly worked them down. Her eyes widened when she saw that the small patch of hair had been shaved off, and she now had an unobstructed view. "Oh my God," she whispered.

Her mouth watered as she went in for a quick taste, but Whitney held her back. "Not yet." She offered her hand and helped Brie up. She led her to the bed and pulled the covers back. "Lie down on your back."

"I'm kinda into this bossy thing," Brie said. "And whatever you're about to do, I'm so into that too." She got on the bed and Whitney stood there, looking at her. "What?" she asked.

"You're just so beautiful like this, with your hair everywhere and your skin glowing in the moonlight. I want to remember it."

Brie rolled onto her side and leaned up on her elbow. "I love that I can see all of you. Did you know you're wet?"

"How could I not be when I'm standing here looking at you?"

Brie ran her fingers down her own stomach. "Let's see if I'm wet too." She jerked when her finger grazed her clit.

Whitney crawled on top of her and pinned her arms over her head. "That's mine tonight." She took Brie's finger into her mouth and sucked the moisture off, then pinned her down again.

Brie could feel the wet heat on her stomach. She desperately wanted Whitney to scoot down so their pussies were touching. Before she could ask, Whitney let go of her arms and moved down there herself. She sat up straight and arched her back while she moved her hips.

It was a beautiful sight. Whitney's breasts were gently moving. Her eyes were screaming that she wanted to be fucked. Her mouth was open and ready for Brie's tongue. But Brie didn't want to move.

Like Whitney, she wanted look at her long enough that she'd never forget the image above her.

When she couldn't wait any longer, she sat up and took Whitney's face into her hands and kissed her. Before long, she was pushed back down. Whitney spread out on top of her and said, "Open your legs for me."

"You realize I'd do anything for you, right?" Brie opened her legs, and Whitney settled in against her.

"All I want right now is for you to come without me using my hands or my tongue."

Brie slid her hand between them. When she said anything, she meant anything. Including getting herself off while Whitney watched. But Whitney grabbed her hand again. "Not with your hand either."

She watched Whitney reach down and open her folds before she pressed herself against Brie. Their clits were touching, and Brie wondered if anything would ever feel as good as this.

It was clear Whitney wanted them to connect in a way that was different from the other times. She didn't want to just fuck. She wanted to make love to Brie. At least, that was what Brie hoped it meant.

Brie slid her hand between them and opened herself up too. The sensation it created when they rocked their hips against each other was incredible. Brie clamped her hands on Whitney's ass and sped up their rhythm. She didn't want to be the only one who climaxed, and by the pleasured look on Whitney's face, she wouldn't be.

Whitney pushed herself up onto her hands, increasing the pressure. Her skin glowed with sweat, and once again, Brie wanted to take it all in so she'd never forget.

"Fuck," Whitney whispered through gasps for air. "Are you close?"

Brie wasn't close; she was there. He eyes slammed shut as the orgasm ripped through her body. She strained against Whitney, wanting to last for as long as she could.

Whitney arched her back and groaned when she came. Her arms shook, and her body jerked until she couldn't take it anymore and collapsed on top of Brie.

The sound of the ocean mixed with their heavy breaths had Brie questioning whether it was even real. She wrapped her arms around Whitney and ran her hands down her back and over her backside. It was real, but was it a glimpse of her future or a fleeting moment in time?

The one thing Brie knew for sure was her own courage had brought them to this moment of pure connection. If she hadn't been in that fateful bar, trying to psych herself up to approach Whitney, she wouldn't be lying under her right now, hearts beating and clits pulsing and hands never wanting to let go.

Whitney lifted her head and kissed Brie's cheek. "How did I do?" she asked.

"You were perfect." Brie pushed Whitney's hair out of the way so she could see her eyes. "I kinda feel like someone just made love to me."

Whitney slid off but kept one leg over Brie and also an arm. She nuzzled in close to her ear and whispered, "She did."

❖

Brie's eyes popped open. "Mom?" She shot up and made sure Whitney was covered by the sheet. Her eyes wouldn't focus, and her brain wouldn't make her mouth shout the words *couldn't you call first?* The only thing she could do was to fall back onto her pillow and pull the sheet over their heads.

She turned and found Whitney on her stomach, shaking with laughter. She shouted, "Hi, Jade," before burying her face in her pillow.

"Hi, Whitney. This isn't awkward at all, so I'm going back to the kitchen to throw back five shots of tequila so the image of you with my daughter will be erased from my brain."

"Good plan, Mom. We'll be down in a minute."

"Save a shot for me," Whitney shouted.

"You know it's eleven thirty, right? It's not like I busted in on you before dawn. Oh, and also, this is my house."

Her mom's voice faded down the hallway. Brie looked at Whitney and snorted. "That's never happened before."

Whitney leaned up on her elbows. "Can I just climb out the bedroom window? Maybe walk my ass right into the ocean and drown myself?"

Brie shook her head. "No can do. We face the music together."

"You realize I'm a celebrated author and public speaker, right? I shouldn't have to deal with mothers. Besides being below my pay grade, it's just not right."

"I guess that's what you get for sleeping with a younger woman."

"You're thirty," Whitney said in a loud whisper.

Brie shrugged. "Hey, at least I get to be under this sheet tent with you when you're all naked and smelling like sex."

"You're not taking me seriously." Whitney took Brie's finger into her mouth and circled it with her tongue.

Brie felt her tummy do a little flip-flop. "I hate my mom so much right now." She wanted more. She wanted that tongue to circle other things. She wanted to be inside Whitney again. Maybe against the shower wall. She also wanted Sunday, even though it was Saturday.

"I hate your mom right now too," Whitney whispered.

Brie rolled on top of her and pinned her hands above her head. "I can't let you go yet. Not if this is the last time we ever—"

"Lunch is ready," her mom shouted from the kitchen.

"Be right down." Brie let go of Whitney's hands. She needed to know where they would go after what she'd just said.

Whitney reached up and caressed her hair. "Our story, no matter how it ends, isn't over. I just need time to get my life back on track."

It wasn't a promise, but it was enough to soothe the ache in Brie's heart. She could hold on to hope for a little bit longer. But she needed to feel Whitney's lips on hers one more time. A kiss that would convey what she was too afraid to say. A kiss that would last forever if she needed it to.

Chapter Eleven

"Y ou're smudging my camera. Who knew your nose was so oily?" Liz didn't really have her nose smashed against Whitney's doorbell camera, but it was damn close. Why did she always insist on a weird closeup?

"I fought off an old lady with a cane to get the last plain doughnut because that's who eats plain doughnuts. You and old ladies. Now open your door."

Whitney tapped the button on her phone and closed her laptop. Normally, she'd be polite and offer Liz something to drink, but she stayed where she was at the kitchen table.

"You're avoiding me." Liz dropped the doughnut bag on the table and pulled out a chair. "And no rude comments about how I'm stating the obvious. Just tell me how to fix it so I can stop stress shopping."

"A new handbag?"

"Try five."

Whitney snorted. "Wow, Liz. I didn't know you cared that much."

"Bullshit. This isn't just a professional relationship, and you know it."

"I thought I did, but then you tried to convince me to take Reece back because it would be good publicity. Should I say it again? You tried to convince me—"

Liz put her hand up. "No need for a repeat. How can I make it up to you?"

"Well, a doughnut isn't gonna cut it."

"Okay. Ask for something ridiculous." Whitney's response was to fold her arms in a protective, stubborn stance. Liz sighed. "Come on, Whit. We always forgive each other for the stupid things we say."

"That wasn't an accidental insult or a slip of the tongue. That was you putting your bank account before my well-being. And since when do you talk to anyone, including Josh, about my broken marriage? What the hell, Liz?"

"I wasn't thinking. I'm an agent. It's in our DNA to do stupid shit. I got excited by the thought of you and Reece together. That sounded bad. Lesbian porn doesn't excite me. I don't even like straight porn that much. The women are too skinny, and the men are not at all like the average man in the length department, but I'm getting off track."

Whitney tried to hide her amusement by glancing at her watch. "It's a little early to be tipping the bottle, isn't it?"

"Not when you feel like you've lost your best friend."

Whitney threw her hands in the air. "You can't say something like that right now, Liz. I still need at least five more minutes of angry glares and mean-spirited retorts. And possibly more doughnuts"

Liz picked up her phone. "I'm setting a timer. Because damnit, Whitney. I miss you."

"Don't act like I fired you, Liz. There's still more than enough work to be done."

Liz leaned back in her chair and scowled. "That's not what this is about, and you know it. I miss my friend, not my client."

This wasn't a side of Liz she saw very often. Being vulnerable, showing true feelings, using labels like best friend, not her usual M.O. It was kind of nice for Whitney to see since Liz had certainly witnessed it all through the divorce. She grabbed her phone and set it in front of them. "It died yesterday. Get me a new one and I might consider forgiving you."

"You want me to buy you a new phone?"

"No. I want you to go down to the Verizon store and spend three hours buying me a new phone and transferring all the data because that's usually how long it takes."

"This is actually great news," Liz said. "It means you weren't ignoring me this morning when I sent five hundred texts begging for this meeting. Ignore the one where I say that no handbag, no matter how expensive, could ever ease the pain of losing our friendship."

Whitney smiled. "Aw, that's so sweet, Liz. But I still need a new phone."

"Or the one where I admit to having a moment of attraction back in 2015. That was just a cheap ploy to pique your curiosity so you'd stop ignoring me."

"Oh, I see. You thought I'd be dying to know the moment when I looked at you, and you looked back at me, and for a split second, there was something we couldn't quite put into words, but it was there, and neither of us could deny it? Yeah, no. Couldn't care less." She tapped the table near her phone. "Get on it."

Liz picked up her own phone. "You won't mind if I delegate this job to my assistant, will you?"

"Whatever it takes, babe." Whitney gave her a not-so-subtle wink and got up from the table to pour herself a cup of coffee. She had a doughnut to savor, after all.

"Hi, Joe. Head over to the nearest Verizon store and call me from there." Liz waited for her to sit back down. "We're on it."

"Excellent. I miss my phone, but the last thing I want to do right now is sit in that damn store with a sales guy who just happened to be watching Falcon the other night."

Liz eyed her for a moment. "You haven't seen Cheese Wedge again, have you?"

"Why do you ask?"

"She posted a song on her blog yesterday. Did you listen to it?"

Whitney's eyes widened. "You follow her blog?"

"Don't you? We have to keep an eye on her. With the current situation, she'd probably get a pretty penny for her story." Liz put up a hand. "And before you say it, I'm fully aware that I'm the one to blame for the hookup, terrible wingwoman that I am."

Whitney wasn't sure if she should trust Liz with the news that she'd seen Brie again, not with the tinge of animosity she'd heard. She wanted to defend Brie, tell Liz she was wrong about her, but that meant they'd have a conversation that no doubt would lead to Whitney having to admit that she'd slept with her again. A part of her wanted to protect that part of them. Keep it special. She didn't know what it was yet, but it wasn't hotel sex anymore.

Yes, she'd listened to the song, which she also happened to love. And yes, she assumed it had been posted for her. Brie wore her heart on her sleeve. Whitney loved that about her. And she wanted to protect that heart. So she changed the subject. "Can I eat my doughnut now?"

"You damn well better eat it. Like I said, it was hard-won." Liz opened the bag and took out her apple fritter before she pushed the bag to Whitney. "It'll be a miracle if I still fit into my clothes after all of this has settled down."

Whitney broke her doughnut in half and dipped it in her coffee. "Someone just won herself a new nickname."

Liz ripped a piece of fritter off with her teeth the way she would a piece of jerky. "Call me Fritter, and it's truly over."

Whitney shrugged. "I'll save it for special occasions."

❖

What did one wear when one was invited onto a movie set? A high-profile movie set. With a friend and part-time lover? And her friend and part-time lover's A-list ex-wife? No pressure. Brie glanced down at her yellow summer skirt. Was it too tight? Maybe she should've gone with something more professional than open-toed sandals. It was too late to worry about that when she was at the studio gate waiting for the security guard to give her a guest badge, but she worried anyway.

What she should've fretted over was why she was invited in the first place. Whitney made it sound like it was nothing, but it wasn't nothing. Reece would be there, dressed up like Piper Kane, no doubt. What was she supposed to say?

Whitney rolled up in a golf cart. Brie breathed a sigh of relief that she wouldn't have to walk in alone. The security guard gave her the badge and let her through the gate. She wanted to rush into Whitney's arms, but it wasn't the place or the time for that.

Whitney looked her up and down and said, "Hello, gorgeous."

"Hi. I'm nervous. Could you say something funny to calm me down?"

Whitney stepped closer, took a lock of Brie's hair in her hand, and lowered her voice to a sexy whisper. "I can't stop thinking about last weekend. Your skin. Your lips. Your…mom."

Brie blushed. "Can we just forget about that last part? Especially since that is decidedly not funny."

"No. Never." Whitney motioned with her head. "Hop on. I'll give you the rundown on the ride over."

Brie sat in the passenger seat. She leaned in and said, "I've missed you."

Whitney's smile turned into a wide grin. "I had to lie to get you on the set. You're my assistant for the next few hours, okay?"

"Well, we've already established that I kinda dig your bossy side. And the whole boss-assistant thing…totally hot. I mean, wildly inappropriate, but hot."

Whitney laughed. "It'll be our own little version of *Jordan's Appeal*."

Brie gasped. She'd never mentioned it to Whitney, but Brie loved that show. Right alongside every other lesbian on earth. "You're right. Hey, do you by chance own any power suits?"

"Several, actually."

"So you know where I'm going with this, right?"

Whitney gave her a sly grin. "I have a strong suspicion, yes."

"Well, let me spell it out for you."

They turned down an alley, and Brie's jaw dropped. Reece stood in what looked like a staging area. She was dressed in a sleeveless camo shirt and army green fatigues. A guy was attaching weapons to her body, and someone else was rubbing some sort of grime on her arms.

"It's the scene where Piper gets caught by the FBI." Brie turned to Whitney for confirmation.

"Wow. That's impressive."

"I know your books by heart. I even know what she says to the first guy who tries to pin her down."

In unison, they said, "Is that a gun in your pocket? If so, it's pointed right at your dick."

Whitney grinned. "It gave Piper the split second of distraction she needed to get away. Unfortunately, the producers didn't want that to be the first words she speaks in the movie."

"Well, that's a damn shame. I laughed out loud when I read that line. Cowards."

Whitney smiled. "I knew you'd have fun today. Just remember, she's not really Piper Kane."

Brie wondered if the reminder was meant to temper her excitement so she wouldn't fawn all over Reece. She turned to Whitney and said, "She's the woman who broke your heart, so I hate her." As they walked over to the group working around Reece, Brie said it over and over in her head. *You hate her. She's evil. You hate her.*

But it was hard to feel that way. Reece was Piper, and Piper was Reece. And Brie loved Piper Kane more than any other character she'd ever read since she'd learned how to read. And there she was in the flesh less than ten feet away.

Reece glanced over at them and did a double take. She gave Brie a good long look before acknowledging Whitney with a smile. "Does it look like I've been crawling through dusty air ducts?"

Whitney walked a circle around her. "You need a little more on the forearms and elbows. Piper was in those ducts for hours."

Reece eyed Brie. "You must be Brie."

"Everyone, this is Brie Talbot," Whitney said.

Reece gave her a nod. "I'm Reece, and this is Bob, the supposed gun expert, and Zoe from the makeup team."

Bob took a step back and put his hands on his hips. "*Supposed* gun expert?"

Reece ignored him and said to Whitney, "He's struggling to teach a left-handed *woman* how to handle a gun."

Bob threw his hands up. "Okay, I'm outta here. Get someone else to help you."

Reece rolled her eyes. "Oh, and he's a quitter too."

Whitney turned to Brie and lowered her voice. "Reece's biggest pet peeve is having a man talk down to her."

"Isn't that every woman's pet peeve?"

"If you met her dad, you'd understand why it's especially frustrating. Give me a minute with her, okay?"

Brie stayed back, but she could hear their conversation due to the echo in the cavernous building. "Shouldn't you have learned that stuff by now?" Whitney asked.

"Yeah, Whit. I should know it by now, but it turns out all that training I had should've been done with my right hand because gee, Reece, I guess we forgot to tell you that. And now, my brain is so confused, I don't know what the hell I'm doing. And all that jackass can do is snicker and shake his head and mumble under his breath."

"It's true," Zoe said. "The dude may be a gun expert, but his people skills suck."

Whitney put her hands up in defense. "Well, it's not my deal. I'm just here for the rewrites and consults."

Reece shook her head. "No. We have a shared goal, remember? I need you here to make sure that when people look at me, they see Piper."

"Oh, they will," Brie said with a big nod. "No question there."

Reece stared at her for a few seconds, then turned to Whitney. "I like her."

Zoe stepped back to look at her work. "You're ready, girl. Go get 'em."

Reece looked like she was about to break down in tears when she said, "I'm not ready. Not at all."

Whitney turned to Brie for what looked like reassurance, so she gave her two thumbs-up to let her know she should do whatever she could to help Reece. She turned back and said, "They'll get another gun expert. Just get through the next few hours, okay? They probably won't even get to the scene where you use the gun. Just lots of crawling around in a tight space. Are you ready for that?"

Reece took a deep breath and shook out her arms. "You know I don't like tight spaces."

"Use it," Whitney said. Acting was probably not her area of expertise, but she knew Piper Kane better than anyone, and she'd no doubt run lines and practiced blocking with this particular actress more times than she could possibly count. "Use that fear. It's hot and dusty. She's trying not to cough out the dust she breathes in. Piper's fighting for her life in there, so don't worry if some of your own fear shows itself. It's perfect."

Reece grabbed her script pages and said, "Okay, let's do this." She gave Brie a nod. "Good to meet you, Brie. I'm sure we'll run into each other again soon."

Brie watched Reece walk away like a boss with a gun on her

right hip and another one tucked in a holster under her left arm. If they'd stayed true to the book, there was a switchblade in her left boot and a photo of her deceased father in the right one. God, how she hoped they'd stayed true to the book.

Whitney stood next to her, and they watched together. "What do you think so far?"

"I'm trying to hate her guts, Whit. I really am. But she's Piper Kane in the flesh, you know? Like, even the way she speaks is Piper. Her attitude. Everything."

"Yeah," Whitney said. "It's almost like the author wrote the character with Reece sitting right in front of her."

A younger guy scurried toward them with what looked like script pages in hand. "Hey, Whitney. Glad I caught you. We might need some rewrites for Agent Thompson. Gary says there's no way an FBI agent at that level would slap a woman, and he refuses to do it."

"Huh," Whitney said. "I guess Gary's an expert on what it feels like to spend three years hunting down the woman who killed your partner and then finally getting a piece of her."

"It's pivotal to the scene," Brie said. "Besides that, he's a dirty cop, and he knows she knows it."

Whitney took Brie by the arm and turned away from the guy. "The audience won't know that until book two," she said under her breath.

"Right. But still, he has to slap her. He has to show that much anger when Piper laughs in his face."

Whitney turned back around. "The slap stays. Do you want to tell Gary, or should I?"

"I pick you." The guy handed Whitney the pages and trotted off.

"Fucking actors, am I right?" Brie quipped. She turned to Whitney and put her hands on her shoulders. "The book is perfect. Make them stick to the story as it was written."

"Sorry to say, that never happens," Whitney said. "There's only so much the screenwriter can fit into a ninety-minute movie."

"Then fight for what's important. That slap sets the tone for their entire relationship. And remind them that it's not like keeping some action sequence that will cost three million dollars. It's a slap from an asshole. No charge. Also, having my hands on your body makes me warm inside." The most she could do in public was give Whitney's shoulders a little squeeze, but she growled under her breath to make it sexier.

"It does things to me too," Whitney whispered. "And although it pains me slightly to say it, I think I'm starting to see why you were so upset when you read the third book."

"Right? Where's my lesbian love scene? I should move my hands before they wander."

"But it was more than that, wasn't it? You could see that I'd lost who Piper really was. I love your wandering hands."

Brie dropped her hands. "I'm so sorry, Whit."

"No, it's okay. I see it now too because I probably would've let that slap slide. And that only means one thing. I need you here with me, Brie. You're a writer. You know the books by heart. You know that if something changes in book one, it could affect book three."

Brie shook her head. "I promised my mom I'd finish my first draft. And on top of that, I work for my dad. I can't just—"

Whitney grabbed Brie's hands. "Talk to them. Make them understand how important this is. They'll be excited about this, won't they?"

"An opportunity in Hollywood? Whit, do you know my mom at all?"

"I do know her. She's fierce like you. Just try, okay? This is a great opportunity for you too. Think of it that way. But mostly, I just need to know you've got my back."

"Whit, I will always have your back no matter what. But working on set with you…" She paused. "It's complicated."

"Try."

With reluctance in her voice, Brie said, "Okay. I'll try." But in her heart, she knew it wouldn't be easy. No way would her mom let her stay in the beach house *and* spend time on a movie set. Brie would have to give up her time on the beach, which broke her heart a little, but she'd do it. She'd do whatever it took when it came to Whitney.

❖

The table was set for four. Getting together as a family wasn't something they did anymore, except for very special occasions. Brie wasn't sure how it would go, but it seemed easier than telling them separately.

Adam and her dad were out on the deck grilling steaks. Her mom walked in the house and said, "Oh, good, you're fully dressed. What a nice change."

Brie rolled her eyes. "Please don't bring last weekend up in front of Dad."

Her mom set her purse down and gave Brie a kiss on her cheek. "I'm just teasing you, baby. Mama knows all about beachy romantic encounters. It's why you and your brother exist."

"Okay, gross." Brie looked her up and down. "But also, wow, you look great." Her mom hadn't worn her usual boho attire. She had on a pair of dark skinny jeans and a white blouse cut low in the front. "Do you have hot a date after dinner?"

"Only with my family. Did you make the sangria? I'm dying for a drink."

"In the fridge." Brie noticed she'd trimmed her hair recently too. Not that her mom didn't always look great, but something was different. The lack of jewelry, for one thing. The chunky silver rings and dangly beaded earrings were gone. No bracelets on her wrists. Her mom had always worn a lot of jewelry that both she and Adam would play with when they were young. Brie just had to put her arm out, and her mom would slide a bracelet on her wrist. Her little arms were so skinny, she could push it all the way up to her shoulder. The thought brought back memories of sitting on the sand in between her mom's legs while they watched her dad surf in local competitions.

Brie wondered why things were so different. Was something wrong? Even though her mom looked fabulous, it was as if she'd stripped herself of her identity. Kind of like that kid who all through grade school and junior high wore red suede Adidas Gazelles. Every Christmas, he'd get a new pair of the exact same shoe, until one January when he walked into school wearing blue Nikes, and everyone freaked out. Brie was pretty sure everyone in the school, including the teachers, wanted to know why he'd changed his signature style, as if it was some sort of tragedy. His answer was simple. He wanted everyone to stop calling him "Red." He was over it.

Maybe her mom wanted a new identity too. Like a midlife crisis or something. Brie's dad walked in and stopped short when he saw her. "Jade," he said with a tone of surprise in his voice.

Her mom turned and gave him a quick nod. "Hey, old man." Okay, something was up. They were never that friendly to each other. Brie watched with fascination as her mom handed him a glass of sangria and said, "I had Gabriela make a special recipe. See if you recognize it."

He took the glass and held it up to the light. "What's my prize if I get it right?"

Her mom shrugged. "I'll think of something good."

Adam, who stood behind their dad, caught Brie's eye and mouthed, "What the fuck?"

Brie wondered the same thing. Were their parents actually flirting? What the hell was going on?

Her dad took one sip and then another. "The summer after the kids were born," he said. "We left them with my folks and went up to Santa Cruz, and right by our motel was this little fish shack with the best damned sangria we'd ever tasted."

Her mom shrugged. "Not bad for a weathered old man. Are you wearing your sunblock?"

"Every day, Jadey." He clinked her glass and said, "Cheers."

Jadey? Cheers? Brie had to look away. She almost felt embarrassed by what was happening. Adam sidled up next to her and whispered, "Why does Mom look like she's ready for a date?"

"Why is Dad calling her Jadey?" she whispered back.

Adam snorted. "Should be an interesting night."

Brie turned back around and mustered up her best cheery voice. "Who's ready to eat? Can't let that sangria go straight to your heads."

❖

At some point toward the end of dinner, Brie thought it would be a good idea to bring up the whole Piper Kane thing. What she said was, "I've been offered the chance to be a story consultant on the Piper Kane movies." What her mom heard was, "Working on set! Hanging out with studio types! Actors, actors, and more actors! Not to mention directors and producers everywhere! Aren't you so excited for me?"

"Did that sangria go straight to your head?" Her mom turned from Brie to her dad. "Talk some sense into your daughter, will you?"

"That never was my strong suit, Jadey. Besides, maybe she's not wrong about it being a good opportunity."

"Well, you just don't understand the complexities of women. And this is a very complicated situation. Not to mention how hard I worked to keep my mom from turning our kids into little Jodie Fosters."

"I understand how damn sexy you look in those jeans." Her dad said it under his breath but loud enough for everyone to hear.

"Okay, whoa," Brie said. "What is going on between you two?"

"Your dad thinks if he compliments me enough, I'll put out tonight."

Brie covered her ears. "I can't hear this right now."

"Oh please, honey. If you can have sex in my bed, you can hear this." Her mom leaned over and whispered something in her dad's ear.

"Are you telling Dad? Mom, you promised."

"That was before you decided to go all Hollywood movie set on me. All bets are off, little girl."

Adam was busting a gut. So was her dad. Brie couldn't do anything but sit back and smile because for the first time in a long time, her family was laughing together, and that felt pretty good. Even though she didn't know what the hell was up with her parents.

❖

After dinner, Brie and her mom stood at the sink rinsing dishes and loading the dishwasher. "Do you think Adam and Dad really went for a walk to talk business?"

"What else would it be?"

"I don't know. Adam said he's going to start dating blond,

short-haired women with big boobs. Maybe he's found the one already and wants some fatherly advice."

"He must've been joking because that is definitely not his type." Her mom put a dish in the cupboard and grabbed another out of the sink.

"We had a weird conversation the other night," Brie said. "Apparently, Adam compares the women he dates to me, and I may have given him a hard time about it."

"Of course you did. You two are so hard on each other sometimes."

"We are. But we also have each other's back when necessary."

"He idolizes you, Gabriela. I know you don't see it, but I do. It's no surprise he wants to find someone with similar attributes. Maybe not the sassy mouth…"

"Hey. A woman has to fight for her place in this world."

Her mom laughed and snapped the towel on Brie's butt. "Preach, daughter. Preach."

Brie rinsed the last dish and dried her hands. "Are you going to tell me what you think about Whitney's offer?"

Her mom leaned against the counter and folded her arms. "I think you want it all. You want me to let you finish out your stay here while you go off to some movie set instead of finishing your book. I think you also want something serious to happen with Whitney, but, baby, she herself said how complicated her life is right now with her wife."

"Ex-wife."

"Fine. Ex-wife. But that ex-wife wants her back, and now, you're telling me that you really want to be around that every day? I worry about you, baby."

"I know Whitney isn't going back to Reece. I know I want more for myself. I want to build a career so one day, I can buy a place like this. Maybe not in Malibu, but I love the ocean. I practically grew up in the sand. It feels like home to me. And if you want me out early, that's fine. But I'm going to work with Whitney."

Her mom leaned against the counter and folded her arms. "I see."

"Don't say it like I'm betraying you," Brie said. "I'm old

enough to handle Hollywood. I'm not going to dive into drugs or get depressed, and fortunately, I won't be in a position to deal with the assholes you've talked about. I won't be in front of the camera. I'll just be one of the crew. And most of my time will be spent with Whitney."

"Uh-huh." Her mom gently took her by the shoulders and looked her in the eye. "Promise me you'll stay true to who you are. You won't let anyone talk down to you. You'll stand up for yourself and report anything that needs reporting."

"I will. Of course I will. Have you ever seen me let *anyone* talk down to me?"

"It can be different when there's such a big power dynamic. I've seen strong women turn into mush if they think it'll get them the role they so desperately want. Growing up in the Hollywood environment, I saw a lot of shit, Gabriela." She waved a hand. "But you know all this. Just be careful. That's all I ask. And you'll be with someone you obviously love who may not be ready to love you back. Do whatever you need to do to protect that big heart of yours, my girl."

"I will. I promise." Brie stepped back and looked her mom up and down again. She honestly couldn't remember the last time she'd seen her wear jeans. "Speaking of staying true to who you are, why aren't you wearing your normal stuff? And why were you flirting with Dad? It was kinda hard to watch since you usually ignore him when we're all together."

"Let's sit." Her mom pulled out a chair for Brie and one for herself, facing each other. She put her arms out in front of her and spread her fingers apart. "It feels strange to not have rings and bracelets to fiddle with, but it's also good to have them gone."

Her mom had tan lines on every finger and one around her right wrist where she'd always worn a leather bracelet Adam had made for her years ago. Brie leaned in and took her mom's hand. "I think this is truly the first time I've ever seen your entire hand. You have such long, pretty fingers."

"Honey, sometimes people need a form of armor to give them a sense of security. I didn't know how much I was using my jewelry and my maxi dresses and my long hair as armor until I started going to therapy. It took me a whole year to shed it all, along with my fears and anger and insecurities."

Brie let go and sat back up. "You've been in therapy? How did I not know this?"

"I haven't told anyone because I didn't want to be asked how it was going or even why I was going. I just wanted to feel better. It had been so long since I'd found any joy in life beyond you and Adam. Being your mother has always been my greatest joy, but when I turned fifty, I realized I needed more. So I found someone I could talk to, and eventually, I started dating again."

Brie gasped. "How could you not tell me you were dating someone?"

"Let me clarify. I wasn't dating anyone. I was going on dates. Just a few. Enough to help me figure out what I was really looking for at this stage of my life."

"And what was that?" Brie feared the answer. Her mom looked so different, maybe she wanted to move to Europe or India or some other far-off place to find herself. Food, God, and sex or whatever that book was called.

But her mom surprised her when she said, "What I had all along but didn't appreciate."

"Do you mean…Dad?"

"He's stronger than I ever gave him credit for. Kinder, more forgiving than I'll ever be. He has a heart of gold, that man. And so much of who you kids are, you got from him. And believe me, it took a lot of therapy sessions for me to realize that. A lot of soul searching. A lot of aha moments."

"I wish you hadn't felt like you had to do all of that soul searching on your own," Brie said. "I would've been there for you."

"I know, honey, but it was important for me do the work myself. And I have. Which is why Jake and I are talking more. And yeah, we flirt some. Sorry it freaked you out."

"It's okay. It was just different, that's all. I guess I should've known something had changed when you so quickly agreed to have dinner as a family. And then you walked in looking all sexy in those jeans. Dad's eyes practically popped out of his head."

Her mom smiled, but it quickly faded into an expression of

sadness. "Yesterday, we talked on the phone, and he broke down. He told me that he never stopped loving me. Even with everything I put him through with the divorce, he still loves me."

Brie's eyes filled with tears. "That's so sweet."

"After we hung up, I thought to myself, today is the day I shed my old skin so I can be deserving of that love. So here I am, with no armor, grateful that he never found someone else. And hopeful that maybe we can find happiness again."

"No armor and looking damn fine, Mom." Brie stood and pulled her mom into her arms. "I'm so happy for you. Will you stay until Dad and Adam get back? We had a failed attempt at s'mores the other night and need a do-over."

They heard the guys coming up the steps from the beach. Her mom pulled her close and whispered in her ear, "Save the double lounger for me and your dad. Maybe he'll make a move tonight."

"In front of his children? Ew." Brie feigned disgust, but really, her heart was so full of love for her mom, she could've cried right then and there. "Oh hey," she whispered. "What if we forget to take the blankets outside, and maybe you'll get chilly and need to cuddle with someone."

Her mom tapped her chin. "Hmm. It does get chilly after dark. Especially if there's a breeze."

"I'll turn on a fan if I have to." Brie gave her dad and brother a little wave when they walked in. "Oh hey, guys. We're going to make s'mores. Get the fire going, will you?"

Adam grinned from ear to ear and said, "I'm on it."

CHAPTER TWELVE

The crate Brie had her laptop set up on had her scrunched over so far, she could've kissed her own knees. Whitney made a mental note to find a better spot for her. She squatted and checked what she was working on. "How's it going?"

"I've almost got the dialogue cleaned up. The screenwriter knows people don't actually talk like this, right?"

"Apparently, he thinks constantly repeating the word 'oorah' is enough to capture Piper's ex-military essence."

"Right? And his understanding of women is...special," Brie added. "He has her speaking in two-word sentences when she's working and rambling away when she's feeling vulnerable. It's kinda sexist."

"Unfortunately, I didn't have a say in who they hired. Let's just be glad Jimmy realized it wasn't working. We may have gotten a lazy writer, but we got a great director." Whitney read of few of Brie's new lines and smiled. "You know, you're really good with this stuff. Maybe you should pursue a career as a screenwriter."

Brie took Whitney by the chin and leaned in close. "I'd kiss you right now if Liz wasn't standing right behind you."

"Hello, Cheese Whiz," Liz said. "Didn't expect to see you here."

Brie gave her an insincere smile. "Well, as you know, I pop up in the most unexpected places."

"That sort of makes you a stalker, doesn't it?"

Whitney got up and took Liz by the elbow. She was miles away from the stalker mindset, so she had to remind herself to go easy on

Liz since the last time she'd seen Brie, she was standing on a bench in Vegas. "Maybe you could lay off the stalker cheese references now that we know her? Whaddaya say?"

"And to think it was just a few weeks ago that we both found it funny." Liz raised an eyebrow. "What's going on, Whit?"

"She's helping me with the rewrites and doing a damn good job at it too. It helps that she knows the characters so well. Better than me, even."

"Okay. I won't get in your way. But maybe we need a hand signal."

"What are you talking about?"

Liz closed her mouth and mumbled through her teeth, "I'm talking about a hand signal that you can use if you want me to call the police. Maybe something like this." She made the jerk-off motion with her right hand.

"I have no idea what you're talking about, but that does not scream *call the police*. That screams…I don't know what it screams other than *I'm so glad I'm a lesbian*."

"Look," Liz said. "I like the girl, but you just told me she knows your books better than you do. Add that to her flying all the way to Fucking Cincinnati just to see you, then pitching up in Vegas, and you have what most of the world would call a rabid-ass fan with possible mental issues."

"Jesus, Liz. That's a bit harsh. She's not the one who camped out on my doorstep for two hours when I wasn't even home."

"I'm still mad about that. You could have told me you weren't there."

"Nah, it was too fun to watch." Whitney glanced back at Brie. "You don't know her, Liz. But I'd like it if you did. Maybe we should have lunch together, just the three of us. You'd see for yourself what a fantastic friend she's been to me. But at the very least, you need to treat her with respect." Whitney hoped her tone would indicate that it wasn't a request.

"Friend, huh? Should I be worried about my status?"

Aha. So that was what this was about. Whitney smirked. "Do we need a hand signal for every time you get jealous? Maybe something like this?" She moved her hands, imitating the way coaches do in baseball. Liz's eyes tried to follow as if she was trying to memorize it, so Whitney kept going.

Liz grabbed her arm. "Okay, stop. I'm getting dizzy. Just reassure me that Cheese Curd back there won't take my place, or I'll turn her into a fine shred before you can say pass me the queso dip."

Whitney suppressed a giggle. "That was an impressive triple play."

Liz shrugged. "Hey, you signaled a home run."

Whitney put her arm around Liz and walked back with her toward Brie. "So we're good?"

"We're good." Liz leaned in and lowered her voice. "Don't be surprised if I use the term BFF a lot so she understands what her place is and what my place is."

Whitney laughed. She appreciated Liz's protective side most of the time. "Your status is safe as long as you don't do anything behind my back when it comes to Reece. Or Brie, for that matter." She put up her hand. "Pinkie swear. Come on. This is what BFFs do."

"Even the middle-aged ones?" Liz huffed, and then her eyes lit up, and her pinkie was shoved into Whitney's face. "Come one, Whit. Do the pinkie thing while she's watching."

"Sorry to interrupt," Brie said. "Just wanted you to know I sent the new pages."

Whitney pushed Liz's hand away. "Thanks, Brie."

Liz seemed to force a smile. "My BFF and I decided it might be nice for the three of us to have lunch together sometime."

"Oh," Brie said. "I'd love to have lunch with you and your B… FF."

Liz puffed out her chest and said, "Good. I'll set it up." She sauntered away as if she'd just shown both of them a thing or two.

"She might be a little bit jealous of you."

"Yeah," Brie said. "I kinda got that vibe. But hey, I'll take a lunch invite."

Whitney smiled. "Good. And before we were interrupted, I meant to tell you that Reece wanted to get your opinion on something."

❖

"Who, me? Why would she want my opinion?" Brie had hardly even spoken to Reece.

It wasn't that she was afraid of Reece. She'd just made a plan to stay as far away from her as possible and wanted to stick to that. Okay, so maybe she felt slightly intimidated by her. Who wouldn't?

"It's a good thing," Whitney said. "Any insight you can give her will only make her performance that much better, which will in turn make the movie better, and that's what we all want and need, right?"

Brie gave her a reluctant nod. "Yes, we all want that."

Whitney put both hands on Brie's shoulders. "You'll be fine. Just be that girl that showed up in Fucking Cincinnati."

So Brie watched from the sidelines while they got Reece ready for the next scene. They'd moved her to a chair where Zoe could do some final touch-ups.

Reece waved her over. "Come and tell me what you think."

Brie flinched when she rounded the chair. "Oh God. I thought it was real for a second there."

Zoe held up her hand for a high five. "I'll take that as a compliment."

Reece had a large knife wound above her right eye. Brie bent down to get a closer look. "That's amazing."

Reece got up. "I hear you're our Piper Kane expert. Walk with me to wardrobe? See you later, Zo. And thanks for the candy bar. I was starving."

"Girl, you need to learn to eat breakfast," Zoe shouted.

Brie took a quick glance at Reece. "Aren't you already in costume?"

Reece adjusted her tactical vest. "All this gear weighs a ton, so I'm trying to get used to it by wearing it all day. Life was so much easier before Piper agreed to work for the FBI."

"If it makes you feel any better, you'll have the lesbians drooling over their popcorn." Brie did her best to keep pace with Reece's long strides. It didn't seem to her as if the tactical gear was slowing her down at all. "Good job on getting in shape for the role. I always pictured Piper with toned deltoids. And abs, of course." She added that last part because she knew how hard a woman had to work to get any definition on her stomach. As she recalled from

Reece's modeling photos, her stomach was flat but not necessarily defined.

Reece gave her a side-eye but kept walking. "Seems like you're madly in love with a character in a book. What about the author? Are you in love with her too?"

Brie wanted to scream yes. But claiming Whitney as her girlfriend wasn't something they'd talked about. She decided to change the subject by pointing at Reece's hair. "Did any of these people even read the book? Piper puts her hair in a ponytail whenever she wears anything that says FBI on it."

Reece stopped and turned. "It's great that you're the world's foremost expert on a fictional character, but movies can't follow every little detail in the book, or it would be twelve hours long. And while I realize that Piper Kane isn't Piper Kane to you unless she has her hair in a ponytail, I can promise you that you're the only one obsessed with her enough to care."

It angered Brie that she had to look up to meet Reece's gaze when she was that close, but if Reece thought Brie would shrink under her hard stare, she was wrong. Because hell, yes, she'd taken a plane to Fucking Cincinnati. "The details make Piper who she is," she said. "Fans—the ones who post on social media and host book clubs and write fan fiction—will notice. But most importantly, if she's not wearing a hair band, she won't have anything to hold the pin in the grenade during the boat chase. So, yeah, I actually do think the ponytail is important."

It took Reece several seconds to back down, but when she did, she put out her hand. Brie gave it a good, firm shake. Reece chuckled. "No, I need something to put my hair up with. Can I borrow yours?"

"Oh. Right." Brie took the hair band out of her own hair and gave it to her. She noticed Reece's hands were shaking. "Are you okay? I didn't mean to get in your face like that."

Reece smiled. "I think it was me who got in your face, but no, you didn't upset me. Whenever I have to pull a gun, I get nervous. I just don't feel like the expert Piper is supposed to be." She tucked her thumbs into her vest. "I don't feel like Charlize, you know?"

"Didn't they find someone else to train you?"

"They're all fucking alt-right jackasses who have a cache of assault rifles in their basements, and I'm supposed to just let them spout their bullshit? No. It makes me sick to even be around guys like that."

Brie thought about it for a moment and said, "I may have a solution for this. Let me make a phone call, okay?"

Reece's eyes lit up. "You know a guy who isn't like that?"

"No, but I know a girl. Good luck with the scene." She turned to walk away.

"Hey, Brie?"

She turned back around. "Yeah?"

Reece grinned and said, "May the best lesbian win."

Oh, it was so on. And Brie didn't know whether to laugh or cry.

It was late, so Brie used the peek-a-boo window before she opened the door. "Thanks for coming."

"Hey, Gabby. I'm really glad you called me."

Brie and her cousin had never really gotten along. No, that was an understatement. Robin had been the bane of her existence for most of their adolescence. She was a bully and a know-it-all. She also happened to be a cop and a gun expert. So, of course, she still chose to use Brie's childhood nickname since everyone in the family knew she preferred Brie.

Robin walked in and took a quick look around. "The place looks great. Mom already sold off her part of the inheritance, but I knew Aunt Jade would keep this place forever." She opened her arms as if she were about to give Brie a hello hug.

Brie folded her arms in a protective stance, sure that Robin would reveal her true self soon enough. "As I recall, hugs were never really your style. More like a good shove when your victim least expected it."

"Ah," Robin said. "Well, you should know I have better manners now. I've also matured enough to know when an apology is in order, and you certainly deserve one, Gab. I'm truly sorry for the way I used to treat you."

Her manners weren't the only thing she'd refined. Her dark hair was parted down the middle and smoothed back into a ponytail, unlike the way she used to wear it, all frizzy and going in every direction like Medusa's snakes.

Her broad swimmer's shoulders filled out the detective suit she wore. Brie laughed to herself for thinking of it as a detective's suit, but Robin looked just like the female cops on TV, right down to the badge clipped to her belt. If she wasn't her obnoxious cousin and just someone on the street, Brie would almost find her attractive. She eschewed the thought and with a not-so-friendly tone in her voice said, "No one calls me Gab anymore. It's Brie now." She went into the kitchen to refill her glass of wine. "Can I get you anything?"

"Maybe just some water." Robin set a small suitcase on a dining chair.

"What's in there?"

"Guns," Robin said in a foreboding voice. "Big ones, Gab."

It was going to be a long night. "Once a smartass, always a smartass, huh, Birdie?"

"Touché. I haven't heard that nickname in a very long time. I'm surprised you remembered it."

"Oh, I remember everything. Just behave yourself with Reece, okay? She's had a hard time with the asshole who was supposed to train her."

"Right. I'll try not to be every cop I've ever worked with."

"Excellent. Reece went outside to take a phone call. Go introduce yourself. and I'll be right out."

Robin pointed at herself. "You want me to introduce myself to Reece Ainsworth? I…I…what would I say?"

"Well, whatever you do, don't hug her."

"Right. Right! I knew that. Don't be silly."

Brie sighed. She couldn't figure out what the hell was going on with Robin. She was always so sure of herself. Even through the awkward preteen years when she'd barely bathed, Robin had walked around as if she owned the world. So confident and so… anti-lesbian. But Brie's gaydar was pinging so hard, her head was ringing. Could it be that Robin was all discombobulated because she was about to meet a beautiful woman? Brie could certainly relate to that feeling. But Robin was married to a man. Unless something had changed.

"Are you still married to what's-his-name?" Brie asked.

"Darren?" Robin waved it off. "Nah. Went our separate ways a few years ago."

"Oh. Okay, um…"

"I know what you're thinking, Gab. I mean, Brie. You're thinking I can't handle the situation with Ms. Ainsworth, but I assure you, I can. I just need you out there to break the ice."

Brie shook her head. "No, that's not at all what I was thinking." She stood up and leaned on the table, grateful something was between them. "I was actually wondering when you were going to tell me that you're gay. Because you fucking bullied the hell out of me for being the little lesbian. And now, here you are…" Brie realized she was talking a bit too loudly, so she lowered her voice to a loud whisper. "We'll talk about this later." She marched over to the sliding glass door and gestured for Robin to step out first.

"Gab—"

Brie put up her hand. "Later, Birdie." She went out to the end of the deck where Reece was just ending a call. "Reece, this is Detective Robin Holmes. She's all yours for the next two hours."

Robin offered her hand. "Pleasure to meet you, Ms. Ainsworth."

Reece smiled. "Call me Reece."

"Make yourselves at home," Brie said. "I'll be inside if you need me."

It felt strange enough having Reece in her home. The last thing she wanted to do was watch Robin fall all over herself to impress her. That would just be gross. So she grabbed her phone and plopped down on the sofa. "Eagle and Robin are in the nest, over."

"Oh," Whitney said on the other end of the line. "Are we doing a walkie talkie thing now, over?"

"You're right. We should save it for sexy times."

Whitney laughed. "Roger that. How's it going?"

"They just started, so cross your fingers." Brie paused. "Oh, wait. I just heard some laughter, so that's a good sign."

"It was very sweet of you to do this."

Brie lowered her voice. "Reece figured it out."

"Figured what out?"

"That we're, you know."

"I see. How'd she take it?"

"Well, she had a smile on her face when she said, 'May the best lesbian win.'"

"Oh God." They sat in silence for a moment before Whitney said, "There's no competition. But be careful with Reece. She's being reckless, and I don't want you in the middle of this."

"I think it helps her having you there every day," Brie said. "I think she had fears about trying to make this movie without your support, and if she knows we're both supporting her, and we all have the same goal, maybe it'll all be fine."

"Talk about taking the high road."

Brie smiled. "I have a good example."

CHAPTER THIRTEEN

Living on the beach created a sense of freedom for Brie. The thought of her small apartment awaiting her made her feel claustrophobic. But that was still a few days away. In the meantime, she had a long holiday weekend to enjoy.

Everything had been going so well on the set that she decided to invite Robin back so she could help Reece practice a complicated gunfight scene they were shooting the following week. Whitney would be there too, of course. Brie hoped she could convince her to stay the night since it would be their last chance to sleep together by the ocean.

It had been a few weeks since the last time they'd made love, and with very little physical contact on the set, Brie felt the loss. She missed touching Whitney's skin and kissing those sexy lips. She wanted more of the closeness they'd shared, even if it was just an innocent cuddle on the sofa. And maybe, she also wanted confirmation that their bond was still strong. It wasn't easy seeing her stand close to Reece while discussing dialogue or whatever they needed to discuss, but Brie did her best to suppress any jealousy. Whitney didn't need that pressure on top of everything else.

After a long week, several glasses of red were in Brie's immediate future. She showered and put on her favorite white linen pants, this time with panties on underneath. It was warm enough that she really only needed a tank top. She chose a white one and dressed it up with a long silver pendant and hoop earrings. A light misting of her favorite body spray, and she was good to go.

Okay, so it might have been the same scent she'd worn when

she'd unexpectedly had sex with her favorite author, but that was neither here nor there. A simple coincidence. Brie picked up the bottle and sprayed a little more on her neck, then went to get that red wine she'd been craving.

The doorbell rang before she could get to the wine cooler. It had to be Robin. She apparently didn't know anything about being fashionably late. Brie opened the peek-a-boo door and said, "Are you packing heat?"

Robin laughed and reached behind her. She pulled out a small pistol and held it up. "I never leave home without my little friend. You smell nice, by the way."

Well, crap. Maybe she'd put on too much body spray if Robin could smell it through the small opening. "Are you sniffing me now? Stop sniffing me, Birdie." She closed the window and suppressed a giggle. Keeping Robin in her place was kinda fun.

She opened the door and was surprised to see her dressed in jeans, a black T-shirt, and Nikes. Her hair was still slicked back in a ponytail, but that was for the best since Brie had vivid memories of how wild and unkempt her thick hair could be.

Robin gave Brie a bottle of wine along with a sincere smile. "Thanks for inviting me back."

Brie glanced at the bottle. "You know your wine. I had no idea."

"Actually, I consulted the experts. Hope you like it."

"Better manners indeed." Brie glanced over Robin's shoulder and saw Reece's Tesla go by. She hoped there would be a spot for her to park along the road so Brie could save the extra spot in the garage for Whitney. She handed the bottle back to Robin. "Would you mind getting that opened? I'm just going to make sure Reece found a place to park." Before she could get out the door, Reece was right there, wiping her feet on the mat. "What did you do, sprint from your car?"

Reece stepped inside and shut the door behind her. "You learn to be quick when you don't want to see yourself all over the internet the next day." Reece leaned in and hugged her. "You have no idea how much I appreciate everything you're doing for me."

They'd never really hugged before. It was so unexpected, Brie wasn't sure how to react. She gave her a light pat on the back. "I'm glad Robin was available to help."

Reece pulled back but kept ahold on Brie's shoulders. "God, you smell good. And you look amazing in all white. You should wear it more often."

"Hmm. Is this a keep your friends close and your enemies closer kind of thing?" Brie joked.

Reece laughed. "Not at all, but way to stay on your toes. You might make it in this business after all. By the way, I'm not sure if I said it last time, but I love this place. Your family is lucky to have it." She stepped away abruptly when she saw Robin. "Oh, hey. I didn't know you were here already."

"Ready to work on your reload speed? I read through the scene, and I think that's where we should focus our efforts."

"Perfect," Reece said. "Hey, I'll meet you out on the deck in a minute, okay?"

"Sure."

Robin gave Brie a questioning look before she left. Once she was out of earshot, Brie asked, "Are you worried about Robin?"

"No," Reece said. "I'm just jumpy, I guess. The paparazzi have been even worse than usual."

Brie could've mentioned that Reece brought this on herself with the tattoo stunt on Falcon, but she stayed quiet about it. "I'll bring drinks out when Whitney gets here. And don't worry, it's a private beach."

❖

Whitney watched from the doorway while Reece and Robin practiced on the deck. Brie stepped up next to her and handed her a glass of wine. "She's getting faster, isn't she?"

"She is." Whitney turned to Brie and took a good look at her. She looked radiant in white. Sexy. Gorgeous. Whitney didn't try to hide the fact that she was enjoying the tight tank top, either. "Thanks for bringing Robin on board. And thanks for wearing that shirt." She took a sip of wine to hide her grin.

Brie stepped a little bit closer. "I miss you."

Whitney turned and leaned back against the door frame. "I miss what's under that shirt."

"Too bad you can't take it off me."

"I can in my head. In fact, you're almost naked right now."

"Don't you dare get me turned on unless you plan on staying the night."

Whitney took hold of the drawstring on Brie's pants. "I remember how easily these fell off you. I also remember—"

Robin cleared her throat and said, "Sorry to interrupt. Mind if I grab a couple of cold ones from the fridge?"

Whitney stepped out of the way to make room. "Hi, Robin. I'm Whitney. Thanks so much for helping Reece out."

"Ah. So you're the one responsible for this story. Whew, it's a workout." Robin wiped her brow for effect.

"Yeah, about that. Would it help any to know that when I wrote it, I never even imagined it'd be made into a movie?"

"It's all good," Robin said. "She'll be ready."

She stepped past them, and Reece was right behind her. She leaned in and whispered, "If you two are going to get it on right here, maybe wait until Robin is gone."

Brie looked at Whitney. "Did she just suggest that we get it on?"

Whitney grinned. "That's what I heard."

"Well, two sets of ears can't be wrong." Brie stopped when she heard Robin coming back their way. She took Whitney's glass. "We're going to need more wine."

Or maybe they should both stay sober, Whitney thought. Even though they'd been on the set together, she'd missed Brie too. And the scent she kept getting little whiffs of reminded her so much of their first amazing night together. And those linen pants, clinging to her ass the way they did…she'd have to give it a nice pat when no one was watching.

She watched Brie and Reece from the doorway, curious to see how they got along off the set. She knew all three of them were putting on their big girl panties every day just to get the movie made. It had worked so far, but she feared that all bets would be off after they shot the last scene. She wondered what that would look like. Not that it really mattered. Reece was her past, and more and more, she felt Brie was her future.

What she saw in front of her was lighthearted, friendly banter. It seemed genuine, but how much of it was just a show? She also had to ask herself that question. How much of what she was doing right now with Reece was forced? And could they ever really be friends?

Whitney realized that day by day, it had gotten easier to see Reece in a more positive light. And that never would've happened if they hadn't been stuck together making this movie. It wouldn't have happened without Brie by her side, either, giving her love and support.

So what did it all mean? For Whitney, it meant that making movies with Reece was possible. And it meant that she needed to go back east to her writing cabin and start working on book four. Because it had become very obvious that Brie Talbot had been right all along. Piper Kane deserved a better ending. And she hoped Brie would continue to be a part of it all.

❖

Brie felt all giggly inside. Wine always did that to her. She rinsed off the last plate and burst into a fit of laughter.

Robin took the plate from her hand. "Everything okay, cuz?"

"I was just thinking about how crazy your hair used to be." She leaned over the sink and laughed even harder. For some reason, the image of thirteen-year-old Robin had popped into her head, and she couldn't let it go.

"Funny," Robin said. "You know what I was doing all through dinner? I was trying to figure out why you had to monopolize the conversation. Can't you leave a little room for your cousin to make a few moves?"

Brie straightened. She wiped her hands dry and turned so they were face-to-face. "Why would I give you even an inch of room to flirt with another woman, Birdie? How do I know you're even out? Maybe we should have that discussion before you try to hook up with my coworker?"

Robin folded her dish towel and set it on the counter. "I came out over a year ago. What else would you like to know?"

Brie had so much pent-up rage when it came to Robin, it was hard to have a civil conversation with her. "I'd like to know if, when you came out, you thought of me and how much you'd bullied me for being exactly what you say you are now."

"We were kids, Brie. Even I got bullied by kids bigger than me. They made fun of my hair, they called me Butch, the guys wouldn't date me, and the girls hated my guts. It wasn't easy for any of us."

Brie deflated. She had no idea Robin had been bullied too. "Sorry for laughing about your hair just now. It wasn't so bad. Also, I'm a little tipsy."

Robin laughed. "It was terrible. I never knew what to do with it, and now, I just throw it in a ponytail every day. Problem solved." She glanced at her watch. "Hey, I gotta run. Say good-bye for me? They're in worse shape than you are."

Apparently, everyone had drunk too much wine. Brie locked the door behind Robin and went back onto the deck. Whitney and Reece were leaning over the balcony, giggling. Brie got in between them and asked, "What's so goddamned funny?"

It came out harsher than she meant it to. They didn't seem to care because they laughed even harder. Brie realized that, much like when she was washing the dishes with Robin, nothing had to actually be funny because everything was when she'd had that much to drink. She didn't need to be jealous; she needed to join in. They all laughed until they got their shit together, and after about three seconds of silence, they burst into laughter again.

Brie put her head back and her arms out and shouted, "I don't ever want to leave this place."

"It's her last weekend," Whitney said to Reece.

"Oh," Reece exclaimed. "That calls for a late-night swim. Last one in buys beer."

Reece scrambled for the stairs. Brie and Whitney stared at each other for a split second, then raced behind. Screams filled the air as they splashed over the waves and fell into the water, fully clothed. The cold water hitting her skin was a feeling Brie had always loved. It made her feel alive and happy.

She was slower to get out of the water. She watched Reece and Whitney walk back up to the house. Whitney turned back, waved her on, and said, "Come on."

Brie was in no hurry. She took everything in. The moon, the

stars, the goose bumps on her skin. She liked this life where she didn't have time to write in her journal or read three books in one weekend. She preferred *this* kind of weekend. But it was almost over, and she wondered how long the three of them would get along this well. How long before Reece would pull out whatever big guns she had and make an all-out run for Whitney, casualties be damned?

But that didn't matter yet. What mattered was that Whitney seemed happier when she and Reece were getting along. Maybe it was dulling some of the pain from the past. But she wasn't going to worry about it tonight. She had her final weekend on the beach. And nothing was going to stop her from making the most of it.

"Damnit, I lost another one." Whitney's marshmallow kept dropping into the firepit. Of course, it had nothing to do with her lack of sobriety. Brie and Reece were already enjoying theirs by the balcony.

"Do I need to come over there and help you?" Brie mumbled through a mouthful of s'mores.

Whitney stood up, got her bearings, and walked over to them. "No, you're going to share yours with me."

Brie held her perfectly melted s'more high up in the air. "No way."

Reece did the same thing. "I worked hard on getting mine just right."

"Oh, I see. You both think you're s'mores experts. Sounds to me like you need an expert s'mores eater to do a taste test. That is, unless you're too scared you won't win."

They looked at each other, then lowered their hands. Whitney took a bite of Brie's first. "Good mix between soft and crunchy. Chocolate is nicely melted. Marshmallow is slightly burned, but I like that." She turned to Reece and took a bite of hers. She tried not to laugh at how seriously they were both taking her. They tasted exactly the same, but she acted like she could tell a difference. "Your marshmallow has a nicely singed outer layer that I find enjoyable. The chocolate is perfect. Just kind of melts in your mouth. It's a tie."

"Damnit, I wanted to win," Brie said in a pouty voice.

"We were played." Reece took the last bite of hers and brushed her fingers clean. Her mouth was so full, it looked like she was having a hard time chewing it. Then again, she probably didn't have much experience with eating, thanks to her line of work.

"Wow," Whitney said. "You really didn't want to share, did you?"

Brie only had a small bite left. "Come and get," she said. And then she held it between her teeth.

Whitney moved in closer and bit off a loose piece of marshmallow. "Mmm. Now, that's what I'm talking about."

Reece slung her arms over both of their shoulders and slurred, "Why the hell didn't I think of that sexy move?" She started to giggle. "Leave it to me to shove the whole thing in my mouth like a piggy." And then she snorted like a pig, which sent all of them into another fit of laughter.

Whitney wrapped her arms around both of them, and they sort of swayed in a group hug. She rested her head on Brie's shoulder and closed her eyes. "I'm so happy tonight," she said. "It's been a long time since I've felt this happy, and I'm so happy. I'm also drunk, so just ignore whatever I say next."

She felt Brie's lips on her forehead. "We're all drunk. I mean, who doesn't share their s'more? It seems like bad camping karma to me."

"Maybe we should sing 'Kumbaya' to reverse the karma." Whitney snorted at her own joke, but she also started to hum and sway.

Reece burst into tears, and in a desperate tone she said, "I'm sorry I didn't share my s'more with you, Whit. Please let me make you another. Please."

Whitney realized it was probably time to call an end to the party when tears were being shed over a stupid s'more. She went to move, but the floor moved instead, and she fell into Reece's arms. "Sorry. The floor, and then my foot, and we should help each other inside." She turned and said, "Hold on, and I'll lead us in."

Sure that they looked like the shortest conga line in the history of the world, Whitney giggled as they shuffled to the door.

❖

The following day, Brie went to the door and opened the peek-a-boo window. "Who goes there?"

Liz rolled her eyes. "The fucking Duchess of Worcestershire Sauce. Now, where can I park my trusty steed?"

Brie grinned. She hadn't asked her grandma's favorite question in quite some time, but Liz took the prize for best answer. "You look good in casual beach wear, Liz. Ready to do some body surfing?"

"I'm here for the shrimp cocktail and Waldorf salad. Oysters on the half-shell would be nice too, if you have them."

"Oh. Well, shoot. This is the Little Fish Shack by the Sea. We only serve grilled fish tacos and homemade guacamole. But we do have a very special sangria that I think you'll enjoy."

"If it'll get me to the other side of tipsy, I'm sure I'll enjoy it."

Brie opened the door and glanced to the right. "Your trusty steed is fine where it is. Hi." She gave Liz what was surely an unexpected hug. It wasn't returned, but she chalked that up to the shock factor. One way or another, she was determined to make friends with Whitney's closest associate. Or her BFF, as Liz would say in solidarity with twelve-year-olds everywhere.

Liz had on wide-legged flowery pants with an orange tank top and matching sandals. Her fancy gold jewelry had been replaced with fancy pink and orange jewelry that perfectly complemented her outfit. Even her large tote bag sported orange and pink stripes. She'd fit in better at one of the ritzy beach clubs, not Brie's humble family beach house, but Brie led her inside. "Make yourself at home. Whit and Reece are out on the deck going over lines. Oh, and everyone has a hangover, so don't talk too loud."

They'd all woken up in the same bed, still fully clothed. Brie wasn't sure how'd they'd even made it to the master bedroom. The last thing she remembered was Reece singing "Islands in the Stream" to the kitchen island.

Liz set her bag on a kitchen chair and eyed Brie's laptop. "Working on something?"

Brie rushed over and closed the lid. "Just a manuscript I've been working on."

"Looked like Final Draft to me." She tilted her head. "What's a book reviewer-blogger-cheesemonger doing with a screenplay?"

Brie tried to keep a cheery tone in her voice when she said, "Those cheese jokes never get old, do they?"

"No, they don't."

Liz stared her down while she waited for an answer, but Brie wasn't about to admit that she'd downloaded the latest version of Final Draft the minute she'd woken up that morning. Whitney's casual comment about how she should pursue a career in screenwriting had her mind reeling with the possibilities. One of which was to write the adaptation for book two herself in the hope that Whitney and the producers would love it. If she handled it right, it could be her way in. Or it could turn out to be a total disaster, which was why she hadn't planned to tell anyone, not even Whitney, that she planned on giving it a try.

Liz turned to go outside, then stopped. "Does Whitney know?"

Brie shook her head. "I was just messing around with it. It's nothing, really."

"Just make sure you give the FBI Director plenty of screen time. I have a strong suspicion she's based on me."

Brie smiled. "Don't tell Whitney. Not yet, anyway."

Liz gave her a wink. "Don't make me wait too long for that drink."

❖

Lunch had been put away, the kitchen tidied up. Whitney poured two more glasses of sangria and went back outside. Reece and Brie were playing frisbee near the surf. She handed Liz another glass of sangria and stood next to her. "Beautiful afternoon, isn't it?"

"Cheez-It throws a frisbee like a boss. Wonder where she learned that."

"Right here. She and her brother pretty much grew up on the beach."

"Looks great in a bikini too. My God, what I'd do to have their bodies again."

"There's nothing wrong with your body, Liz. Go put on a suit and have some fun."

"You're right. It's pretty good for my age. Hell, if I can still get a hunk under forty to sleep with me on a Wednesday night, it must not be too bad, right?"

"Just one this week?" Whitney quipped.

Liz held up her glass. "It's a damn good thing I'm here with three other women, or this evil elixir would raise that number to four."

"An orgy? My God, Liz. Say it isn't so."

"I had no idea you were such a prude. What's your limit? Two?"

Their phones went off at the same time. Whitney chose to ignore hers but not Liz. "We're at the beach, Liz. Can't they live without you for a few hours?"

"And that's why I don't have a husband." Liz looked at her phone, then took off her sunglasses and peered at it closer. "Well, well. It looks like I just got my answer. Get those girls off the beach. I need to call Josh." Liz headed for the door.

"Liz, what's going on?"

She stopped and turned around. "Does a threesome on this very deck ring a bell?"

"A what? Oh God." Whitney ran down the steps and shouted until she got their attention, then waved them in.

❖

Whitney leaned on the table near Liz's phone. "It's not what it looks like, Josh."

Brie zoomed in on the grainy photos on her own phone. A gossip site had just posted them with the subtitle, "Reece and Whitney Ainsworth reunite, but they're not alone. Who is the mystery woman they're getting cozy with somewhere in Malibu?"

Josh's voice came booming through the speaker phone. "I told you to let me know first, didn't I? And who is this mystery woman I'm looking at?"

Whitney glanced over at Brie. "She's a friend."

She couldn't use a different word? Something a bit more endearing? A really good friend? A special friend? Even a lady friend sounded better than just friend. Brie tried not to pout about it.

"Your hand is on her ass, Whitney."

"She's someone who's special to me," Whitney said. "That's all you need to know. Please try to keep her name out of this."

"That's not up to me. If they want to find her, they will. Gotta run. I've got a tomahawk steak on the grill. Enjoy the rest of your day, ladies. Preferably in private."

Whitney straightened back up and put her hands on her hips. She glared at Liz, who was leaning against the counter sipping on sangria. "Stop with the smug look, Liz. We did not get it on last night, okay?"

Brie cleared her throat. "Well, Reece may have fallen in love with the kitchen island, but I'm not sure if they had sex."

"Oh, my God," Whitney said. "I woke up with that image in my head. I thought it was just the hangover."

Liz's eyes went round. She stepped away from the counter. "I'll just be over by the table."

They had a photo of Reece in Brie's arms. Taken out of context, it could easily be assumed that they were about to kiss, and that Whitney was there for it. Brie tried to hide her amusement when she said, "While it would give me an outrageous amount of satisfaction to be able to brag to my straight twin brother about the threesome I had with these two, it would be a lie." She tilted her head. "Just out of curiosity, how awful would it be if I let him believe it? I need to think about the pros and cons because God, how I would live for that moment when he'd have to admit that he could never, not in a million years, top this." She could tell all three of them were stifling a laugh. "Sorry. Our sibling rivalry is real."

Reece joined them in the kitchen. "How awful would it be if we let the whole world believe it? I mean, I'll do whatever you want, but like Brie said, maybe we should consider the pros and cons."

"There are no pros," Whitney said. "The only thing this will do is make Brie's life ridiculously complicated. She'd have no privacy. Are you really willing to throw her under the bus for your own benefit?"

"I was thinking it might benefit all of us."

"Maybe make the world think that tattoo wasn't an epic mistake? God, Reece. Stop being so selfish and consider for a moment how this might affect me and Brie. Can you do that?"

Whitney's harsh tone silenced Reece. It silenced everyone.

Brie felt bad that she'd joked about it now. She didn't really see the harm the way Whitney seemed to, but what did she know? This public life thing was all so new to her.

Liz finally stepped forward. "Can I say something?"

"No, you may not."

Whitney went outside in a huff, leaving Brie alone with them. "Say it to me, Liz. You're the one who brought me into this world, so say it to me."

"This world of debauchery? First of all, you're welcome." Liz pulled out a chair and sat. "I'm just sorry you couldn't experience it for yourself because I'll never forget the special night I had with Mrs. and Mrs. Ainsworth. Talk about kinky."

"In your dreams, Liz." Reece went to the fridge for more sangria.

"Oh, come on, peanut butter cup. You couldn't give me five minutes before you blew it up? I could've had Queso Blanco here eating out of my hand while I described our bedroom exploits in fine detail."

"Can't wait to hear who was on top," Brie said. "And the cheese jokes need to stop if you want me to listen to what you have to say about this."

Brie held her own during the five-second stare down that ensued. Putting Liz in her place felt like a victory all on its own. The icing on the cake was Reece's obvious appreciation for the slap back.

Even Liz cracked a smile eventually. "Fine. No more cheese jokes. But for the love of God, do something about that logo."

"I have someone working on it."

"Good. Then here's my advice for all three of you: if you want this to work in your favor, and I'm guessing you do, then take control of the narrative. Get on the same page. Strategize. And use it for all its worth to promote yourselves and this movie you're making. Hell, if it were me, I'd let the world speculate for a while because nothing, and I mean nothing, sells like the sweet scent of *are they or aren't they?*"

Later, Brie went onto the deck and took in the view one more time before she had to move out of the beach house. She knew so-called private beaches weren't actually private past a certain point in the dry sand. Nobody owned the wet sand or the ocean beyond it. But she and her neighbor's strip of the beach didn't have any public access. That particular stretch of beach was blocked by rocky cliffs on both sides. The only way to see them would have been from the neighbor's house or by boat. The more she thought about it, the more she wondered if someone she knew had taken the photos. What she couldn't figure out was why.

Whitney wrapped her arms around Brie's waist from behind and rested her chin on her shoulder. "Are you sure about this?"

Brie turned around in her arms. "Are *you* sure?"

"My concern is you. Reece is a big girl. She can handle anything. And all I have to do to escape the madness is go back east to my cabin once we're done filming. But you live here. Your family is here. There's no escape for you."

"I might feel differently if I hadn't already spent so much time on the Piper Kane set," Brie said. "Maybe I could've hidden out in my apartment until it all died down, but one quick call to any of the crew and the press will have my name." She put her hands on Whitney's chest. "Like Liz said, let's use this for Piper Kane."

Whitney sat on the end of her bed and turned up the volume on the TV. This was it. In a few minutes, Reece would be on with Johnny Falcon. Brie was on her way to her mom's house. She wanted to be there to explain in person. How that conversation would go, Whitney had no idea. She feared the worst. A part of her wanted to text Reece and tell her not to go on. It was only because Josh was fully on board that she'd decided to go through with it. Like he'd said, she needed some good publicity. If you could call what they were doing that.

"Everyone, please welcome Reece Ainsworth to the show. Welcome back."

"Thank you. It's good to be back."

"Any more tattoos you'd like to show us?"

"Not at this time, but I promise, you'll be the first to know if I do get another one."

"You'll see it here first, folks. You're currently shooting the

Piper Kane movie, correct? For those who don't know, Reece's next movie is based on a book series her ex-wife wrote, which is a great segue into my next question. How was your Labor Day weekend? Oh, wait. Wait. Don't answer that yet. Guys, let's see the photos from Reece's weekend."

The first photo came up, and the audience cheered and whistled. Reece asked Johnny, "Do you mind if I poll your audience?" She turned to them and shouted, "How many of you have, drunk or sober, accidentally slept with your ex?" Several hands went up. "Okay. And how many of you have been lucky enough *and* drunk enough to have a threesome?" Several more hands went up. "And how many of you just failed to answer that question truthfully because you think it's none of my damned business?" She turned back to Johnny while the crowd cheered her on. "Now, back to your question. My weekend was fantastic."

Whitney turned the volume down a bit after the crowd had settled down, and Reece went on to describe how terrible she was at throwing a frisbee. Johnny offered to show her how and just happened to have a hundred frisbees on hand which he and Reece threw to the audience members. She breathed a sigh of relief that it had gone so smoothly.

Her phone vibrated. It was a text from Brie.

Just got to my mom's place. Wish me luck.

❖

As the gate slowly opened, Brie could see her dad's truck in the driveway. It was good news on several levels. Hopefully, her mom would stay calmer during the conversation, and even more importantly, maybe her parents were getting back together. She just hoped they weren't scrambling to put their clothes back on since she preferred to think they only snuggled.

She got to the top stair, and the front door opened. "Hi, Dad. You're here late."

"I was just about to leave." He leaned in and kissed her cheek. "Good luck."

Surely, he knew she was smarter than that. "Oh no. I need you here for this, which is why I parked behind you."

She stepped into the house, and he closed the door behind her. "This isn't really my area of expertise."

"Mine either. Just back me up, okay?" She took him by the hand and led him into the great room.

The TV was on, and her mom was in the kitchen pouring herself a glass of wine. Normally, she'd be in her robe at that time of night, not short shorts and a loose button-up that was open to her cleavage. The new and improved Jade seemed to be sticking. She set her glass on the kitchen island and stared Brie down. "At least you didn't make me come and find you. Thank you for that."

Brie sat on a barstool. "It's not what it looks like."

"Don't lie to me, Gabriela. I gave you the beach house in good faith, and now it looks like you've been using it to get your freak on. What am I supposed to do with that? And how the hell are you going to protect yourself when you don't even live behind a gate? Your life as you know it is over."

"I hope so," Brie said. "Because I want the life that's ahead of me, not the one that's behind me. I want to be more and do more and experience everything life has to offer."

Her mom threw her hands in the air. "Apparently so."

Brie shook her head. "I didn't mean it like that. I mean, I wasn't referring to women in the plural sense. God, Mom. You have me all flustered now."

"That makes three of us," her dad said under his breath.

"I warned her," her mom said. "Whitney was warned, and now, all bets are off. I know people, Brie. Important people."

Her dad sat next to her. "Honey, all we care about is your well-being. We don't want to see you get in over your head and become a victim of the Hollywood media machine."

"You might need to look closer to home, Dad." She turned to her mom. "I can't prove it, but I think it might've been Robin who took those photos and sold them to the highest bidder."

Her mom slid the wineglass out of the way and leaned on her elbows. With a piercing stare, she said, "Now why would Birdie do that?"

"Jealousy, I guess. Reece was struggling with her gun skills for the movie. I asked Robin if she could help, and she did. She was there that night. The photos were taken after she left. But before she left, she'd made it clear to me that she'd tried to flirt with Reece, but for some reason, she thought I was getting in the way of that."

Her mom straightened back up. "Birdie put in a request for the beach house yesterday. She'd like to use it this weekend, even though she hasn't stayed there since Grandma died."

Brie huffed. "It's probably a ploy to get Reece all alone with her under the guise of another training session."

"And how would you feel about that?"

"It's not about me, but I think it was a mistake to involve Birdie. I should've known she'd still be the same mean person she always was. So the answer is, I would hate it if you gave her the weekend."

"Maybe it's time," her dad said. "You've wanted to cut the family off for a while now."

Her mom let out a big sigh. "I fear the longer I let them have access to the beach house, the more they'll start to believe it's their God-given right to use it. It'll get ugly for a while, but both of my sisters inherited enough money to buy their own." She picked up her glass and took a long sip, then set it back down. "It's decided, then. I'll send out an email tomorrow. Right after I find out if Birdie benefited financially by betraying her cousin. And God help her if she did."

Brie's dad got up and kissed her on the forehead. Then he rounded the island and said, "I'm proud of you, Jadey."

Brie lowered her gaze when he went in for a kiss. It was something she hadn't seen in years, and she felt a blush creep up her neck. "Gross, you guys." She said it in a whiny voice, but she didn't really mean it. They both looked happier and somehow younger. Especially her mom. It was as if an invisible weight had been lifted from her shoulders, and she could smile again. Laugh again and mean it. Her phone buzzed with a text message from Adam.

Two hot women? I should just kill myself right now.

"Anything important?" her mom asked.

"It's just Adam. Turns out he's a bit jealous."

Her dad laughed. "His sister is living his best life for him. He must be crushed."

Brie took a screenshot of the text for posterity. "Hey, we don't have to tell him it didn't really happen, do we? I mean, can't we just let him think I'm better at this than he is? Like, all I have to do is snap my fingers, and women gather around me like I'm Snoop Dogg?"

Her mom turned to her dad and said, "Are you buying this innocent act?"

Her dad shrugged. "She hasn't convinced me it didn't happen."

Brie laughed and put up her hands in defense. "Okay, believe whatever you want. I'm going to go back to my apartment and hope no one has found out where I live yet."

"No. No, you're not," her mom said. "Go back to the beach house. Use the alarm system at night, and don't let any family bother you. Especially not Birdie. If she did this to you, she's going to pay for it. That much I can promise you."

It seemed like an ominous statement. "That's nice of you, Mom. But I could just stay here with you if you want."

Her mom gestured with her head toward her dad. "I think I'd prefer to leave my options open when it comes to house guests."

Brie slid off the stool and went over to her parents. She gathered them into a hug and said, "I'm sorry about that comment earlier. It's not gross when you two kiss. And by all means, get your freak on whenever you want." She gave them both a quick kiss and headed for the door, excited to get back to her beach house. "I love you both," she shouted over her shoulder.

As she rounded the corner of the living room toward the door, she heard her mom whisper, "There's no way she had a threesome."

Brie paused to hear her father's reply. "Brie? Please. That girl barely has any experience with twosomes."

Brie closed her eyes and took in the sounds around her. She'd been watching the sunset for long enough that her feet had sunk into the wet sand. How many times had she and Adam done the same thing only to push each other until one of them fell over? She smiled at the memory. He was a good brother. A good man.

She took her phone out of her pocket and replied to his text.

Try to keep up, bro. And come for dinner sometime soon. I

miss your mediocre face. Oh, and did you know Mom and Dad are getting it on?

Whitney walked up and stood on one side of her with Reece on the other. "Everything good?" Brie asked.

"Johnny's had his own share of run-ins with the media," Reece said. "I knew he'd be down with our plan."

Brie repeated the plan out loud. "Don't confirm. Don't deny."

"Because they won't believe your denial anyway," Whitney added.

"Well, my parents believed the denial. Apparently, they think I'm too much of a prude for a threesome." Her eyes darted between them. "I'm not, by the way. Not that you're offering or I'm offering, I'm just saying."

Reece laughed. "We get it. You're not a prude."

Whitney grinned. "I can attest to that. Now, can we talk about why you're back here at the beach?"

"My mom thinks I'll be safer here. More privacy. I think she and my dad are so busy falling in love all over again that neither of them wants to worry about me fending off paparazzi at my apartment, although it's hard for me to believe it would ever come to that."

"We're hoping it won't," Whitney said. "But I'm also glad you'll be here."

"Writing a screenplay," Reece said with a wink.

"Starting immediately," Whitney added. "We'll get someone to help you, if you need it, but we want you to write it. That means you won't go back to the set. You'll stay here and write. And once we're done shooting this one, I'm going to work on book four because if we put it off for too long, Reece will be too old."

"Hey." Reece gave Whitney a slug in the arm. "Don't be ageist. But go easy on the car crashes and repelling off fifty-story buildings, would you?"

"I vote for less car crashes and more love scenes," Brie said. "That way, Reece can just lie on her back like the pillow princess she is and...hey." Reece gave her a nudge, and because Brie's feet had sunk into the sand, she almost tipped over. That was when she realized she was also much shorter than both of them. She looked up at Whitney and said, "It's probably hard to take me seriously, given my current situation, but I'll give it a shot as long as you promise me that if it's terrible, you won't let anyone else read it."

Whitney gave her a thumbs-up. "You got it, shorty."

They walked away, and Brie shouted, "Hey, a little help here?"

CHAPTER FOURTEEN

Whitney knocked on Reece's trailer door and opened it a crack. "You wanted to see me?"

"Come in and lock the door behind you." Reece tossed her copy of the script on the coffee table and put her feet up. The table creaked under the weight of her heavy military boots.

"Let me guess. You called me all the way over here because you want Piper to wear Chucks in book four?"

Reece folded her arms. "I called you all the way over here because I need to talk some sense into my ex-wife."

Whitney chuckled. "Oh, no. You lost that right a long time ago." She went to unlock the door.

"I get that, Whit. But you need to give it back to me for five minutes. Please just sit and listen."

Whitney took her hand off the lock and sat. She knew what was coming. It was the same thing every time. "I know what you're going to say."

"You're gearing up."

"We're not married anymore." Whitney held up her left hand. "See? No ring."

Reece sighed. "This is part of it. A few weeks before you leave, you get distant and defensive because you know how I feel about it, but I'm not talking about me, Whit. I'm talking about Brie."

Whitney stood and went to the kitchen sink. She leaned on the counter and looked out the small window at nothing but another trailer. "I haven't told her yet."

She and Brie had grown so close, she couldn't imagine her

being anything but hurt when Whitney told her she'd have to go back east to her cabin to write book four. *Oh, and by the way, Brie, you're not welcome there.* She'd told Brie in the past that the cabin was her place for solitude, that no one ever joined her there. But Brie wasn't just anyone. They'd built a bond, and she knew it would hurt Brie to know that Whitney had no plans to let Brie into that part of her life. It made her stomach roil just thinking about it.

"Can we talk about last weekend?"

Whitney turned and leaned against the counter. "Anything to change the subject."

"It's not really a subject change. I just want you to go back to that moment when the three of us were this close to making those photos a reality. I know you considered it, even if it was for the briefest of moments. Am I wrong?"

Whitney folded her arms across her chest. "What are you doing, Reece?"

"Trying to save our future. The future of this franchise we're hoping to create. Our working relationship. My friendship with Brie." Reece stood. "Whit, look at me. I know you don't trust me. And why should you? But don't forget that I know you. I know your moods. I know your habits. And I know that you're already gone. You're up in that cabin with Piper. Can't you see how much you've shut down in less than a week? And if you think I'm the only one who sees it, you're wrong."

"I know where this is going," Whitney said. "You want to blame the writing cabin for the fact that you had an affair."

"I'm not trying to make excuses for anything. I'm being honest. When we were married, I hated that cabin. I would lose you for weeks. Months sometimes. And it wasn't just a physical loss. You would check out emotionally too."

"It'll be different this time. I'll check in with Brie every day. Not every few days, every day."

"Don't make that promise to her because you'll break it. And just so you know, your check-ins almost made it worse for me. I could hear it in your voice, how annoyed you were that you had to drive down the mountain and make the call."

"That's not true. I was probably just frustrated with the writing. You got to strut down a runway for a living. Just put on a dress and walk. I have to create something. I have to spend hours on research. I have to pull ideas out of thin air and turn them into something people will want to buy. But none of that means anything to you, as you proved to me the last time I was up there. So excuse me if your opinion doesn't mean shit."

Whitney unlocked the door and turned back around. "Brie isn't you, Reece. She wouldn't cheat on me when I'm trying to finish a goddamned book." She slammed the door shut and pulled her phone out of her pocket. "I need to vent in private."

❖

Liz opened her door. "You got here fast. What did you do, drive on the sidewalk?"

Whitney brushed past her. "How fucking dare she?"

"As long as the *she* isn't me, I'm all ears." Liz closed the door and went into her kitchen.

Whitney threw her purse on a chair. "I'm talking about Reece. How fucking dare she?"

"We're back to that? I thought you two were getting along swimmingly. Tea or coffee?"

"We were until this week. Tea is fine."

"Lover's quarrel?"

Whitney dropped into a chair at the dining table. "We're not lovers, Liz. She's my ex-wife. Period."

"I was kidding. But, wow, do you three have the world thinking that you are. In fact, we should drink to your success."

"The world can fuck off," Whitney said. "It's none of their business, and it will continue to be none of their business."

It was all so insane from start to finish. It was starting to feel as if Whitney couldn't make good choices anymore. Random sex with a stranger? Thinking she could make a movie with her ex-wife? Being coy about a threesome that never happened for publicity? Where would it stop?

Liz set two cups on the table and sat. "I took the liberty of choosing the stress-relieving tea. It works great with a vodka chaser, but you're driving."

"How many ex-husbands do you have? I lost count after three."

"Very funny. You know I stopped counting after two, but if memory serves, which it often doesn't, the last one was Pierre. He was number four, and I only remember that because he only had four toes on his left foot. It seemed like a good omen to me, so I married him."

Maybe she'd spent too much time with Liz and the bad decision making had rubbed off on her. Whitney would have to give that some serious thought. In the meantime, she really needed her BFF. Yeah, Liz's silly abbreviation had grown on Whitney. "Reece is trying to blame our divorce on my writing cabin. Can you believe that shit?"

"Ah. Hence the how fucking dare she," Liz said. "Well, she's right." She tossed back her shot of vodka and slammed the shot glass on the table. "Thanks for giving me a reason to drink."

Whitney sat there speechless. She was sure Liz had just said the divorce was her fault, but that couldn't be possible. Because BFFs didn't do that.

Liz blinked at her several times. "Shit. I just said that out loud, didn't I?"

"You just lost your title." Whitney shot out of her chair and went for the vodka bottle. She grabbed it and rifled through the kitchen drawers until she found a pen. In big letters, she wrote BFF on the label.

"Hey, now. Just slow down, hon." Liz took the pen and bottle from her and set them on the counter. She pushed Whitney's hair off her face and held her chin so they were eye to eye. "I just made you want to cry a fucking river, didn't I?"

Whitney bit her lip to keep it from quivering and nodded. Liz wrapped an arm around her and led her to the sofa. She sat and patted her shoulder. "It's a good thing I'm not wearing Chanel."

❖

Whitney grabbed a bottle of wine and two glasses before she went into Brie's bedroom. She set them on the bed and stripped her clothes off, then sauntered into the bathroom. "I'm looking for a sexy woman covered in bubbles."

"You found her." Brie pushed a clump of bubbles to the side. "Care to join me?"

Whitney set the bottle and glasses on the edge of the tub and leaned down for a kiss. "Hello, beautiful. God, am I glad to see you."

Brie looked gorgeous with her hair piled on top of her head, bubbles up to her neck. She'd lit a few candles that were flickering in the breeze from the open window, and the sounds of the ocean mixed with the R&B coming from the speaker. It was all so beautiful. Too beautiful to be real. It wasn't their beach house, and Brie—beautiful, persistent, sexy Brie—wasn't even officially Whitney's girlfriend.

She'd thought about making it official with just a few words, but with her looming departure, she wasn't sure if that was the best idea. And now, with Reece's unfortunate and hurtful comment, she was even less sure what to do.

"Tough day?" Brie asked. "You sounded kind of sad on the phone. And your eyes are puffy. What's wrong?"

Everything was wrong. Nothing made sense, but she didn't want to discuss it again. Not when she could sink into the tub between Brie's legs and let the world fall away for a while. She got settled in the warm water and said, "Just tired. Give me your hands." She interlocked their fingers and kissed each knuckle. "You have such beautiful hands."

She'd first noticed Brie's hands the morning after their first night together, before it all went to hell. She'd noticed the thin gold ring with the small moonstone that she wore on her right middle finger. She gave that ring another kiss.

Brie kissed the top of her head. "I'm glad you're here. I've missed you all week."

"I've missed you too." Whitney did her best to keep her tears at bay. Could this last forever? Could they make a life together? It seemed so crazy given their start. But she'd come to rely on Brie in a way that she hadn't with Reece. Brie seemed to get Whitney in a way no one else did. She'd been avoiding the subject of leaving, but maybe she didn't have to. With Brie also being a writer, she'd probably understand her need for solitude. Tonight wasn't the night to find out, though. Tonight she wanted to stay in what felt like a perfect moment between them.

Whitney turned and took Brie's face in her hand. "Kiss me," she whispered.

❖

It was a no-brainer to have the wrap party at the beach house. Reece had suggested it. She wanted to give everyone on the crew a special gift, and what better place to do that than a private beach? Brie was more than happy to host. She looked forward to seeing everyone again, and Reece had promised that she wouldn't have to do a thing.

She locked the door behind the last of the caterers and went into the kitchen where Whitney was wiping down the countertops. "I'd say that was a success."

"Everyone loved it." Whitney gave her a kiss on the cheek. "You'll have to thank your mom for us too."

"Oh. Yeah, that. I might have told her it was going to be a small gathering. Just a few people."

"Well, I'm glad I'm leaving the state," Whitney quipped. "I really don't need another count against me." She stopped short and froze, her eyes locked on Brie's as if she'd just revealed something she hadn't meant to.

Brie wouldn't have thought anything of it if it wasn't for the look of panic on Whitney's face. "Is there something you forgot to tell me?"

"Can we talk about this later? When we're alone?"

She went back to wiping down the countertops. Brie glanced around. "We are alone. Everyone left." Now Brie felt a sense of panic. Whitney had been so busy the last few weeks, they hadn't had much time together. She so looked forward to getting into a normal groove where they saw each other every day and did normal things like go to lunch and buy groceries and fall asleep watching the late news. Normal couple stuff.

Whitney put the dishcloth in the sink and stayed on the other side of the island. "I've been meaning to talk to you about it. I just haven't found the right time."

Shit. This didn't sound good. Not at all. Brie pulled out a barstool. Whatever this was, she wanted to be seated for it. Were they breaking up? Were they ever really together, or had it all been a fantastic dream that she was bound to wake up from?

Whitney rounded the island and sat next to her. She put a hand on Brie's arm. She wasn't comforted by that gesture. It scared her even more because it told her that Whitney had bad news. News that would cause pain. Brie wanted to get up and put as much space between them as she could, or even better, run away before Whitney could say a word. She wasn't ready for this news. She was too smitten. Too in love.

"I have to go to my writing cabin," Whitney said. "I know it's far away, and the phone service sucks, but I don't see any other way if I'm going to write book four."

Brie didn't dare breathe yet. "And?" she asked.

"And, nothing. Like I said, I was waiting for the right time to tell you."

Brie exhaled. Whitney hadn't said the breakup words, that was a good thing. But why had she kept it a secret? "Am I the last to know about this? Does Reece know? Liz?" She needed room to figure this out so she stood and went to the other side of the island. "What were you going to do, just leave and not say good-bye?"

"Of course not," Whitney said. "I have to do this, Brie. It's the only place I've ever been able to write. I need my trees and birds and my grandfather's old leather chair and the faint smell of cigar smoke. It was his fishing cabin before I inherited it, and for some reason, I write well there."

"Are we talking months? Because I really could've used some time to adjust to the idea."

"Three. Maybe four."

It was devastating news. Brie tried to quell her emotions. Three or four months was a hell of a long time to leave someone you loved, especially when the relationship was so new. Sure, people did it all the time, but only if they were going off to fight a war or whatever. She couldn't think of any other good reasons, but they had to be better than Whitney's excuse. They didn't have to leave the beach house yet. What better place to write than that? And the fact that Whitney wasn't even willing to try made Brie feel both mad and sad.

She sucked in a breath and said, "Okay."

Whitney's eyes widened. "Okay?"

"What else can I say? I mean, it's not like I was ever going to get an opinion on the matter, right?"

Whitney lowered her gaze. "I'm sure Reece would be happy to tell you that she didn't have a choice in the matter, either, which is why I'm giving you one. I won't go if you don't want me to."

Brie threw her hands in the air. "Oh, now it's up to me? Five minutes ago, I didn't even know it was happening." There was no way Brie would fall into that trap. She shook her head. "I'm not going to keep you here when you'd rather be somewhere else."

"Please, just tell me that if I go, you'll still be here when I get back."

"Where else would I be? I'm going to be busy writing the screenplay and, apparently, missing you."

"I'm sorry I didn't tell you sooner. I should have. I just didn't want to ruin the time we had left. And I will be back, Brie. You understand that, right?"

Would she be back? Brie couldn't be sure of anything. Whitney had lied about this, so what else was she hiding? "I'm sorry you didn't trust me enough to tell me sooner," Brie said. "I could've made plans to go with you. I could've—" As soon as she said the words, Brie realized that was never an option. She wasn't invited. She walked out of the kitchen and said, "I'm going to bed. Let yourself out or stay in the guest room. I really don't care."

❖

Brie had been lying there for a while, listening to small noises like doors opening and closing that told her Whitney hadn't left yet. She'd shed a few tears that she'd managed to hold back during their conversation. This wasn't how she'd imagined the evening would go. After everyone left, she'd hoped they'd snuggle by the fire pit and ask silly questions like, "What was the best day of your life when you were a kid?"

There was so much they didn't know about each other. All the little details and stories that only a new lover would find enthralling. But it wasn't to be, not when Whitney wouldn't have internet or phone service. Brie rolled onto her side and hugged a pillow.

Knowing that she'd be the only one to shed any tears over this was hard to take.

She heard her bedroom door open. Whitney took her by the shoulder and urged her onto her back, then straddled her. She said, "I'm not leaving, and I'm not sleeping in the guest room."

"You *are* leaving. For four months. And you can't fix this with sex."

Whitney shut her up with a kiss. Brie tried her best to resist giving in. She didn't want a farewell fuck; she wanted Whitney to stay and write her book there. They could write together. Support each other. Why did she have to be incommunicado on the other side of the country?

Whitney took Brie's hands and interlocked their fingers, then slid them above her head. She kissed her again and worked her way over to Brie's ear. "Let me make love to you," she whispered.

Brie whimpered. She felt Whitney's tongue on her neck, and that whimper turned into a groan. "This isn't fair."

Whitney pulled back and looked her in the eye. "Was that a yes?"

Brie realized the answer would always be yes. She couldn't fight it. She wanted Whitney on top of her, inside her, loving her. She wanted her tongue and her lips and her hands. She wanted that voice to whisper in her ear again.

There was too much in between them. Too many blankets and clothes, but Brie's hands were pinned above her head. She nodded. "Yes."

Whitney sat up and pulled her shirt over her head. Brie sat up too. She reached around and unhooked Whitney's bra, then dragged her nails down her back. Whitney gasped and pushed her back down on the bed. Their eyes locked for a few seconds before their lips collided in a passionate kiss. Brie held on to Whitney's head and deepened the kiss.

Would it be the last time their tongues explored? The last time her hands would grip those hips? The last time she'd keep herself from saying too much? The last time she'd try to convey without words how in love she was? Did it even matter to Whitney what she felt?

Brie's eyes popped open when Whitney rolled off her to take

off her pants. Her chest heaved for air. Her eyes filled with tears. She mouthed the words at first. Then whispered them. Then said them out loud. "I love you, Whit."

The bed stilled. Brie squeezed her eyes shut. She shouldn't have said it. Not right before Whitney planned to leave. This was supposed to be their farewell, right? Brie wanted it. Even if that was all it was, she wanted it.

Whitney took Brie's face in her hand. "Look at me," she whispered.

Brie opened her eyes and tried to blink away her tears. Whitney wiped away the few that escaped before she whispered, "I love you too."

CHAPTER FIFTEEN

"How long has she been gone?"

If Brie answered Adam's question accurately by saying Whitney had been gone twenty-nine days, four hours, six minutes, and approximately thirty-seven seconds, he'd try to be a supportive brother by offering to stay the night and watch old movies or something, but Reece had already made that offer, and Brie had gladly accepted. She'd made the mistake of telling Adam, who suddenly found the time to stop by for a visit.

"A few weeks," Brie said. "And you're going to make a fool of yourself, you know that, right?"

Adam leaned back and put his feet up on the ottoman. "I think it's important that I meet her. And believe me when I tell you that I'll know if you're sleeping with her."

"Ha. You just want to drool on her flip-flops and grind against her leg like a miniature schnauzer."

"You're so gross sometimes, sis. And where do you come up with such random dog breeds?"

Brie went back into the kitchen. "Adam, you're dressed in metrosexual business bullshit casual at the beach. At least untuck your shirt tails."

He shot up out of his chair. "You're so right." He kicked off his shoes and rolled his trousers up a bit, then untucked his shirt. "Is this better?"

Brie grimaced. "No. Now you look like you've been on a three-day bender. Tuck your shirt back in and lose the sweater vest."

"You just told me to...never mind."

She set a small bucket of beer on the coffee table and sat opposite him. "She'll come through the garage door, so come over here if you want to see the grand entrance."

Adam got up and sat in the chair next to her. "Do I smell okay?"

Brie leaned in and sniffed, then scrunched her nose. "Polo?"

"I'm doing a retro thing."

"I think it's called dating cougars, but retro works too. At least you moved on from the big-breasted blonde thing."

Reece came through the garage door with a giant watermelon in her arms. "Where can I unload this?"

Adam shot up and rushed over. "I've got it." He put it on the counter and offered his hand like a goofy thirteen-year-old. "Hey, I'm Adam. Brie's older brother."

"By five minutes. So I've heard. Nice to meet you, Adam."

Brie wanted to get up and give Reece a fist bump for keeping Adam in his place, but she stayed where she was. "I have a bucket of 805s ready and waiting for you."

Reece dropped her purse and went over to Brie. She leaned down and kissed her cheek. "This is why I adore you."

Brie grinned at Adam, which garnered her his signature flip-off disguised as a head scratch. She laughed under her breath and said, "Come join us, Adam."

Reece spread out on the sofa and took a long swig of beer. "So, big brother, I hear you're pretty good on a surfboard."

Adam sat back down. "Breezy said something nice about me? I'm shocked."

"Breezy, huh? That's cute. I like it. Maybe I'll start using it. What do you think, Breezy? Can I call you Breezy?"

Brie winked at her. "You can call me anything you want."

Reece gave her a quizzical look, so Brie winked at her again. That seemed to be enough for Reece to realize that Brie wanted to have a little fun with her brother. Reece rolled onto her side and posed like Elvira on her red velvet sofa. Never mind that she had on jeans and a crew-neck T-shirt. Poor Adam wouldn't get even the slightest glimpse of cleavage.

Brie had to hold her breath to keep from laughing when Reece said, "Did you hear that, Adam? I have permission to call her Breezy, but I think I'll stick with Lucious Lady Lips."

"Stop. I can't take it." Brie leaned back and threw her hands over her face while she giggled. As much as she wanted to keep up the charade, Reece was laying it on a little bit too thick.

"Hey. I was just getting started," Reece said in protest. "Do you have a gun, Adam? Breezy can't resist my charms when I have a cocked gun in my hand." She raised her hand and shot Brie with a finger gun, then gave her another wink, this time in slow motion.

"This isn't funny," Adam said. His voice an octave higher than normal. "Do you even know the hell I'm going through with all of my friends believing that my sister is getting it on with Reece Ainsworth? I've had to resort to dating older women just so I can get some respect back."

Reece shrugged. "I guess that explains the Polo cologne."

Brie burst out laughing. "My bro is a cougar hunter. Grr."

Adam went to stand, but Brie caught him by the arm. "No. Don't go. I'm just messing with you. Please stay for lunch. I'd really like it if Reece could get to know you better."

"What are you making?"

"That's a very good question," Reece said. "Because I'm starving, and I'm gonna need more than watermelon if I'm going to learn to surf today."

Adam scoffed. "Uh, Brie isn't that great on a surfboard. She can't really…you know…stay up for very long."

Reece grinned. "I guess that leaves you, then, Adam." She turned to Brie. "Now, how can I help with lunch?"

Brie got up and headed for the kitchen while Adam made an obvious attempt to not explode with joy, but Brie heard his little whimper.

She opened the fridge and pulled out a package wrapped in brown paper. She set it on the island and put her hands on her hips. "Surf and turf, anyone? Bro, you're on the grill. Reece, get your ass in here and help me peel some shrimp."

Adam gave her a salute and headed outside. Reece stood next to her and flung an arm over her shoulders. "You were right. Your brother's a sweet guy. And he's almost as pretty as you but not quite."

"Don't tell him that. He'll be devastated." Brie turned to face Reece. "I'm really glad you called. It's nice to have company." She wrapped her arms around her and tried not to think about what, or who, was missing.

❖

Reece came out of the water looking worn out. She plopped facedown on the towel next to Brie's. "Your brother's a taskmaster. Or maybe it's just that I'm not used to getting pummeled by wave after wave."

Brie shaded her eyes. The sun was low in the sky, making it hard to see him clearly out in the waves. "I'm sure he'll talk about the day he taught Reece Ainsworth how to use a boogie board for years to come. Maybe write a memoir. Have it engraved on his headstone. Oh! And don't forget about the tattoo. No doubt, he'll put your name on his ass." It wasn't until Reece didn't respond that Brie realized what she'd just said. "I'm sorry. I wasn't making fun of your tattoo."

"It's okay. It wasn't the smartest thing I've ever done." Reece rolled over and sat up. She wrapped her arms around her legs and rested her cheek on her knees.

Brie grabbed another towel and wrapped it around Reece's shoulders. She noticed the look of concern in her eyes. "What's wrong?"

"Do you miss her?"

The question took Brie aback. Was Reece asking because she missed Whitney too? It would make sense, considering how much time they'd spent together on the set. Brie hoped it wasn't anything more than that. She hoped Whitney hadn't kept something from her, and she certainly hoped that Reece wasn't somehow communicating with Whitney when Brie couldn't. "I miss her like crazy," she said. "It's only been a month, but it feels like a lifetime. I honestly don't know how you did it."

Reece lifted her head and turned away. "Beautiful sunset tonight."

It wasn't that beautiful since there was cloud cover. Not beautiful enough to warrant a comment. She'd deflected, and Brie needed to know why. "That was a quick change of subject. Did I say something wrong?"

Reece shrugged the extra towel off her shoulders and got up. "I'm getting cold. See you inside."

Adam ran up and shook his wet hair out on Brie like he'd done a thousand times before. Brie got up and slugged him, then turned and watched Reece run up the stairs to the house.

"God, she's gorgeous," Adam said. "Just look at that…oof!"

Brie elbowed him in the stomach. "Have a little respect."

Adam grabbed a towel and dried his arms off. "Did something happen?"

"Maybe. I'm not sure."

"Need a minute? I can hang out on the deck. Get the fire pit going. Find my fishing pole for s'mores."

Brie's first instinct was to make Adam think he was losing some of that thick hair on his head with one of her snide remarks, but she stopped herself and said, "I know we give each other shit on a daily basis, but you're awesome, and I love you."

Adam smiled but didn't reply. He picked up all of the towels and trudged through the sand with Brie. When they were almost to the stairs, he said, "Love you too, sis. Now, is there any chance you could befriend a straight version of Reece? Because I flexed my guns and she didn't even notice. It was the weirdest sensation."

Brie huffed. "You're so transparent, covering up your inability to share a tender moment with your sister by making a lesbian joke."

"It was that or burst into tears." They got to the bottom of the steps, and he handed her the hose they used to wash off the sand. "Just kidding. I haven't cried since seventh grade. Now, rinse off and go apologize for whatever awful thing you said so I can share the double lounger with Reece."

Brie grabbed the hose and furrowed her brow. "Is your hairline receding? It is, isn't it? Oh God, Adam. Whatever will you do?"

❖

Brie found Reece in the guest room getting dressed. She tried for a casual tone when she said, "Hey, wanna help me cut up that humongous watermelon?"

Reece pulled on her jeans and buttoned them up. "I want you to go see her."

"Who?"

Reece stopped and glared at Brie. "Who do you think?"

Brie sat on the bed. "Why?"

"Because this is what she does. She disappears." Reece turned away and untied her bikini top. "I'll give you the address. It'll take two planes and a rental car to get to her." She pulled a T-shirt over her head and sat next to Brie on the bed.

They both stared at the wall for what felt like minutes. Brie wanted to believe Reece had good intentions and that this wasn't some ploy to get between her and Whitney. She turned to her and said, "Tell me why you really want me to go."

Reece took in a deep breath and sighed. "You just need to trust me on this one."

"I want to," Brie said. She could list out all the reasons why she had doubts, but Reece had to know. The tattoo alone was enough.

Reece stood and paced for a moment. At times, Brie would look at her and wonder why Whitney hadn't already taken her back. She had so many great characteristics to go with the total hotness. She was kindhearted, funny, affectionate, and down to earth, considering what she did for a living. Brie really liked Reece and was happy to keep her in their lives. She found herself wondering if Reece felt the same way or if she was just biding her time. Waiting for the right moment to get Whitney back.

Reece stopped pacing and stood in front of her. "If I could go back and do it differently with Whitney, I would speak up instead of letting the bitterness build inside me. I would force her to listen and to take my needs into consideration. I would use my voice instead of trying to find comfort in someone else's arms. Why are you still sitting there when you could be booking a flight?"

It was all too sudden. Brie needed time to think it over. She'd already chased Whitney across the country, did she really want to go back to stalking her? Showing up without any notice? Liz would never let her live it down. Whitney might go back to not trusting her. And what about Reece? Were her motives genuine? Brie looked her in the eye. "Does this mean you've given up on ever getting Whitney back?"

Reece sat back down. "I gave up a long time ago, Brie. This isn't me pretending to be your friend and Whitney's friend, for that matter. I came to realize that even if you weren't in the picture, I could still never get back what she and I had. I broke that bond of trust. But if you're asking if I still love her, I always will. And I know I hurt her beyond measure. I fucked up. And the only way I can make that up to her is by making sure she has a chance to be happy. From where I sit, you're her chance at happiness. And while it's not always easy seeing the two of you together, I can't imagine seeing her with anyone else. You're good for her, Brie. So go let her be good for you too."

Brie wrapped her arms around Reece and whispered, "Thank you."

Two planes. Scratch that. One plane. One puddle jumper. One rental car. One flat tire. Zero cell phone service, and two people pointing Brie in completely opposite directions made for a level of grumpiness that could only be cured with a stiff drink and a two-hour massage, neither of which seemed to be in her near future.

She slowly climbed the dirt road in her compact rental car, ready to turn around when she found a spot wide enough to do so safely because surely, this road would only lead her to a painful and gory death at the hands of a sadistic prison escapee.

She hit a deep rut that caused the car to veer to the left. She pulled hard on the steering wheel and overcorrected right into another rut. She slammed on the brakes and took a few deep breaths. There was so much growth along both sides of the one-lane road, she wasn't sure how far she'd have to go to find a turnaround point.

She looked behind her and considered reversing back down the mountain, then thought better of it considering her bad track record in the Whole Foods parking lot.

She peered through the front window at the road in front of her. There seemed to be fresh tracks in the dirt. "With my luck, they're from a four-whe...*aah*!" She screamed at the top of her lungs and pushed the gas pedal to the floor. "Bear," she screamed. "That was a fucking bear." She'd only seen it out of corner of her eye, but the damn thing was huge and up on two legs, ready to eat the car with her in it. The steering wheel pulled left and right. The car bounced like the shocks had broken, but she didn't take her foot off the gas until she saw a narrow turn-off to her right with a No Trespassing sign nailed to a tree. She decided she'd rather die at the hand of a serial killer than be torn limb by limb by a grizzly bear.

A cabin came into view through the thick vegetation. She slammed on the brakes, skidding to a stop just before she plowed through the front porch. She opened her door and screamed for help, hoping she'd scare the bear away long enough to get inside. She made a run for it, screaming and looking behind her. Her foot caught on something that sent her flying toward the porch stairs where she landed face-first.

It stunned her enough that she had to shake off the dizzy feeling before she tried to stand. She grunted as she tried to push herself up, but her arms collapsed underneath her. She cried out in pain and decided it might be best to roll over and try to sit up that way.

She was sure her chest would be black and blue from hitting the edge of a step. Not the sexiest look when she hadn't seen her lover in a while. She managed to roll onto her back, but pain shot up through her arm. She grimaced, held it to her chest, and shouted, "What the fuck?"

"That's exactly what I said a minute ago. What the *fuck*?"

Brie opened her eyes and smiled. "Hey, Whit." But her smile faded, and her eyes grew big when she remembered what she'd seen. "Bear." Her breathing grew shallow. She started to panic because she couldn't say more than "Bear." She pointed behind Whitney. "Bear."

"That was me. Do I look like a bear? And what were you thinking bringing that little car up here?"

Brie was thinking that the damned stairs she was lying on were not designed with ergonomics in mind. She grimaced as she tried to sit up. The lack of core work had suddenly become an issue. *Note to self: do some sit-ups once in a while.*

Whitney helped her stand. "A four-wheel drive barely makes it up that road. I'm not sure how you even got that far."

"It's amazing what you can accomplish when a bear is chasing you." Brie grimaced again. "I think I hurt my wrist."

"Let's get you inside." Whitney opened the cabin door. "Sit on the sofa so I can assess the damage."

Brie glanced around. "You mean, I drove right to your cabin?" She would've offered her hand for a fist bump if it didn't feel like it would fall off. But what a relief that she'd actually made it. Her smile faded when she noticed Whitney didn't seem the least bit impressed.

The cabin was small. A leather sofa took up most of the space in front of the fireplace. A small table, barely bigger than a TV tray, sat under a window with only one chair. The kitchen took up a corner by the table. Everything looked original, except maybe the fridge.

The only decoration on the wood-panel walls was an old fishing pole and a framed map of some sort. A rocking chair took up the corner opposite the kitchen near the fireplace. Brie loved old rocking chairs, but she imagined it would creak loudly if she sat in it. That was only a concern because of the dead silence that almost felt oppressive after being near the ocean where the crashing waves were a constant, never ending sound.

She felt embarrassed when she realized Whitney had just hung a red and black plaid jacket on a hook. Everyone knew bears didn't need jackets. She had a red thermal shirt on underneath, and Brie thought she was the most beautiful lumber-jill she'd ever seen. She smiled and said, "Feel free to chop some wood while I watch."

"Maybe save the jokes until we figure out if you broke anything." Whitney pushed her sleeves up and sat on the coffee table. She let out a sigh that screamed disappointment and said, "Hold still."

Brie rested her good hand on Whitney's knee. She needed some sort of reassuring contact to offset the cold tone in Whitney's voice. "How does it look, Doc? Will I live?"

"You could've seriously injured yourself driving like that. You could've high-centered or gone off the road or taken out my front porch with a goddamned Kia or whatever the fuck it is." She held up a hand and said, "How many fingers?"

"I prefer two. Sometimes three."

"How many am I holding up?"

Brie blinked a few times and said, "Three."

Whitney dropped her hand. "You hit your head pretty hard on the step. Any dizziness or nausea?"

"I was dizzy, but it went away."

She pushed Brie's sweater up her arm. Her hand and wrist had started to swell. "It might be broken."

"Does that mean sex is out of the question? Because that's kinda why I came here. You know, cozy cabin sex where we get it on in front of the fire?"

Whitney got up and put her coat back on. "It means a trip back down the mountain."

Brie's jokes were falling flat. She wanted to protest driving back down that road, and she wasn't sure if the emotions bubbling to the surface were due to the pain in her wrist or the even bigger pain in her heart because Whitney, the woman she'd driven to the end of the earth for, had yet to even say hello. "Can't you just pop it back into place? I really don't want to leave now that I'm here."

"You can't stay, Brie. What were you thinking? Never mind. Just get in the car."

Whitney stood there with a hand on her hip, holding the door open again. She didn't seem interested in even looking Brie in the eye. It reminded her so much of the morning after their first encounter, when Whitney couldn't get Brie out of her hotel room fast enough. Great. She'd managed to create an even worse encounter than their first one. At least the first time she'd been kicked out, it was after a night of unforgettable sex.

She stood and took a final look around the little cabin she'd probably never see again. Why in the world had she ever listened to Reece?

❖

"Can you turn down the lights?" Brie threw an arm over her eyes and knocked her wrist against something. "Ow. Motherfucker."

"The pain meds must be wearing off," Whitney said. "I'll go get the nurse."

Brie opened her eyes again. Her arm was in a cast, but it still hurt like hell when she hit it on those metal bars hospitals used to keep people from rolling out of bed. Her mouth felt like a sandbox, and she felt sticky all over, like she'd been sweating. She didn't dare lift her arm again in case a gaggle of skunks had set up house. Was it a gaggle or a herd? She'd have to look it up later.

Whitney came back into the room. She looked so cute in her jeans and hiking boots that it made Brie smile. "Hello there, mountain girl."

Whitney put her hand on Brie's forehead. "How are you feeling?"

"Like a big bear took a swing at me."

"You'd be dead if a big bear took a swing at you." Whitney moved her hand to Brie's cheek. "You scared the shit out of me back there."

Brie's lip quivered. She tried to be brave and not cry. Whitney obviously wasn't in the mood for her antics. "I guess I overreacted," she said. "The woods aren't really my safe place. Like, when you're meditating and they tell you to go to your safe place, I'm a gazillion miles away from bear country."

Whitney finally cracked a smile. "No, you're not in Malibu anymore, Princess."

"No. I'm in the land of hot lumber-jills, and I gotta say, I'm digging this rugged look."

Whitney stepped back when the nurse came in. She stood off to the side with her arms folded and a deep furrow in her brow. Brie wasn't sure if she was angry or worried. "I'll be okay," she said. Whitney shook her head in what was clearly disgust and moved out of her line of sight.

❖

Brie waited in the car while Whitney paced in front of the little country store. Apparently, this would be their last chance to get phone service before they headed back up the mountain. She'd already called her mom to let her know she'd be fine. She left out the part about the possible concussion since the doctor didn't seem too worried about it.

She didn't know who Whitney was talking to, but she figured Reece was probably getting an earful for giving Brie directions to the cabin. She opened her door and got out of the SUV. Whitney dropped the phone to her side. "Where are you going?"

Brie pointed at the store. "Just want to look around." She went inside and gave the cashier a nod that caused pain to shoot through her neck. Thinking she might have given herself whiplash too, she picked up a jar of pain relief cream that was fifty-percent more effective than competing brands. She set it back down and picked up the competing brand because even in her compromised state, she didn't want to be swayed by fake statistics, especially when those statistics weren't taking her mind off the fact that this was not the Whitney she knew and loved.

This was the Whitney who had flipped out after their first night together. Angry and impatient Whitney. Frustrated and feeling like she'd been lied to Whitney. And that made Brie wonder if Whitney thought she'd been deceptive by showing up on her front porch. Well, splayed out on her front steps, but still. Was that why she seemed so upset?

She picked up a few candy bars and a bottle of water and set it all on the counter in front of the cashier. "That looks painful," the woman said. "What happened?"

Brie glanced at her swollen black and blue fingers sticking out from the bright pink cast. "I was running away from a bear."

"She was running away from me, who she thought was a bear. Hey, Mirna." Whitney brushed past her and went to the coffee machine.

Mirna laughed under her breath, then cleared her throat. "That must've been scary." She choked back another laugh and covered her mouth with her hand. "Sorry. Must have a little tickle in my throat."

Brie threw some cash on the counter. "I'll get the grumpy bear's coffee too." She managed a fake smile and said, "Thanks, Myrtle."

"It's Mirna."

"Got it." She rushed out of the store and got back in the car. Her cheeks felt hot from embarrassment, and her body ached so badly, she felt like she was constantly on the verge of tears. With a shaky hand, she dabbed some cream on her neck and rubbed it in.

Whitney opened her door and put two cups of coffee in the holders. "Get everything you need?"

"You didn't have to embarrass me like that in front of Myrtle."

"Her name is Mirna. And I wasn't trying to embarrass you." Whitney got in the car and buckled her seat belt.

Brie gave her a once-over, hoping she'd see someone she

recognized. But all Whitney gave in return was a hard stare. "Why are you so angry with me? I didn't mean to fall on your porch and sprain my wrist."

"You have three screws in your wrist, Brie. Three. So don't call it a sprain, and for God's sake, stop making bear jokes. It stopped being funny at least twelve hours ago."

Brie wiped a tear from her eye. "If I didn't know better, I'd say you weren't exactly happy to see me."

"I'm just frustrated. You should've called before you tried to come all this way, and now you're injured, Brie. How are you supposed to write a screenplay with your hand in a cast?"

Brie didn't dare answer. She'd say something she'd regret. But at least she knew what Whitney was most concerned about. "Who were you talking to?"

"It doesn't matter."

"It matters to me if it was about me," Brie said.

"I was talking to Liz. She's coming to get you."

"What?" Whitney tried to put the car in drive, but Brie grabbed her arm before she could. "Why can't I stay here with you?"

"You need care. The cabin is too far up the mountain for emergencies." She threw her arm over Brie's seat so she could reverse. "Put your seat belt on."

❖

Whitney's fingers had stiffened up. It often happened when she got on a creative roll and typed for hours on end. She swirled a teaspoon of honey in her tea and wrapped her fingers around the hot ceramic mug.

She'd insisted that Brie sleep on the sofa so she could watch her. The sound of her head hitting the wooden step had Whitney worried about a concussion. The whole scene kept playing out in her mind. Brie's ear-piercing screams. The tires trying to get traction in the soft dirt. The engine revving as she flew up the road. And none of it made a bit of sense in the moment and still didn't.

Then there was the race back down the mountain. And pacing in the hospital waiting room while they tried to repair the damage

Brie had done to her wrist. And then waiting again for her to wake up. Whitney felt traumatized by all of it. And she was furious with Reece. Boy, would she get an earful the next time they spoke.

She took a sip of tea and realized Brie was staring at her over the back of the sofa. "Hi," she said. "I thought you were sleeping."

"Do you realize that's the first time you've said hello to me?"

Brie's voice sounded weak. Whitney got up and went over to her. She sat on the coffee table and rested her arms on her knees. She hadn't noticed it before, but Brie's lips looked chapped. And her beautiful hair was a tangled mess. And she still had on the same clothes she'd arrived in yesterday. The same sweater. The same jeans. Her shoes were even still on her feet.

The nurse must've dressed her in the same stuff while Whitney talked to the doctor. Yes, of course that was it. Then she realized that she hadn't taken any other clothes for Brie to change into. She hadn't even washed the dirt off her forehead where she'd hit it on the step. She reached out and pushed her hair back and saw that there was a little bit of dried blood just past her hairline. She didn't even know if Brie had bruises anywhere else because she'd been too wrapped up in her own anger and frustration to look. She shot up and headed for the door.

Brie's rental car was still unlocked. She grabbed her purse off the passenger seat and a carry-on bag from the back seat. She stood with them in hand and stared at her little cabin. She hadn't ever spent time there with her grandfather, even though she'd begged him to take her and teach her how to fish. It wasn't a place for a little girl, he'd say. Once she grew up, she understood better that it was his special place where he could drink and smoke cigars and fish all day, and no one was there to tell him otherwise.

It also became clear that her grandmother had never been invited to join him. No one ever had, as far as Whitney knew. It was his place. He'd built it for one. And she'd chosen to continue that tradition.

Reece only knew where it was because she'd insisted Whitney give her directions in case of an emergency. She remembered making Reece promise they'd never be used for anything other than an emergency. Evidently, her ex-wife thought this situation qualified.

She felt ashamed that she'd been so unwelcoming. So cold. So numb to the reason Brie had shown up there in the first place. She lowered her gaze when she realized she hadn't even asked.

Reece was right. Whitney shut everything else out when she was there. Everything and everyone. That was why it had angered her when she heard a car on the road just as she was coming off her hiking trail. And then she saw what kind of car it was and thought she'd be stuck helping some idiot find their way back down the mountain.

She'd come up behind the car and was about to bang on the roof to get their attention when they'd screamed and sped up the mountain like they'd just seen a…bear. Whitney sat on the edge of the porch. She needed to gather her thoughts before she went back inside and made things worse. They'd talk about it when Brie felt better. She was too weak and too medicated to have a rational conversation. And Whitney was too…numb. And she didn't understand why. Why couldn't she take Brie in her arms and comfort her? Tell her she'd missed her. Why had it seemed like such a huge invasion of privacy to have her show up there?

It startled her when the door opened, and Brie stepped onto the porch. She'd pulled her hair back into a ponytail. That couldn't have been easy with only one good hand. She'd washed her face too. Those were things Whitney should've done for her before they'd even left the hospital.

Brie went down the steps, keeping her injured wrist close to her body. She took her purse from Whitney's hand and opened the car door.

"Where do you think you're going?"

"I'm not welcome here."

"You can't leave," Whitney said. "It'll be dark soon."

"Then I better leave now while I can still see the road."

"Brie."

"You. Don't. Want. Me. Here."

Whitney grabbed the car door. "Okay, I'll admit that this is my special place, and I'm not used to visitors, but the way you—"

"What, Whit? The way I crashed your party of one?"

"I was going to say that the way you arrived was upsetting, to say the least."

"For both of us. But I'm going to take my inconvenient injury and let you get back to your tea. I noticed there's only one mug, which is probably why you didn't offer me any. Or maybe it's because you're angry that I'm still stalking you, is that it? There's old Cheese Head, popping up where she doesn't belong again. Make sure you have a good laugh about it with Liz over an expensive bottle of wine. I'm sure she'll snort it through her nose when she hears about the nonexistent bear sighting."

Whitney held on to Brie's carry-on with two hands. "You can't drive. You're on heavy pain meds. Please. Just come back inside."

Brie glared at her for a moment, then grabbed her bag and slammed the car door shut. "I'll leave first thing in the morning." She brushed past Whitney and headed back up the steps.

"It was a good exit speech, though. It hit all the right notes," Whitney said, hoping to lighten the moment.

"Oh, now you have your sense of humor back?" Brie went back into the cabin and let the screen door slam behind her.

Whitney went back in and found her sitting at the little table. "I'm stealing your mug," Brie said. She took a sip of what had to be lukewarm tea by then.

Whitney set the bag by the door and took the cup from Brie's hand. "Let me make you a fresh cup." She set the tea kettle on the stove and went into the bathroom. Luckily, she had an extra bath towel. She set it by the tub and turned on the hot water. "I'm running a bath for you," she shouted. She stood there in a bit of a daze and watched the tub fill.

She should've done some shopping while she was in town. With only one electric hot plate, cooking more than some scrambled eggs or a grilled cheese sandwich took too much effort. She wasn't there to make elaborate meals anyway. Breakfast cereal, fruit, tuna sandwiches, canned soup; those were her staple foods. There was a good chance Brie might not be that hungry anyway. She might want to go straight to bed after a hot bath. Whitney could sleep on the sofa so she wouldn't disturb her during the night. She had enough blankets to keep both of them warm. Maybe even an extra set of sheets. She hadn't bothered to sort through the linen closet in a while. She always took her sheets down to the laundromat when she needed clean clothes and put them right back on the bed. Life was simple at the cabin. Too simple for most people, which was another reason she told herself she never had guests.

She snapped her fingers when she remembered she had some bubble bath in the medicine cabinet. The tub was almost full, so she poured it right under the faucet so it'd foam up quickly. She tested the water. It was a little bit too hot, so she added more cold water.

Once Brie was clean and comfortable, Whitney would sit and try to explain things. She'd explain her writing process and all of the reasons why the cabin worked so well for that process. She'd explain how hard it was to write with distractions all around her. Phones going off and muffled music and the nightly news, or even worse, the canned laughter of a sitcom, all of those would yank her out of Piper's world and slam her back into reality.

The cabin was different. Distant bird calls, the sound of a breeze blowing through the trees, and occasionally, the pitter patter of rain on the roof was all she ever heard. That and the sound of a tea kettle whistling. "Brie, could you get that," she shouted.

She turned the water off and made sure the sink looked clean. The roll of toilet paper was running low so she changed that out. But the kettle kept whistling. A sense of panic rose in her chest. She rushed out into the living room. "Brie?"

She took the kettle off the stove and opened the front door. She rushed down the steps only to find that the crappy little rental car was gone.

CHAPTER SIXTEEN

The candy bars had come in handy. Same with the pain relief cream she'd rubbed on her neck several times on the way home. Brie cleaned the empty wrappers out of her purse and tossed them in the trash can. She'd have kept the cream except she knew the distinct medicinal aroma would only remind her of that time she'd made the worst trip of her life, so it went in the trash too.

Her wrist ached. Her whole body ached from the fall, but she was clean and safe and ready for a hot cup of coffee and a date with her journal. She hadn't written in it for a while, but she figured if ever she needed to work through some shit, the last few days would beat everything that had come before.

She poured herself a cup, sat at the kitchen table, and started typing.

Dear Journal,
I should've stopped chasing her after fucking Cincinnati.

A knock on the door startled Brie. She went to the door and opened the peek-a-boo window. Liz took her sunglasses off and said, "This won't take long."

Brie wanted to make her say whatever she had to say through the window, but she opened the door and waved her in. "I just poured myself a cup of coffee. Would you like one?"

"Like I said, this won't take long."

"Have a seat." Brie got her coffee and joined Liz in the living room.

"How was your trip home?"

"It was hell," Brie snapped back. "Are you asking for Whitney? Because I seriously doubt she gives a damn."

"I would've gone with something more neutral. Neon pink is very limiting."

"Like I had a fucking choice, Liz. I wasn't exactly coherent when they put the cast on. Besides, don't you have a handbag this exact color?"

Liz put her hands up. "Okay. I can see you're not in the mood for foreplay, so I'll get right to it. Reece fucked you. She set you up. And don't tell me she had nothing to do with it because she's the only person who knows where that cabin is. Hell, I don't even know where it is, and I'm her BFF."

Brie waved her good hand. "Okay, you can stop beating the BFF drum. I have absolutely no desire to oust you from that particular throne."

"Good. Because I'd fight you to the death to keep it, and I'd win. In fact, you're lucky I'm not a lesbian, or I'd own that throne too."

"Oh, for God's sake. Don't be ridiculous." Liz's arrogant expression made Brie want to burst out laughing. Also, she made a mental note to never ever let Adam meet Liz until he'd gotten past the dating older women thing. "Why are you here, Liz?"

"Look, I'm not saying Reece wanted you to get injured, but she knew what Whitney's reaction would be if you showed up unannounced."

Brie didn't believe it. This was a ploy of some kind. But it didn't matter anyway because she was done. Done with the chase. Done with playing the fool. Done with all of it. "I appreciate your concern, but I'm not feeling great, Liz. I'd like to go lie down."

"I understand." Liz stood and went to the door. "I'm really sorry this happened to you. Think about limiting your contact with Reece until Whitney gets back. And don't forget that a woman who's willing to tattoo a name on her body probably won't stop until she gets the girl." She lifted an eyebrow. "Or maybe it's you she's after. Either way, be careful."

Brie closed the door behind her and locked it. She really did need to lie down before she collapsed.

❖

The nap helped to clear Brie's mind. She'd felt so fuzzy-headed from the pain meds, it was a miracle she'd made it home in one piece. She craved an ice-cold beer, but she grabbed a soda from the fridge instead and took her dinner out on the deck.

Whitney had gone back down the mountain again, which meant there were more texts Brie had avoided looking at. She wasn't ready for apologies or explanations. They'd just be excuses as far as she was concerned. Fine. Whatever. She was done.

She set her turkey sandwich and soda on the balcony ledge. It was a beautiful evening. There were a few people on the beach. A paddle boarder in the water. A dog barking in the distance. And the sound of Brie's beloved ocean. She was just about to take a bite of her sandwich when she heard someone in the house. "I'm out on the deck, Mom."

Reece appeared in the doorway. "It's me. You didn't answer when I knocked, so I used the garage code." She stepped onto the deck and walked over. She scanned Brie from head to toe and gently touched her bruised fingers. "I'm so sorry this happened." She reached up and pushed Brie's hair back to inspect the bruise on her forehead and said it again. "I'm so sorry. I should've mentioned the bad road. I should've taken you there myself. I should've—" She paused for a moment and shook her head.

Brie reached for her hand. "Hold me?"

❖

Whitney parked in front of the store and grabbed her phone. She sent a text to Liz and then to Brie. They had thirty minutes to call back before she headed up the mountain. She got a cup of coffee and a newspaper and sat in the small dining section of the store.

"Hey, Whit." Mirna sat at the table with her.

"Hey. I didn't see you behind the counter."

"I was in the back, stocking the milk. It's the one item we sell out of every week due to the large family of boys staying in the Millers' cabin. Did you know Bob Miller? He was good friends with your grandpa. They fished together every summer, but since Bob passed away, his kids rent the place out all summer. Make a pretty penny doing it too."

"It must be a much nicer cabin than what Grandpa built."

"Well, Bob was a family man. Your grandpa, not so much."

"No. I guess he wasn't."

"It must be thirty years on now, but I still remember the day your grandma came up here. She wanted to surprise your grandpa on his birthday, so she loaded up a picnic basket with all kinds of goodies, and before she walked out of the store, she asked me if she looked pretty. I complimented her dress, and that seemed to make her happy."

Whitney stopped her. "Mirna, where are you going with this story?"

"Oh, I was just reminiscing. Glad your friend got home okay." She got up slowly. "Oh, these old bones of mine. I sit for two minutes, and it takes me twenty to get going again. Oh, well. I'll leave you to your newspaper."

"Mirna, what was that about my friend?"

"Oh, saw on the interweb. She's back at the beach with Reece. Will you be joining them soon?"

"Not for a while." She forced a smile and pulled her phone out of her pocket. She did a search for Reece Ainsworth, and the latest images came up. Her heart sank. Her stomach roiled. Her anger flared. Someone needed to fucking call her back ASAP.

Brie's mom set her phone down. "It wasn't Robin. Nothing I could find pointed to her."

"No," Brie said. "It was a guy on a paddle board. I remember seeing him right before it happened."

"The timing couldn't have been coincidental. Someone knew Reece would be on that deck with you. I told you, honey. You can't trust these people."

Brie shook her head. "Please don't lecture me right now. I can't take it. My wrist is broken, but so is my heart. I just want to go back to my little apartment and hide from the world."

"You can't. They know who you are now. It's time to hunker down with me or your dad. We're going to insist, honey."

Her mom was right. Brie needed to stay out of the public eye for a while. She needed to heal. She needed to sleep in late and go to bed early. She needed to get back on track with her yoga routine. She needed to read books and find some normalcy in her life. "No offense to you, Mom, but I'd rather stay at Dad's place. He's hardly ever there."

Her mom reached for her hand. "If you really want to escape this mess, disconnect yourself from all of it. Write your book and forget them."

It was good advice, but at the same time, heartbreaking. She'd have to let go of all of those dreams she had. She'd have to let go of Whitney and Piper Kane. She'd have to find a way to live without them, and that didn't seem possible. But she'd try. She had to try.

❖

There was a chill in the air. Whitney started her car and turned on the heat while she waited for Liz to answer her goddamned phone. Suddenly, no one was available when she'd drive down the mountain. Apparently, they didn't care to get an earful every time.

It was ridiculous that Liz couldn't find Brie. People didn't just disappear anymore; they left digital trails everywhere. Her phone rang. "Tell me you found her."

"Her family isn't talking, Whit. They won't tell me where she is. Maybe you should consider respecting her desire for privacy. Let it go and move on. God knows I tried to warn her about Reece."

"Stop," Whitney said. "I already told you that I don't believe your little theory. Reece knows that she and I are over."

"Then maybe the photos are real, and she's moved on to Brie. God, I hate that I ever brought that woman into your life. I'm so sorry, Whit."

"Just find her." Whitney tossed her phone on the passenger seat and covered her face with her hands. If only she could turn back time and do it all differently. Why did she have to be so stubborn? She loved Brie. But she hadn't said so in the hospital. She should've said it over and over. She should've taken her to a hotel with a big comfy bed and room service. She should've insisted on traveling back home with her. She should've chased her back down that mountain when she left. That was her biggest regret. She'd stood there like an idiot on the porch when she should've jumped in her SUV. God, she could be a stubborn SOB at times.

Her phone buzzed again. She put it on speaker and said, "Please tell me you didn't fuck me over again because I don't remember discussing the part of the media strategy where you and Brie make out on the deck while I'm a million miles away."

"I have no idea how anyone would've known I'd be there," Reece said. "I went there to apologize. We hugged, and some paparazzi asshole took a pic. That's it. Look closely and you'll see that it was nothing, okay? Whit, tell me you believe me."

"Fine. I believe you. But I'm just about out of reasons to give you the benefit of the doubt, so you better have a fucking good reason for sending Brie up here alone."

"Believe it or not, I did it for you. All I wanted was for her to fly back there to you and do what I never could."

"And what's that, Reece? What could you never do?"

"Make you see that you can't just disappear on the people you love. You find another way. Take a look at those photos again, and maybe you'll see that it's Brie hanging on to me, not the other way around. And ask yourself why, Whit. Why would she cling to me for the comfort she so obviously needed from you?"

"Oh, here we go again. This is where you tell me that your affair with Kat was all my fault."

Whitney's anger flared. Her heart pounded in her chest. She was about to let loose on Reece and start screaming at her when she heard her say, "No. That was my mistake."

"What was that? Can you say that again, please? I didn't quite hear it the first time."

"You heard me. And you need to hear this too. I saw in Brie's eyes the same hurt I felt every time you left me for that cabin. Which tells me you did one hell of a job letting her know she wasn't welcome there. Will you ever learn, Whit?"

Whitney's eyes shuddered closed. Reece was right. She'd made Brie feel as unwelcome and unimportant as she could. It was selfish and cruel and something she might never have the chance to make up for. She opened her eyes again. "Is she okay, Reece? Just tell me she's okay."

"Of course she isn't okay. She loves you, dummy. And you rejected her."

"Take care of her until I can get there." Whitney ended the call. She saw Mirna inside the store stocking the shelves. She got out of the car and went inside.

"Hey, Whit. I have your order ready, minus the canned tuna. Ted forgot to set some aside for you before that family of boys came in and bought us out."

"That's fine, Mirna. I just wanted to ask a question."

Mirna stopped what she was doing. "Is everything all right?"

Whitney shook her head. "Not really, but I need to know how that story you told me ended. The one about my grandmother coming up here to visit my grandfather?"

"Right. Well, about an hour after she'd filled that picnic basket, she came back in looking rather distraught. She set the basket on the counter and told me to give it to someone who needed it. I never saw her again, and let me tell you, it was difficult for me to look your grandpa in the eye after that. I'd usually have Ted ring him out so I wouldn't say something I'd regret because it was clear he'd broken his wife's heart."

Whitney sucked back her emotions and gave Mirna a hug. "Thank you. And don't worry about the food order. I'm leaving tomorrow."

"Going back to the beach?"

Whitney stopped at the door and turned around. "Going to find a different way."

❖

It was a bachelor pad in every sense of the word. A poor man's Jimmy Buffet penthouse. The beach was several blocks away, but if she got on the roof, Brie could still watch the sunset over the water. Her parents had bought the three-story house years ago as an investment. They'd split it into two units and rented it out to their surfer friends. After the divorce, her dad had moved into the top unit. He'd built stairs up to the roof, along with a deck. It was big enough for two sling chairs and a small end table.

Brie went up there every evening. And every evening, she contemplated whether to make the phone call. She'd tucked her phone into her dad's safe when she'd arrived over a week ago. It had been the hardest week of her life. She'd hated every minute of the isolation. No phone calls, no visits. "How does she do it?" she whispered.

Her dad had been there once to check on her and fill his duffel bag with clothes. He'd told her that he and her mom were going to take a road trip up to Santa Cruz and to call if she needed anything. He looked happier than she remembered ever seeing him before. Happy and in love. Jake and Jade were back together again. It was nice to see love blooming somewhere. God, she felt lonely. Her wrist had stopped aching, and her bruises had faded. But the rest of her ached for some connection. But not just any connection. She ached for Whitney.

Her ears perked up at the sound of Adam's voice. She got up and looked over the edge of the house. "Hey. Come on up." And then someone else appeared. She took a step back. Her heart rate increased. Her breaths got shallow. Her eyes filled with tears.

She heard someone running up the stairs and took another step back. Whitney came into view. Brie put up a hand to keep her from coming any closer. "I can't," she said through her tears.

Whitney stayed where she was. No longer the lumber-jill, she looked like a California girl again in her cropped jeans and sandals. Adam stepped up behind her looking guilty as hell. "She begged me, sis. Like, down on her knees in my office begging to know where you were."

"Don't blame Adam. Blame me. For everything."

Brie sucked up her emotions enough to say, "It's fine, bro. You can go." He backed away and made the *call me* sign with his hand. She gave him a nod. Whitney started to take a step closer, but Brie put up her hand again.

Whitney said, "Okay. I'll stay here. But please just hear me out. I have a lot to say."

Brie wanted to shout, "You sure didn't have a lot to say in the cabin. Or the hospital. Or your car. Oh, but in the store, you sure as hell made time to make fun of me in front of Mirna."

A strong gust of wind caught her summer dress and nudged her a step toward Whitney. Was God telling her she should give in already? Just let go of the past and embrace whatever future they might have together? Was that even what Whitney wanted to say? Brie leaned against the wind so she could hold her ground.

"I'm going to sell the cabin," Whitney said. "I can't be there anymore. It reminds me too much of that time I forgot what was really important and let the woman I love drive back down that mountain and leave me for what might turn out to be forever."

The wind died down. Brie brushed her hair out of her face. "I waited for you at the bottom. Did you know that? I waited because I wasn't sure if I could get back home by myself. But you never came, Whit. I chased you all over the country, and you couldn't even follow me down that mountain. I think that says it all, don't you?"

Whitney shook her head. "No. All it means is that I'm an idiot. But I'm your idiot, Brie. You own my heart. And yes, I can be stubborn and selfish, but I can also own it and admit how wrong I was. Please, Brie. Let me make it right."

She took a step closer. Brie didn't stop her that time. But she needed more. "I don't know how to get back to a place where I know you'll be there for me, no matter what." She looked at the sky in an effort to keep her tears from falling. When it didn't help, she went to wipe her eyes with the back of her hand, forgetting there was a cast in the way. "Ouch. Damnit."

Whitney grabbed the napkin from under Brie's beer and handed it to her. "Are you okay?"

Embarrassed, Brie slapped the napkin over her now irritated eye. "Sometimes I wake up with the grid pattern of the cast imprinted on my cheek. I can't seem to get used to it being there."

Whitney took her hand and kissed her bruised fingers that had faded to a nauseating shade of yellowish green. "I wonder if you could get used to waking up with my arms around you." She kissed the last finger and met Brie's gaze.

"I..." Brie stammered. Her heart told her to jump in with both feet. Her head told her the physical wounds were the least of her worries.

"This cast is like you, Brie. You're imprinted on my heart. And I'd give anything to hit reverse and go back to the moment when I knew it was you in that car and that it was my fault you were so scared. I would do it all so differently."

Brie took the napkin away from her eye. "Maybe…you could tell me what you'd do differently."

Whitney smiled. "Well, first of all, I'd take you in my arms and kiss your cheek and tell you how happy I was to see you because I wouldn't have even been up there writing if it weren't for you."

"Well, that's probably true," Brie said. "I think you owe me a spot in the acknowledgments section of book four."

Whitney took both of Brie's hands. "I owe you so much more than that. How about the dedication spot? And maybe an exclusive interview for your blog."

"I'd like that," Brie said. "What else are you offering?"

"Long walks on the beach. Lots of snuggling by the fire pit. My heart, if you want it."

"Did you really get on your knees in Adam's office?"

"I did. And then your dad walked in. It was awkward for everyone."

Brie laughed. "I can't wait to hear my dad tell the story."

"Oh, good. Because I told them that if I won your heart back, we'd barbecue at the beach house this weekend. So, no pressure or anything, but they're really looking forward to it."

Brie took Whitney's face in hand. "My love. You don't have to win back what was always yours. You just have to take good care of it from now on."

Whitney put her hand over Brie's heart. "I'll protect it with my life."

Brie turned around so they were both facing west and leaned against Whitney. "This is my favorite time of day, when the sun is just hitting the horizon. I love to watch it disappear."

"I didn't know that. But I guess there's a lot we don't know about each other."

Brie grinned. "We'll learn."

❖

Six Months Later

Brie checked for the paddle boarder before she went out on the deck. They knew who he was thanks to Adam's sharp eye and a pair of binoculars. The guy lived a few doors down from her mom's beach house. A down-on-his-luck actor who knew how to make a quick buck.

She wasn't living there anymore, but doing a quick check of her surroundings had become a habit. She leaned on the balcony and took in a deep breath of the ocean air. She was a beach baby. Always had been. Always would be.

Her mom came up behind her and squeezed her shoulders. "I can't believe my babies turn thirty-one today." She turned away from the beach and leaned against the railing, her face lit by the interior lights. She had a glow about her that Brie wasn't used to seeing. The tan lines on her wrists and fingers were fading, and the maxi dresses hadn't made a return. The smile lines around her eyes seemed more prominent, but that was a good thing. "You look so happy, Mom."

"I am. Happier than I've been in a long time."

There was no hesitation in her reply. No questioning the accuracy of Brie's statement. And that smile lingered again. "So maybe this thing between you and Dad is going to last?"

Her mom motioned with her head. "I was just going to ask you the same thing about Whitney."

Brie turned around. Whitney and her dad were chatting at the kitchen table. She'd blended right into Brie's family as if she'd been there forever. Every once in a while, Adam would drop to his knees and beg her for something mundane like a beer or a marshmallow for his s'more. If he wasn't teasing her, he was doting on her like a lovesick idiot because he did love her. They all did.

Brie turned back to the ocean, and back to her doubts. Could she hold on to a love that was so special? It was a question she asked herself every day. "I'm so in love with her, but—"

"But what?"

"I don't know. I guess I'm waiting for the next thing to come along that'll tear us apart again."

"Have you made any kind of commitment to each other?"

Brie shook her head. "I can't be the one to make that move to the next level. I need it to come from her. After everything we've been through, it has to come from her."

"It will. Gabriela, look at me. It will. She adores you and thinks you're so talented and feels lucky to have met you. So it's time for you to stop doubting and start embracing what you have. Go to her. She has a birthday surprise for you."

"She does? How do you know? Have you been conspiring behind my back?"

"I plead the Fifth." Her mom took her hand and led her inside. "I think it's time for the big reveal."

Whitney waved her over. "Come and sit by me."

Brie sat and rested her hand on Whitney's leg. "What's going on?"

"Something I hope you'll like."

Her mom sat across from them. "Whitney's been campaigning, and she finally wore me down."

Her mom pulled out some papers from a large envelope and set them in front of Brie. Her jaw dropped when she realized what they were. "You're going to let us buy the beach house from you?"

Whitney wrapped her arms around Brie's shoulders. "Remember that time you told me that you missed the things we didn't have? One of those things was to hear a book being written from the other room while you made dinner. And I can't think of a better place for that to happen than right here in your favorite place on earth."

Brie grabbed Whitney's face and kissed her, something she hadn't done in front of her parents before. She got up and rounded the table. "Are you sure, Mom? This was your inheritance."

Her mom stood. "And I can't think of a better way to keep it in the family. Besides, this old man and I want to see the world together."

Her dad stood too. "Who you calling an old man? I'm three weeks younger than you."

Brie wrapped her arms around both of them. "I promise to cherish this place until I die." She went back to Whitney, jumped up and down and squealed in delight before she grabbed her and pulled her into her arms. "For real, babe?"

"I think your mom is probably sick and tired of all the begging, and that's why they've decided to travel, but yes. For real."

"Oh God. You didn't get on your knees again, did you?"

Whitney laughed. "I have no shame when it comes to making you happy. Zero."

Brie glanced at her parents. Her mom had tears in her eyes, and her dad was beaming. Brie also burst into tears and giggles because how could her life get any better than this?

Adam walked in with balloons and said, "Are you ready for thirty-one birthday spanks, Breezy?"

Brie put her arms out and said, "Welcome to our house, bro."

Brie had never seen her dad wearing a suit before. Adam had obviously helped him shop for it because it fit his trim body like a glove. She went up to him and straightened his tie. "You look good, Dad. Kinda rugged like Jeff Bridges."

"More like a fish out of water."

She patted his chest. "Just act like this is another typical Thursday night. That's what I'm trying to do."

It was anything but another Thursday night. Even though she'd been preparing for it, Brie was nervous as hell to talk to the press. It would be an onslaught when they walked out there. Cameras flashing, people shouting their names. A flurry of questions, some of which would probably get personal. She had her canned answers memorized; she just had to pull them from the back of what would surely be a stunned, frozen, empty brain.

He took her hand and said, "You look stunning, honey. And you do belong here. Remember that when you go out there."

"She does," her mom said. "Much to my chagrin."

Brie laughed. "Well, at least you kept Adam from crossing over to the dark side."

"Oh, he's looking for a sugar mama as we speak." Her mom pointed at Adam chatting with Liz. "But I get the feeling that woman goes through men faster than she does handbags."

"Oh God," Brie said. "Is he still dating older women?" She noticed Whitney waving her over. "Gotta go, guys. I'll see you inside." She gave them both a kiss on the cheek and whispered in her mom's ear, "You should wear that dress when you marry Dad again. He can't stop looking at you."

It was a simple dress. Long sleeved. Fitted. A pretty shade of deep purple. Not really a wedding dress, but for some reason, as Brie looked at her parents all dressed up for her big day, she could envision them at the altar, repeating new vows to one another. It was a beautiful image that she hoped would become a reality one day soon.

"It's time," Whitney said. "Are you ready?"

Brie blinked back her tears and took Whitney's hand. "Don't my parents look amazing?"

Whitney gave them both a light hug and said, "I have to steal her away now."

"Go," her mom said. "We'll be right behind you."

Those words meant everything to Brie. She wanted to share this moment with the people she loved most, including her gigolo brother who'd just offered his arm to Liz. But Brie couldn't worry about that now. Not with Reece waving them over. It was time. She took a deep breath and looked at Whitney. "Let's do this."

Whitney raised their joined hands and kissed Brie's. "Let's do this."

They'd decided to wear designer pantsuits instead of dresses. Reece in red, Whitney in gold, and Brie in white. Power colors, the designer called them.

The three of them stepped onto the red carpet to oohs and awes from the crowd. Brie waved to the cameras the way Reece had demonstrated to her. She felt a bit silly, but she also felt the power of her new position in life. She had a bigger voice in the world, and she planned to use it.

Together, they stopped to be interviewed by someone from the E! Channel. "Hello, ladies," the reporter said. "You all look gorgeous tonight. Now, tell me how this female power trio of author, screenwriter, and actor came about?"

Reece smiled at Brie and Whitney. "I think we all realized we were stronger together than apart."

EPILOGUE

"Where is he?" Reece set a watermelon on the kitchen island.

"What am I, chopped liver?" Brie gestured with a knife at the watermelon. "And where the hell do you find such gigantic watermelons?"

Reece gave her a kiss on the cheek. "I know a guy. Now, where is he?"

"Probably burying his mom in sand."

"Perfect. I'll help him. And whatever you're making smells delicious."

Brie waved her off. "Yeah, yeah. Go play with your boyfriend. He's been asking about you all day."

Reece gasped and swooned as if she'd just been told that her celebrity crush had mentioned her on Johnny Falcon. Brie laughed and said, "Go. He's been waiting for you."

Reece rushed out the back door and down the steps to the beach. Brie set the knife down and wiped her hands dry. She grabbed her phone so she could take some pictures and stood next to Liz on the deck. "Has he buried her yet?"

"Not even close. Give that kid a backhoe or something. Watching him throw one baby handful at a time on her is torture."

"He's one, Liz. It doesn't matter if he actually buries her, only that he wears himself out trying."

"Well, thank God Auntie Weece showed up. Now we'll get somewhere."

"One of these days, Auntie Whiz is going to give in to those cute little dimples, and then it'll be all over. He'll have you right here." Brie held up her little finger.

They watched Reece pick him up and throw him in the air, then kiss his chubby cheeks. Liz huffed. "I'm not a sucker like Auntie Weece. He'll have to negotiate with Auntie Liz."

"Don't you mean Auntie Whiz? As in Cheese Whiz?"

"I don't think that's what your child means when he says my name. I think he recognizes that he's talking to a very intelligent woman."

Adam rushed onto the deck. "Where is he?"

"What am I, chopped liver? He's down on the beach burying his mom in the sand."

Liz leaned in and said, "You need a new line."

"Or maybe they'll all get sick of hearing it and say hello first. Or was I just the vehicle that brought them an apple for their collective eye?"

"I can respect that theory." Liz straightened and turned to Brie. "By the way, I'm still waiting for my thank you."

"For what?"

"For what? Look around you, honey. You have a beautiful wife, a new career, an adorable little boy who everyone but me is in love with. And all because I spotted you in a hotel bar."

"Should we kiss? I feel like we should kiss because I'm just that grateful."

Liz shrugged. "I sowed my wild lesbian oats in college, but by all means, lay one on me while I pray to God that there's a paddle boarder out there with a camera."

Brie had grown to love bantering with Liz. Hell, if she were honest, she'd have to admit that she'd grown to love her as a person too. She'd witnessed glimpses of her softer side, and she knew Liz had Whitney's back. She truly was her BFF, and for that, Brie was grateful.

She leaned in and said, "You can pretend all you want that you don't love our little guy, but I've seen you talk to him when you thought no one was watching."

Liz shrugged. "I was just letting him know I'm taking on new clients. He has my card. He'll call when he realizes he could rule the world with those dimples."

"My mom will have your head on a platter."

"Whose head will be on a platter?" Whitney dusted the sand off her legs before she sidled up next to Brie. "Hello, beautiful."

"Aw. Thank you for saying hello to me." Brie wrapped her arms around Whitney's shoulders. "Liz was just telling me about her plans to make our son the next big child star. What do you think, honey?"

Whitney gave Liz a glare. "I think you'll have to get through me, Jade, Jake, Adam, and Reece to do that. Besides, Liz, aren't you about ready to retire? We could teach Kane to call you Granny. Or Mee Maw."

Brie gasped. "Or Nana."

Liz huffed her disgust and backed away. "You two aren't the least bit funny. I specifically did not have children for this very reason. I'm Auntie Whiz. Period. And I need another martini."

Brie waited until Liz was inside the house before she burst into laughter. "Well done, honey. Somehow, you just forced Liz to embrace her nickname."

Whitney wrapped her arms around Brie's waist and asked, "Are you as happy as I am?"

Brie tapped her chin. "Well, let's see. I have an incredibly sexy wife who I'm madly in love with, and an adorable healthy son. Oh, and a house on the beach. And a new career." She shrugged. "Eh. Life is just so-so."

Brie's parents rushed through the door. "Where is he?" they asked in unison.

Brie laughed and pointed with her thumb. She turned back to Whitney and said, "Wanna make out while we have babysitters?"

"Yes." Whitney grabbed Brie's hand and led her into their home.

About the Author

Elle Spencer is the author of several best-selling lesbian romances, including *Casting Lacey*, a Goldie finalist. She is a hopeless romantic and firm believer in true love, although she knows the path to happily ever after is rarely an easy one—not for Elle and not for her characters.

When she's not writing, Elle loves working on home improvement projects, hiking up tall mountains (not really, but it sounds cool), floating in the pool with a good book, and spending quality time with her pillow in a never-ending quest to prove that napping is the new working.

Elle and her wife live in Southern California.

Find out more at www.ellespencerbooks.com.

Books Available From Bold Strokes Books

A Woman to Treasure by Ali Vali. An ancient scroll isn't the only treasure Levi Montbard finds as she starts her hunt for the truth—all she has to do is prove to Yasmine Hassani that there's more to her than an adventurous soul. (978-1-63555-890-6)

Before. After. Always. by Morgan Lee Miller. Still reeling from her tragic past, Eliza Walsh has sworn off taking risks, until Blake Navarro turns her world right-side up, making her question if falling in love again is worth it. (978-1-63555-845-6)

Bet the Farm by Fiona Riley. Lauren Calloway's luxury real estate sale of the century comes to a screeching halt when dairy farm heiress, and one-night stand, Thea Boudreaux calls her bluff. (978-1-63555-731-2)

Cowgirl by Nance Sparks. The last thing Aren expects is to fall for Carol. Sharing her home is one thing, but sharing her heart means sharing the demons in her past and risking everything to keep Carol safe. (978-1-63555-877-7)

Give In to Me by Elle Spencer. Gabriela Talbot never expected to sleep with her favorite author—certainly not after the scathing review she'd given Whitney Ainsworth's latest book. (978-1-63555-910-1)

Hidden Dreams by Shelley Thrasher. A lethal virus and its resulting vision send Texan Barbara Allan and her lovely guide, Dara, on a journey up Cambodia's Mekong River in search of Barbara's mother's mystifying past. (978-1-63555-856-2)

In the Spotlight by Lesley Davis. For actresses Cole Calder and Eris Whyte, their chance at love runs out fast when a fan's adoration turns to obsession. (978-1-63555-926-2)

Origins by Jen Jensen. Jamis Bachman is pulled into a dangerous mystery that becomes personal when she learns the truth of her origins as a ghost hunter. (978-1-63555-837-1)

Unrivaled by Radclyffe. Zoey Cohen will never accept second place in matters of the heart, even when her rival is a career, and Declan Black has nothing left to give of herself or her heart. (978-1-63679-013-8)

A Fae Tale by Genevieve McCluer. Dovana comes to terms with her changing feelings for her lifelong best friend and fae, Roze. (978-1-63555-918-7)

Accidental Desperados by Lee Lynch. Life is clobbering Berry, Jaudon, and their long romance. The arrival of directionless baby dyke MJ doesn't help. Can they find their passion again—and keep it? (978-1-63555-482-3)

Always Believe by Aimée. Greyson Walsden is pursuing ordination as an Anglican priest. Angela Arlingham doesn't believe in God. Do they follow their vocation or their hearts? (978-1-63555-912-5)

Courage by Jesse J. Thoma. No matter how often Natasha Parsons and Tommy Finch clash on the job, an undeniable attraction simmers just beneath the surface. Can they find the courage to change so love has room to grow? (978-1-63555-802-9)

I Am Chris by R Kent. There's one saving grace to losing everything and moving away. Nobody knows her as Chrissy Taylor. Now Chris can live who he truly is. (978-1-63555-904-0)

The Princess and the Odium by Sam Ledel. Jastyn and Princess Aurelia return to Venostes and join their families in a battle against the dark force to take back their homeland for a chance at a better tomorrow. (978-1-63555-894-4)

The Queen Has a Cold by Jane Kolven. What happens when the heir to the throne isn't a prince or a princess? (978-1-63555-878-4)

The Secret Poet by Georgia Beers. Agreeing to help her brother woo Zoe Blake seemed like a good idea to Morgan Thompson at first…until she realizes she's actually wooing Zoe for herself… (978-1-63555-858-6)

You Again by Aurora Rey. For high school sweethearts Kate Cormier and Sutton Guidry, the second chance might be the only one that matters. (978-1-63555-791-6)

Love's Falling Star by B.D. Grayson. For country music megastar Lochlan Paige, can love conquer her fear of losing the one thing she's worked so hard to protect? (978-1-63555-873-9)

Love's Truth by C.A. Popovich. Can Lynette and Barb make love work when unhealed wounds of betrayed trust and a secret could change everything? (978-1-63555-755-8)

Next Exit Home by Dena Blake. Home may be where the heart is, but for Harper Sims and Addison Foster, is the journey back worth the pain? (978-1-63555-727-5)

Not Broken by Lyn Hemphill. Falling in love is hard enough—even more so for Rose, who's carrying her ex's baby. (978-1-63555-869-2)

The Noble and the Nightingale by Barbara Ann Wright. Two women on opposite sides of empires at war risk all for a chance at love. (978-1-63555-812-8)

What a Tangled Web by Melissa Brayden. Clementine Monroe has the chance to buy the café she's managed for years, but Madison LeGrange swoops in and buys it first. Now Clementine is forced to work for the enemy and ignore her former crush. (978-1-63555-749-7)

A Far Better Thing by JD Wilburn. When needs of her family and wants of her heart clash, Cass Halliburton is faced with the ultimate sacrifice. (978-1-63555-834-0)

Body Language by Renee Roman. When Mika offers to provide Jen erotic tutoring, will sex drive them into a deeper relationship or tear them apart? (978-1-63555-800-5)

Carrie and Hope by Joy Argento. For Carrie and Hope, loss brings them together but secrets and fear may tear them apart. (978-1-63555-827-2)

Detour to Love by Amanda Radley. Celia Scott and Lily Andersen are seatmates on a flight to Tokyo and by turns annoy and fascinate each other. But they're about to realize there's more than one path to love. (978-1-63555-958-3)